WISH

Rock
& ROMANCE
Stars

A.K. EVANS

ISBN: 978-1-951441-22-7

Cover Artist
cover artwork © Sarah Hansen, Okay Creations
www.okaycreations.com

Editing & Proofreading
Ellie McLove, My Brother's Editor
www.mybrotherseditor.net

Formatting
Stacey Blake at Champagne Book Design
www.champagnebookdesign.com

WISH

PROLOGUE

Beck

"I CAN'T DO THIS."

"What exactly do you mean by that, Bill?"

Something was wrong.

I didn't understand it; I just knew they were angry. They weren't shouting, though. My mom and dad never really shouted. But they did get angry. And when they were angry, I could always tell by the way their voices sounded.

And they always used each other's real names.

They didn't know I was watching. Listening.

I was supposed to be in bed. I had school tomorrow, and it was past my bedtime.

"I want a divorce, Sandy," my dad told my mom.

Divorce.

I didn't know what that was. It didn't sound like a good thing.

"A divorce?" my mom said. "Why?"

"This isn't what I want," he told her.

"What about the kids? Sadie is only two. And Beck? Beck is just six, but Bill, he adores you," she said.

That's when I knew a divorce was definitely a bad thing.

"He'll be alright," Dad said. "They both will. You wanted them; I know you'll give them everything."

My mom didn't say anything for a long time. Then she said something that proved I was right about divorce being bad. "Everything except a father."

Why wouldn't we have a father? Where was our dad going?

"I'm not cut out for this."

"What are we going to tell them?" she asked.

I heard him take in a breath and let it out. "You can tell them whatever you want. I've already packed a bag, and I'm leaving tonight."

"Bill."

Her voice sounded strange. She sounded scared. Sad.

"I'm sorry, Sandy."

"How am I going to do this on my own?" she asked him. "How do I teach Beck about being a man?"

Now I understood what divorce was. Dad was leaving.

And he was going to do it right now because I heard the chair move on the kitchen floor.

"Bill, wait." Mom was begging him. "We can work this out."

"We can't. I'm done."

I scooted back on the stairs to hide behind the wall because I didn't want them to see me. Then they were at the front door.

"Please don't leave us. We love you."

Say it back, I thought.

He didn't say it back. And he wasn't going to.

I knew that because I heard the front door open and close. Then I heard my mom crying.

I didn't know what to do.

Anytime I was upset, she always hugged me until I felt better. I thought I should do the same for her.

So, I got up off the stairs and walked to the front door. My mom was crying so hard she didn't even hear me. She was sitting on the floor with her knees up by her chest, her arms wrapped around her legs, and her face was resting against her knees.

I moved closer to her.

Then I sat down beside her, put my arms around her, and said, *"I love you."*

My mom hugged me back and cried harder.

I used to think my dad was the coolest guy in the world. Now I didn't think that at all.

In fact, I hated him for making my mom cry.

CHAPTER 1

Chasey
Twenty-six years later

GUT INSTINCT.

I had to trust it.

For far too long, I'd been doing my best to ignore what I knew in my heart was happening. But my priority had been different then. I had done what I needed to do to make sure she was okay.

My daughter.

My beautiful, newborn baby.

I'd overlooked what I believed was happening because I didn't have a choice. I wanted her healthy. I wanted her safe.

And that's what mothers do; they sacrifice for their children.

Or, they were supposed to.

Mine never did.

I'd never be the kind of mother to my child that my mother was to me.

So, I sacrificed. Every time I even considered bringing my concerns about what was happening to the table, I'd feel my daughter moving in my belly, and I'd push my worries to the back of my mind again.

I couldn't do that any longer.

She was here, she was healthy, and she was safe.

More than that, *she* deserved better than she was going to have if my instincts were telling me the truth.

I wasn't even sure if I should call it instinct any longer. I already knew the truth. There was far too much evidence, far too much proof, for me to believe otherwise.

I had a feeling it was that small part of me that wanted to be wrong for the sake of my daughter. She didn't deserve any of this. She deserved a happy, healthy family. She deserved to have her mom and her dad in her life.

I guess she still would. It's just that... we wouldn't be together.

Because while there were sacrifices mothers made for their children, this wasn't one that I'd make. In the end, it would be better for her, anyway.

My husband was cheating on me.

While I hadn't specifically caught him in the act, I knew it was happening. Today, I was finally putting a stop to it.

There was a small part of me that wondered if this was a smart thing to do. After all, I had to take my daughter with me. The only person in the world I could depend on was my best friend, Mara. But she was at work. Plus, I wasn't exactly keen on going anywhere without my baby just yet.

For weeks, I sucked it up. I put attention on my daughter and making sure she was taken care of.

Now, I had the proof staring me right in the face, and I couldn't suck it up any longer. I closed the laptop screen, gathered up the diaper bag, my purse, my keys, and my daughter in her car seat.

Minutes later, I was out the door.

Fortunately, I only needed to make a seven-minute drive to the hotel.

By the time I pulled into the parking lot, I said a silent prayer of thanks that my daughter hadn't gotten fussy on the ride and simply remained asleep. I got out of the car, got her nestled against me in the fabric baby carrier, and made my way to the front door of the hotel.

I'd already come up with my plan on the drive.

"Hello. How can I help you?" the woman at the front desk asked when I walked through the sliding doors.

"I'm so sorry, but I forgot my key in the room," I started. "Is there any way you could make another one for me?"

"Sure. Do you have your ID on you?"

I hated lying to this woman, but I had no choice. I needed to do this for myself and for my daughter. "Oh, yes. Sure," I replied. Then, after I pulled out my ID, I realized Aaron might have put it under his name, so I added, "I wasn't paying attention when we checked in. My husband might have put it under his name, which is the same last name, but we used my credit card."

It hit me then just how foolish he was. Who uses their wife's credit card to book a hotel not even ten minutes away from their house? Did he think I wouldn't find out?

Maybe he'd been hoping I'd be too distracted with taking care of the baby that I wouldn't notice.

And now that I was standing here waiting for a copy of the room key, I started to feel a bit of panic take over. Even though I knew what I was going to find, I still didn't think anyone could properly prepare for something like this. I was trying to remain calm, but I could feel my insides beginning to tremble.

"Room 632?" she asked, interrupting my thoughts.

Nodding, I answered, "Yes, that's correct."

When the woman at the front desk, who I now knew from her nametag was Demi, handed my license back to me, she said, "Here you go. I love your name, by the way. Is it pronounced Chasey?"

"Yep, that's correct," I confirmed. "And the connotation is correct. I'm always the one doing the chasing."

6

Shit.

I hadn't meant to add that last part. That was the nerves taking over.

Calm down, Chasey.

The next thing I knew, I had the room key in my hand and was heading toward the elevators. I stepped on, pressed the button to the sixth floor, and kept my hands wrapped around my baby.

She was the only reason I wasn't having a total meltdown yet. I needed to stay calm for her.

The elevator came to a stop, and I stepped off. I followed the signs in the hall that pointed to the room in which I knew I'd learn the fate of my marriage. I made it there, took a deep breath, and waved the key card in front of the lock.

I heard the faint sound of the door unlocking and opened it.

Seconds later, I wished I would have simply trusted my instincts. Why did I need the visual proof?

Not only that, I couldn't seem to move either. With one hand still cradling my daughter, the other was holding the door open.

And I couldn't stop myself from assessing the scene in front of me.

There was my husband, on his back with his underwear pulled down to his knees, his socks on his feet, and a tank top covering most of his torso.

He didn't see me.

That was because there was a woman sitting on his face. And with just one look at that woman, I could easily see that she hadn't had a baby five weeks ago. She was trim, fit, and attractive.

Her hands were holding the back of my husband's head, and I started to feel sick. It seemed I had arrived just in time for the show.

She started to pant and moan like she was auditioning for

a role in an upcoming porn flick. Just when I thought I could take no more, she was flipped to her back, and her head was now resting at the foot of the bed.

Without a condom on, my husband wasted no time shoving his dick inside her.

How I didn't throw up was beyond me?

My hand started to slip on the door, and I moved slightly to catch it. That's when Aaron's eyes came up, saw me standing there, and he stopped.

"Baby, what—"

That was all the woman beneath him got out before she followed the direction of his eyes toward me.

"Chasey," Aaron began.

Coming into this, I wasn't sure how I'd react. Now that I was here, I had to admit, I was surprised at how calm I was.

"You just lost your family," I seethed.

He hopped off the bed and started pulling his underwear back up his legs, but I moved out into the hall and walked as quickly as I could back to the elevators.

"Chasey," I heard him shout.

I was silently willing the doors to open so I could get away before he caught up to me. Thankfully, they did.

And just as they started to close, he ran up to the doors. Unfortunately for him, he needed to wait for the next elevator.

All I could think about was getting myself out of there as quickly as possible. I would not break down here. I wouldn't let him see me cry. He didn't deserve my tears.

Relief swept through me when the elevator doors opened on the main floor. I was going to return the key and get out.

As quickly as I could I rushed to the front desk.

"Are you okay?" Demi asked.

I shook my head, placed the key card back on the counter, and rasped, "Thank you for your help. I'm sorry I lied."

My declaration caught her by surprise. "Lied?" she repeated.

WISH

I nodded. "I didn't check into the hotel, but I saw my credit card was used here. My husband wasn't home, so it wasn't hard to figure out."

The moment I got the words out, I heard, "Chasey!"

My calm demeanor had vanished and rage filled its place. I spun around and demanded, "Don't you dare come near me, you piece of shit."

Apparently, Aaron didn't care what I had to say. He begged, "Wait. We need to talk about this."

"There's *nothing* to talk about. I *never* want to speak to you again!" I yelled.

Yep. Calm, cool Chasey had fled the building. Enraged Chasey wasn't far behind. I began moving back away from Aaron. I just wanted to get out of there.

But suddenly, I stopped.

I realized, I didn't want to do that just yet. I needed him to know exactly how I felt. And I didn't care who was standing around to watch it unfold. Let him have a dose of humiliation. It would never compare to how embarrassed I felt right now.

"You son of a bitch," I shouted. "I can't believe you. While I'm at home struggling to take care of our five-week-old daughter on my own, my husband is here screwing some bimbo."

"He did not," Demi seethed from behind the desk. "Tell me he did not do that."

My eyes never left Aaron as I stood there with my hands on my daughter and confirmed, "He absolutely did."

"Bastard," she clipped.

"Baby, please," Aaron said, taking a step toward me.

"Don't you 'baby' me," I demanded. "I just saw something that no wife, let alone a new mother, needs to see her husband doing. You just lost me, so I hope it was worth it."

"I promise it was just sex," he declared. "It didn't mean anything. Please, Chasey, we're a family."

9

"You've got to be kidding me," I countered. "Just sex? Just sex?! Are you serious right now?"

"Chasey, baby, it's been a long time," he reasoned.

I wanted to scream. If it hadn't been for the fact that I had my little girl in my arms, I would have allowed my new gut instincts to kick in. Those instincts were telling me to claw his eyes out.

"A long time?" I repeated. "Oh, I'm so sorry, Aaron. I was put on pelvic rest for the last eight weeks of my pregnancy and then managed to push a baby out of my vagina just five weeks ago. I should be more understanding of everything *you've* been through over the last thirteen weeks. What was I thinking? How insensitive of me, during all of that, not to be concerned about you getting your dick wet."

I couldn't believe him.

Did he think this had been fun for me?

I wasn't happy about it any more than he was, but I made the sacrifice I did for our daughter. It was heartbreaking to think he couldn't do the same.

"Excuse me, miss?"

My head snapped to the left, and my lips parted as my eyes widened.

Maybe I'd just made all of this up in my head. Maybe having a baby made new mothers so exhausted that once they fell asleep, dreams took over and played tricks on their minds.

Beck Emerson was there.

He was just standing there.

Beck wasn't some long lost friend or anything like that.

Nope. He was the man who played the keyboard and synthesizer for the world's biggest industrial rock band, My Violent Heart, and he was just standing right there beside me.

What was he doing here?

Better yet, why was he talking to me?

I had been stunned into silence.

WISH

The only thing I could do other than stare at the gorgeous specimen beside me was gently stroke my hands up and down my daughter's backside. I'd always done that as a way to comfort her, but now I had to wonder if I was doing it to comfort myself.

Unfazed by my reaction, Beck asked, "Is there anything I can do to help?"

God, his voice was so gentle, so caring, I wanted to cry.

I hesitated briefly, but ultimately shook my head. "No. I just found out my husband is cheating on me. Actually, correction. He's now my soon-to-be ex-husband."

"Do you want me to kick his ass?" Beck offered. Judging by the look on his face, he was hoping I'd give him my blessing.

Unfortunately, before I could do that, Aaron shouted, "Hey! You can't do that! I'll have you arrested for assault."

Beck looked in Aaron's direction and ordered, "Shut up, dickwad. I'm talking to your wife."

I completely understood the intention behind his words and truly appreciated them, but I had to correct him. I leaned closer and said, "Soon-to-be ex-wife."

Beck returned his gaze to me, and his lips twitched. "Why don't we go for a walk outside?" he suggested. "You don't need to be around this douchebag any longer, not when you've got this sweet little baby in your arms."

No, I didn't.

And at the mention of my daughter, I felt the reality of the situation hit me. This was going to be a nightmare.

"Okay," I rasped, turning fully toward him.

Beck shifted his body, reached his hand behind me, and allowed it to settle at the small of my back.

Tingles shot up my spine as he urged me in the direction of the exit.

Once we were outside, he asked, "Are you okay?"

"No," I answered honestly.

"How can I help you?" he pressed.

I shook my head as we made our way through the parking lot. "I wish I knew the answer to that," I said. "I knew this was happening, and despite it, I still wasn't prepared to see it in action."

"I'm so sorry this happened to you," Beck lamented.

"Yeah," I murmured.

We came to a stop beside my car, and I turned to face him again.

"What's your daughter's name?" he asked.

For the first time all day, I smiled. "Luna," I said.

Beck returned my smile, glanced down at Luna, and replied, "She's adorable."

"Thank you. She's my whole world," I shared.

I don't know what compelled me to tell him that. Maybe it was that he was who he was and had just witnessed what took place inside the hotel lobby. I don't know. I just wanted him to know that I wasn't some woman who went around starting fights in public places with her husband.

"I'm sure she is," he responded. "And did I hear correctly inside? Your name is Chasey, right?"

"Yes."

He grinned at me and said, "It's really nice to meet you, Chasey. I'm Beck."

I let out a laugh. "Yeah, I knew that," I told him.

He shrugged. "Hey, I never like to assume that people know who I am," he returned.

I knew who he was. And if my life hadn't just imploded, I might have considered what could be, even though it would only be a dream.

But that wasn't the case.

So, I said, "Well, I should probably go and get her home."

Something flashed in his face, but as quickly as it was there, it was gone. "Right. Yeah."

I worked to remove the carrier from Luna's tiny body while I kept a firm hold on her. Beck stood there watching me.

I didn't mind, though. If I was able to get one last look at him before I pulled out of the lot, I'd take it.

After what just happened, I felt I deserved at least that much.

Once Luna, who was thankfully still asleep, was securely fastened in her car seat, I moved to open my door.

"Chasey?" Beck called.

I stopped with my hand on the doorframe and turned to look back at him. "Yeah?" I answered.

"Can I give you my number?" he asked.

"What?"

"Do you have your phone on you?" he questioned me. "I'd like to give you my number."

I had no idea what was going on.

"You… you would?"

He nodded and explained, "I just want to know that you've got a way to get in touch with me if there's anything I can do to help you. I know that whatever is going to happen now isn't going to be easy for you. If I can help, even if it's just to lend a listening ear, I'm happy to do it."

"Oh, uh, wow," I marveled. "That's really kind of you."

When he didn't respond to that, I realized he was waiting for me to get out my phone. I reached into my purse, pulled it out, unlocked it, and held it out to him. He took it, programmed his number in, and handed it back to me.

"Anything you need, Chasey, I'm serious," he deadpanned. "Don't hesitate to reach out to me."

I didn't know what to say, so I simply nodded my understanding and rasped, "Thanks."

"Go ahead and get your baby home," he urged.

With that, I folded into the car and turned it on. Beck closed my door for me and waited in the parking lot as I pulled away.

Just before I turned out of it, I glanced in the rearview mirror and saw that he was still standing there watching my car.

I liked the way that felt too much.

What just happened?

I got the phone number of the hottest man in the world just minutes after finding my husband cheating on me. I thought things were bad when I walked into that hotel room. Even though I knew I'd never call him, having Beck's number programmed into my phone took a bit of the sting out of my day.

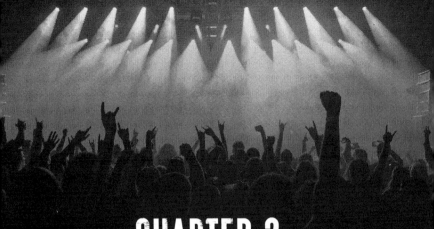

CHAPTER 2

Beck

I THOUGHT BY THE TIME I STEPPED ONTO THE ELEVATOR THAT I'D feel just a little less angry.

I wasn't so lucky.

There was still so much anger coursing through me, and I quickly came to the conclusion that it was going to take me a long time to calm myself down.

As I rode the elevator up to the floor Cash just texted and told me our room was on, I couldn't avoid recalling the scene we walked into not even thirty minutes ago.

My Violent Heart, the band that started without that name when I was thirteen, had arrived in New Hampshire to play a couple of shows. We'd ended up in this small town, and I was surprised that it seemed to have more excitement than some of the bigger cities.

Being a member of a rock band that toured all over the country and the world, I'd certainly seen my fair share of drama.

But this took the cake.

Because it wasn't just some stupid lover's quarrel.

This was about a woman—a new mother—catching her husband in the act of cheating. This was about an innocent little girl named Luna who was going to have to grow up in a world where her parents were divorced.

And as much as I hoped Chasey followed through on her declaration that the asshole who stood down in the lobby trying to convince her to work things out would be her ex-husband, I hated what it meant for her daughter.

In the back of my mind, though, I was slightly comforted by the fact that Chasey would make it so her daughter didn't feel the sting of her father's infidelity. How that woman managed to not completely break down when she saw what she did and heard the things her husband said to excuse his behavior was beyond me. There was no denying just how strong Chasey was.

And that asshole?

What kind of man cheats on his wife five weeks after she's given birth?

The ride up to our floor along with the walk through the halls to the two-bedroom suite I was sharing with Cash didn't do much to calm me down. I was just as livid now as I had been when I was standing in the lobby watching the scene unfold.

I was only grateful for the fact that I managed to keep it together long enough not to freak Chasey out.

But now that she'd left, I could deal with the frustration I felt.

Since I hadn't been there when Cash got our room keys, I knocked on the door to the suite and waited for him to open it.

Once he did, he made his way back to the couch in the main space and sat down. I stood there, continuing to think about what Chasey just went through.

It wasn't until Cash spoke that I snapped out of it and moved to sit on the chair off to the left of the sofa.

"Is everything alright?" he asked.

"Yeah, it's fine," I lied.

Instantly, I noticed Cash assessing me and knew that he knew I'd just lied. Considering we'd known each other since we were in kindergarten, that was no surprise. It also wasn't a surprise when he called me out on it.

"You're lying," he declared.

"Yep," I replied, not taking my eyes off the television. I wasn't paying attention to what was actually on; I was still just trying to calm myself down. I hadn't managed to do that before I clipped, "That guy is a fucking asshole."

"I can't say I don't agree," Cash remarked.

"Shit. That baby was only five weeks old," I muttered.

Way younger than I had been. Way younger than my sister had been. Our father walked out when I was six and Sadie was two. Our mom worked her tail off to take care of us, and she did it. But I knew things would have been easier for her if our dad had stuck around.

"Are you planning to do something about this?" Cash asked. "How was... what was her name, when she left?"

"Chasey," I answered. "And I talked with her for a while to make sure she was okay. I mean, how good can a woman who's just recently given birth to a baby feel when she *walks in* on her husband cheating on her? Anyway, before she got back in her car and took off, I gave her my personal number and told her to call if there was anything I could do to help her."

Of course, those were my words to Cash because I didn't understand how it was possible that a new mother would feel anything but devastation if she witnessed what Chasey had just witnessed. Despite what I thought, Chasey managed to keep it together surprisingly well.

Maybe it was a mom thing.

They just kept going. No matter what happened, no matter what things came along and tried to knock them down, they'd get right back up. Moms were the real superheroes.

Cash cocked an eyebrow at me. I knew exactly what he was thinking. He thought I had made a mistake in giving Chasey my number.

"Do you think that was smart?" he asked.

I knew Cash was just looking out for me. It wasn't uncommon, given our lifestyle, that a woman would come along and attempt to exploit us for money. Or sex.

More often than not, it was the sex they were after, which I guess worked for everyone in most cases.

There was no doubt Cash wasn't referring to Chasey being after sex. He was worried that she just landed herself in a shitty situation. We obviously didn't know anything about her or her finances, but divorces were rarely cheap. Not only that, the life of a single mother wasn't typically easy.

Cash knew that I had a soft spot in my heart for single moms, and the last thing he wanted was for me to get taken advantage of.

Oddly enough, this was one situation where I would not have minded being used.

Even still, I doubted Chasey was the kind of woman who'd do something so grimy. That was why I shot back, "I don't give a fuck if it was or not. I can always change my number, but she might not have anyone there to have her back. To me, it was worth the risk."

And it was.

If that woman needed help, and I could give it to her, why wouldn't I?

Cash nodded his understanding and accepted my choice.

That was about what I would have expected, too.

Because the truth was that when it all came down to it, that's how things worked with any of us in the band. We'd been together for so long—Cash, Killian, and I had started it all—that it went well beyond just making music together. It went beyond touring.

It was about family and friendship.

Yes, we partied hard, we had good times together, and we enjoyed the life we built together.

WISH

But deep down, I'd always look out for Cash, Killian, Walker, Holland, and Roscoe the same as they'd look out for me. That's just what you did with people you cared about, people who were just like your family. Cash, Killian, Walker, and Roscoe were like brothers to me while Holland was like a second sister. I couldn't imagine turning my back on them, and I was certain they felt the same.

So even when they did things like Cash just did by asking if what I'd just done in giving Chasey my number was smart, I tried to understand that it was always coming from a good place, even if I snapped at him when giving him my response.

But that was part of it, too. Your family knew who you were, how you reacted, and they'd allow you the opportunity to vent those frustrations when you needed it. They also knew when you needed time alone to decompress.

After sitting there for a long time thinking about it all, I stood and said, "I'm jumping in the shower. Maybe that'll help cool me off. Who would have thought some small town like this could have so much drama?"

"Well, it's only Thursday, and we don't leave until Monday, so there's plenty of time for more to be had if that's what you're looking for," Cash noted.

I grunted, feeling frustration wash over me.

As I walked away toward the second bedroom in the suite, the only thought running through my mind was that I wasn't looking for any more drama. Having the chance to see Chasey again would have been great, but I knew better than to think that I'd actually see her.

A new mom who just learned that her husband was cheating on her wasn't going to have the time or probably even the energy or desire to go out for a night of fun.

I might have wanted it for her, but this was life. I'd learned a long time ago that life didn't always go the way I wanted. All anyone could do was suck it up and roll with the punches.

A few minutes later, I was standing in the shower and couldn't stop my mind from drifting to Chasey.

Even as tired as I knew she was, I still thought she looked beautiful. Obviously, I couldn't speak about what it had been like while she was pregnant, but there was no denying that motherhood looked good on her.

Chasey had been wearing a pair of shorts, which showed off her long legs. I didn't know if she worked out regularly or what, but it was evident her legs were strong. Her long, blonde hair with loose waves was pulled back away from her face and fastened together at the nape of her neck with a band.

And curves.

The woman had a gorgeous ass, something I noticed immediately after I walked into the hotel.

Just thinking about her ass and her legs, I felt myself growing hard. As the water ran down my body and thoughts of the gorgeous woman with long blonde hair, gorgeous legs, and the kindest eyes I'd ever looked into that were a mix of varying shades of yellow and green, I tried and failed to avoid giving in to the urge to make myself come.

After lathering up one hand and gripping my cock firmly, I pressed the other palm to the wall of the shower and started to stroke myself.

Maybe it was wrong to feel this way about a woman who'd just experienced what Chasey had. I was sure that sex was the last thing on her mind right now.

But the thought of her legs alone was enough to have me forgetting all about right and wrong. I continued to stroke and envisioned having those legs wrapped around me, having her thighs thrown over my shoulders while I buried my face in her pussy.

It didn't take me long to get myself worked up to the point of no return. Before I had even expected it to happen, all the muscles in my entire body clenched, and I came hard. I found it surprising that after being around Chasey for not even an hour that I was already reacting to her like this.

Just one short conversation was all it took.

Despite the physical release I'd just had, I could still feel the remnants of anger over Chasey's situation lingering behind. In the blink of an eye, there was about to be another single mom in the world.

I fucking hated it.

On that thought, I finished in the shower and turned the water off.

Once I got myself dressed, I sat down with my phone in my hand and looked out the window of the hotel room.

Visions of a pretty blonde with gorgeous legs danced in my mind.

I shook my head in disbelief and a bit of frustration.

All that Chasey was in just the physical sense was exquisite. The fact that her husband, or soon-to-be ex-husband as she liked to refer to him, had her and thought he could step out on her just showed how ridiculously stupid he was.

Looking the way he did, it was a wonder how he even managed to score a woman as beautiful as Chasey. He didn't even compare.

And maybe it shouldn't all be about looks. But the truth was that any man with half a brain would have taken one look at her and realized how lucky they were that she'd even give them the time of day. I couldn't imagine why her husband would risk losing her.

I realized I didn't understand the inner workings of their relationship, but in my opinion, there was nothing that justified his behavior. Even if he no longer wanted to be with her, even if he no longer loved her, he could have respected her as the mother of his child and been honest with her.

He clearly thought she was the one who was lucky to have

him. That whole idea made me laugh. If that was what he thought, he was obviously clueless.

It was at that point when I realized I couldn't focus on that guy. It was only making me angrier.

I sighed as I returned my thoughts to Chasey. I really hoped she was going to take me up on my offer and call me. Even though I'd just jerked off in the shower thinking about her, this wasn't about sex for me.

There was this overwhelming urge and desire in me to help her. I knew, especially if she followed through with a divorce like she should, that it was going to be tough.

Hell, it was going to be tough for her if she didn't follow through with it.

Either way, I knew Chasey would spend her days doing her best to raise her daughter and give her what she needed. The only difference would be whether she'd have to do it with him by her side and the reminder of what he did staring her in the face every day, or if she'd be doing it on her own.

Neither situation would be easy, and if I could help her simply by giving her a shoulder to cry on or just a listening ear when she needed to vent, I'd do it.

I'd do it not only for Chasey but for her daughter, too.

Because I was once that kid. The kid who had the mom that had been betrayed and let down by the man she loved. If me stepping in to help Chasey made it so that she was a little less stressed, or a little less burned out, it was worth it. If she had that, it might give her whatever she needed to be an even better mom; it might help her shield her daughter from what I witnessed as a kid. Luna wouldn't have to see her mom exhausted and defeated.

So, I'd do it for Chasey, and I'd do it expecting nothing in return, even if I'd silently hope for more.

Even though she had just left the hotel not that long ago, I gripped my phone in my hand a little tighter, willing it to ring.

WISH

The logical part of my brain knew that she had a five-week-old baby. That alone was enough to keep her mind occupied. Add to that the realization that her husband was cheating, and there was no doubt I was the last thing on her mind.

But there was the other part of my brain that wanted things to be different. For me, yes, but mostly for her. I knew I wasn't going to get my way.

Not liking the way I felt, realizing my shower did little to help how I was feeling, I knew I needed to find another way to bring myself back down and cope. And I knew there was one of two ways to make that happen. Talking to my mom. Or talking to my sister.

I was very close with the both of them, and I was very protective of them.

It didn't matter that I was on tour. I still tried to talk with them regularly. They both still lived in Pennsylvania, and whenever I was home, I always made the effort to visit and spend time with them.

For now, after today's events, I settled on calling my mom. In the back of my mind, I figured it'd be better for me to hear her voice, know that she was happy, and remind myself that no matter what life threw at her, she got through it.

My hope was that in the same way I was always there to look out for them that my mom would be able to make me feel better about what happened today. She'd give me the reassurance that just like her, Chasey would come out of this on the other side and would be happier than ever.

On that thought, I rested my heels up on the coffee table, found my mom's name in the list of recent calls on my phone, and tapped on the screen.

It wasn't going to be the same as talking to Chasey, but I knew I'd feel better in the end.

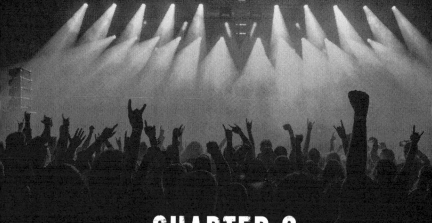

CHAPTER 3

Beck

"**I** CAN'T BELIEVE I FORGOT WHAT THAT WAS LIKE."
I looked over at my best friend since kindergarten and said, "Yeah, me too."

Cash didn't hesitate to share, "It kind of makes me want to rethink what we're doing. I mean, I'm not saying we should stop doing the bigger cities and venues, but last night felt good."

He was referring to our impromptu performance last night at Granite, a bar in the small town of Finch, New Hampshire. The same town that I'd met Chasey just over two weeks ago.

Last night's show was the first time in a very long time that we played for such a small crowd. It was definitely reminiscent of the early days of being a member of My Violent Heart.

I loved it.

Cash loved it.

I had a feeling the rest of the band did, too.

But there was one thing I didn't like about any of this.

It had been just over two weeks since we left New Hampshire to continue with our tour. I'd made progress since we left. My days had been filled with traveling and performing, so there wasn't a whole lot of time for me to be caught up in anything else.

Okay, that wasn't entirely true.

Ever since we left, I had thought about Chasey. But those thoughts were typically when I was in bed ready to go to sleep.

She never called me after I gave her my number in the parking lot of the hotel, and I started to accept the cold hard truth that she wasn't going to call, either.

I hated it, but I couldn't say that I didn't understand it. There was, undoubtedly, a lot on her plate right now.

For the most part, I'd been doing okay. We were touring and playing shows several times a week for crowds of thousands. Life was good.

But all the progress I'd made in trying to forget the woman who caught my attention in this small town had come to an abrupt halt.

We came back here following our show on Wednesday evening. It was now Sunday, and we were in the middle of a week-long break. None of us had any familial ties to the area; we'd done it for Cash.

As it turned out, he'd been having a hard time forgetting the woman he'd met during our first trip here, Demi. I couldn't say I didn't understand that feeling just a bit, and since I knew how much it was affecting him, I had no problem agreeing to the trip back.

I could have gone on to the next destination on the tour and done a bit of relaxing in a different location, but I didn't really want to. There was some small part of me that I think was secretly hoping I'd somehow run into Chasey again while I was here.

But it had been a few days now, I hadn't seen her, and I was no longer feeling as unaffected as I had been while we were out touring.

I was willing to do anything I could to distract myself. And if I could get that distraction by talking to Cash about music, I'd take it.

"It really did," I responded. "It was a nice change of pace to be able to play for a smaller crowd."

"Yeah, and being able to interact with them after the show was even better," he added.

I rolled my eyes. "You didn't exactly stick around as long as the rest of us to do that, though, did you?" I countered.

Cash shrugged and grinned at me. "I didn't want to risk Demi leaving before I had the chance to see her again," he explained.

"And did you?" I asked.

He nodded. "Yeah."

I was glad for that. It was the whole reason we'd come back here, so to know that he was taking advantage of every opportunity while we were here to show her how serious he was, particularly when the woman had made it clear she wasn't interested in him, was a good thing.

"How did it go?" I asked.

"It's definitely getting better," he answered. "She's still holding herself back, but I'd say she's softening just a touch toward me. At least she's not sneering at me every time she sees me now."

I let out a laugh. "Well, that's good news then."

"Yeah," he returned. "What about you? Have you tried searching for Chasey since we've been back?"

Tipping my head to the side, I asked, "Why would I do that?"

Cash shot me an incredulous look. "Do you think I'm an idiot?" he countered. "Beck, I've known you since we were just kids in elementary school. You think I don't know that you're just as hung up on that woman as I am on Demi?"

"I'm not hung up on her," I lied.

"You gave her your number," he pointed out.

"Yes, I did," I confirmed. "Because she just found out that her husband was cheating on her, and she has a brand-new baby. I was just trying to be nice and help her out."

"Are you saying that since you haven't heard from her that you're not even remotely concerned with how she's doing?" Cash asked.

It was one thing to deny the overwhelming attraction I felt to Chasey, but it would have been something else entirely to act like I didn't care at all.

"Of course, I'm concerned," I told him. "But I'd be concerned about any woman who went through what she did. That's all it is."

Cash shot me an assessing look. In his expression, I could see that he didn't believe a single word that had come out of my mouth this entire conversation.

"Deny it all you want," he finally declared. "You know you hate the fact that she hasn't called. If I were you, I'd talk to Jagger. He might be able to help you locate her."

Jagger.

I hadn't considered that.

Jagger was one of the guys on rotation as part of our security. He worked for Harper Security Ops, which was a private investigation and security firm located in Pennsylvania and was owned by Killian's cousin, Royce.

Cash had a point. If I wanted to find out where Chasey was and how she was doing, Jagger could probably help me do that.

But because I didn't want Cash getting any crazy ideas and spreading them to the rest of the band, I simply replied, "I'm not a stalker, man. I gave her my number to call if she needed anything. That's all it is. Nothing more, nothing less."

At that, Cash decided to let it go.

"Alright, Beck. Whatever you say," he returned.

I returned my gaze to the television in front of me. I wasn't paying attention to what was on, though.

Instead, I was replaying the conversation I'd just had with Cash in my head. I didn't want to act like Chasey was nobody special, but I also didn't want to act like it mattered to me if she called.

The truth was that I didn't want to get my hopes up.

After watching my father walk out the door when I was just six years old, I tried not to ever really expect anything in life. For a long time, we struggled. My mom did everything she could to take care of Sadie and me and give us a good life. She did. And because she worked so hard, my sister and I both grew up to be successful.

Sadie and I were both creative souls. But where I was into music, my sister preferred a much quieter and simpler life. She was an artist and loved to paint. Though she wasn't living the life I was, Sadie still did very well for herself.

And we owed that all to our mom. She'd poured all of her energy and effort into caring for us and making sure we had everything we needed to live comfortably and pursue our dreams.

But I knew it came at a cost to her. My mom would never admit that, though. She'd tell me I was crazy for ever thinking that what she did for her children was anything other than her heart's deepest desire.

I guess in a way it was; however, there was no denying that she never had any time or extra money for herself. My sister and I appreciated her more than I think either of us could ever tell her with words.

If nothing else, I was grateful that we both managed to do something good with our lives that made her proud. There wasn't a mother on the planet who could come close to having the same level of pride for her children as Sandy Emerson.

Yes, even after her husband walked out on her, my mother kept his last name. That was just another sacrifice she made for her children.

So, although life turned out better than I could have ever imagined for myself, it came at a great cost.

I didn't want to have any preconceived ideas or notions about anything as it pertained to Chasey because I refused to allow myself to feel disappointed. I'd been dealt a lot of fortune in my life, and I didn't think it was right to expect I'd get more.

Or, at least, I didn't think I'd get more without some incredible sacrifice.

The problem with that was that in this situation with Chasey, I wasn't sure I would be the one sacrificing. That wouldn't be fair to her.

On that thought, I came to one conclusion. There was someone I needed to talk to today. From there, I'd figure out how to proceed.

"Everything okay?"

That came from Jagger.

"Yeah," I answered. "Can I come in and talk to you a minute?"

Jagger stepped back and allowed me to come inside his hotel room. It was about an hour after my conversation with Cash, and I'd managed to discreetly locate which room Jagger was in. The last thing I needed was anyone else in the band knowing what I was doing just yet.

"What's going on?" Jagger asked after I stepped inside the room and the door closed behind me.

"I wanted to ask you about the services Harper Security provides that go beyond personal security," I started. "Specifically, I'm curious to learn about the investigative services you offer."

Jagger shot me a questioning look. "What do you want to know?" he asked.

"I want to know what's involved in finding someone," I told him.

"Someone?" he repeated. "Does this someone have a name? Do we know it?"

I nodded. "Yes. But this is purely hypothetical right now," I insisted.

Quite frankly, I didn't know why I was being so secretive. Maybe it's because I was standing here talking to Jagger about locating a woman I'd spoken to only once in my life.

"Alright," he responded. "So, that's a good start. Any information you have on the person is beneficial. Obviously, things like date of birth and perhaps a location would be a huge benefit. If you know where they work, that'll really narrow things down."

"And what happens once you locate the individual?" I asked.

Tipping his head to the side, Jagger countered, "What do you want to have happen?"

I stared at him without answering. I didn't know. Truthfully, I didn't even know if this was something I should follow through on. I mean, was I really going to take it to this level?

Chasey had my number, and she hadn't reached out. Maybe that told me all that I needed to know.

"I'm not sure yet," I admitted.

Nodding his understanding, Jagger explained, "Well, if it's simply about finding someone, we can do that. We locate the individual, give you the information we find, and you get to decide what you want to do with it."

I swallowed hard. Having that information might be too tempting. "What if..." I trailed off. I couldn't believe I was actually going to ask him this.

"What if what?" he responded, urging me to continue.

"What if I didn't want that information? What if I just wanted you to locate the individual and report back to me on their current situation?"

Jagger's brows pulled together. "Their current situation?"

"Yes. If I just wanted to know that this person was doing okay and not struggling, would you be able to find that out and tell me?" I wondered.

"I don't see any reason why we couldn't," he said. "Unless there was some extenuating circumstance, that shouldn't be a problem at all."

I dropped my gaze to the ground and thought a moment. When I lifted my eyes to Jagger again, I asked, "How long would it take?"

He shrugged. "That depends on the information we have," he answered. "It could be a few days, or it could take months."

I nodded. I had to imagine that it wouldn't take Jagger or the rest of the team at Harper Security very long to locate Chasey. I mean, how many Chasey's could there be in New Hampshire?

After taking a bit more time to consider everything, I said, "Thanks for the information, Jagger."

"That's it?" he asked, cocking an eyebrow.

"Yeah."

The expression on Jagger's face indicated he was certainly intrigued by the discussion we just had. Despite it, he never gave into the curiosity by pressing me further. He simply offered, "If you decide you want any help, don't hesitate to ask."

"Thanks."

With that, I turned and walked out of his room.

I couldn't do it. As much as I might have felt a pull to her and wanted to know that she was doing alright, I decided against having Jagger and Harper Security do anything.

For now, anyway.

It felt creepy.

And I thought that the last thing Chasey would need or want is to feel like she had some crazy stalker on her hands.

So, it was difficult to turn it down, but I knew I had to do it. I would trust that she was doing alright because she hadn't called.

If our paths were meant to cross again at any point in time, they would. Until then, knowing I'd be leaving here in a couple days, I'd go back to touring, living, and enjoying the life I had. If I was meant to have more good in my life, I'd take it as it came.

But I had to be honest with myself. I'd already received a lifetime of bounty. What were the chances that more was waiting out there for me?

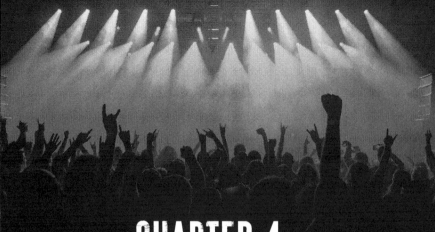

CHAPTER 4

Chasey

TODAY WAS THE WORST DAY OF MY LIFE.

Considering it had been two months since I walked in on the act of my husband cheating on me, that was saying something.

The truth was, as horrible as that had been to witness, I expected it. Of course, I never could have imagined what I'd actually see, but I had certainly anticipated some form of intimacy between him and another woman.

Perhaps that was why I hadn't cried much about it. I knew what was coming.

Obviously, it hadn't been easy. I struggled every day to cope with my new reality. I was now a single mom, only a few more weeks away from having my divorce finalized.

There were times now when I thought about how much had happened since that day at the hotel.

I drove back to the house I rented with Aaron, the home we had intended to grow our family in until we could save up enough to buy our own. About an hour after I had gotten there, he returned. I cringed every time I thought about what he did in that hour.

Luckily, I was prepared when he walked through the door.

"I'll be sleeping in the guest room for the next few weeks," I started. "And I'll be taking steps to start divorce proceedings immediately."

"Chasey, we need to talk about this," he begged. "I made a mistake."

Shaking my head, I disputed, "A mistake is not remembering to get the oil changed on the car. Knowingly paying for a hotel room so that you could have sex with another woman is the very opposite of a mistake. It was intentional, it was calculated, and it was utterly disrespectful to our marriage."

"I know. I know," he insisted. "I'm so sorry. What can I do to make this right?"

"You can make sure to not fight me on the impending divorce," I started. "And you can be the father your daughter deserves. That's it. There's nothing else I want from you."

"But we're a family," he reasoned.

My brows shot up as my eyes nearly fell out of my head. "Really, Aaron? Because you could have fooled me. Family means love, respect, and loyalty. You have none of that for me or our marriage. All I want right now is for you to leave me alone."

"That's why we're in this position," he clipped as he rolled his eyes.

"Excuse me?"

"All you've wanted is for me to leave you alone," he argued, his voice getting louder. "I'm a man who has needs, you know?"

God, he was such a disgusting pig. "I know. You already made that *very* clear," I returned.

"What did you expect me to do? It's been so long."

"I expected you to stick by my side through this," I informed him. "I expected you to put aside your own selfish needs for the sake of your daughter."

"Luna was born weeks ago."

"And? The doctor said I shouldn't be having sex for a

minimum of six weeks after delivering her," I reminded him. "I'd love to know how quickly you'd be *up* for the job if you had to push a baby out of your equipment."

Aaron huffed. "Oh, come on. I'm sure it's not that bad."

He had no idea. He'd never know. And I honestly didn't have the patience or energy to deal with him.

"You know what? I'm done with this conversation. You're unbelievable. Even if I had been cleared for it sooner, I wouldn't have done it. I'm exhausted, Aaron. I'm here doing my job as a mother and taking care of Luna while your only concern is your dick. I'm done." Waving my hand between the two of us, I continued, "Screw who you want because this is over."

With that, I turned and walked away. Seconds later, the front door slammed shut.

Aaron never came back that night. He did return the next day to pack a couple of bags. Without so much as a second glance at Luna or me, he took his things and left.

I cried that day.

But I didn't do it for me.

I did it for my daughter.

How had I been so blind to who Aaron really was? I didn't need his apologies. I didn't want his excuses. But Luna didn't deserve this. Her father didn't even care.

And even if I had wanted to believe that he was just taking time to cool off, I would have gotten my proof that wasn't the case as time went on. Aaron never returned.

In fact, he never even called. As it turned out, the relationship he had with the woman I had caught him with wasn't just about sex. They were seeing one another. He was living with her now.

If I hadn't been raised by a woman who did just enough to ensure that I survived, I might have been surprised by Aaron's lack of action, concern, and attention for his child. But I had a mother who didn't care about me. I had two parents who didn't care. I never met my father, and my mother hated me because my father left not long after I was born.

Anyone else might think that history was repeating itself, but I knew better.

Luna wouldn't know anything but love and care and compassion from me. I'd do anything in my power to be the mom she deserved. I'd be a better mother to her than the one that I had for myself. That was all I ever wanted anyway.

But now, two months after it all happened, I realized I wasn't going to get my wish. Today proved that.

The days leading up to today had been filled with anxiety and sadness as I prepared to do the one thing I told myself I'd never do once I had children.

Then I woke up this morning and took Luna to a babysitter. It was the most gut-wrenching and heartbreaking moment of my life having to leave her. It was the first time I had been separated from her since she was born. I hated every single minute of it.

My dream had always been to be a mom. Today, I wasn't that. Or, at least, I wasn't the version of a mom that I wanted to be.

But I had no choice.

The money ran out, and I needed to be able to keep a roof over our heads. I moved out of the house that Aaron and I had shared. It had more space than Luna and I needed, and I couldn't afford it.

At the very least, I was grateful for the fact that my best friend, Mara, was going to watch Luna for me on her days off. If nothing else, I was relieved to know that I was handing over my daughter's care for a few hours to someone I could trust. Not only that, Mara wasn't going to charge me. On the days that my best friend had to work, I had no choice but to put Luna in day care. I didn't know how I was going to survive that.

WISH

Thankfully, Mara was off today. I pulled up outside her townhouse, threw my car into park, and ran to the door.

A moment later, I was lifting Luna out of Mara's arms and smothering her with kisses. "I missed you so much, baby," I told her.

Luna didn't fuss at all. She took all the love I had to give to her and gobbled it up. That's what I was telling myself she was doing, anyway.

After giving her a bunch of attention, I looked up at Mara and asked, "How was she?"

"Perfect, as always," she told me. "She's honestly the best baby in the world."

I smiled and looked down at my girl. She really was the best.

"I can't even tell you how much I missed this little girl," I said.

Mara let out a laugh. "I have a pretty good idea," she returned. "How was your first day?"

"I hated it."

"Was it that bad?" she asked.

I continued to pepper kisses to the side of Luna's head as I considered how to best answer Mara's question. Eventually, I shrugged and explained, "It's not the job itself that's the problem. I just hate being away from Luna."

When things started to get to a point where I needed income, I had no choice but to take the first job that would pay enough to cover my expenses. Through the divorce proceeding, Aaron was ordered to pay child support. But the problem was that it was only a percentage of his meager income. There was no way we could survive on that alone.

That meant I ended up working my first day today as a mail clerk at the local post office. It would be steady income and set hours, which is precisely what I needed.

"It'll get easier," Mara assured me.

I wasn't sure I believed that. I couldn't imagine not feeling like my heart was being ripped out of my chest every time I left Luna to go to work.

"I don't know," I murmured.

"Listen, I was thinking about this today. If you want, I can come over to your place to watch her on the days that I'm off. This way, she'll be in her own crib for her naps. It wasn't bad here today at all, but I think it'll be better for Luna in the long run to be in her home," Mara offered.

"That would be a huge help," I said. "Are you sure you don't mind?"

Mara tipped her head to the side and smiled. "Not at all. You know I love this girl as if she were my own," she answered.

"Thank you, Mara. I really appreciate that. For now, I should probably get going, so I can get her home and have enough time to cuddle her until I have to go back to work tomorrow."

At that, Mara turned and gathered up Luna's diaper bag. After zipping it up, she held it out to me. "Call me if you need anything," she said.

Taking the bag from her, I slung it over my shoulder and promised, "I will. Thank you, again. Today would have been so much harder if it hadn't been for you."

"You know I'll always do whatever I can to help," she returned.

I did. She'd been the only person I could depend on throughout all of this. I had no siblings, I didn't know my father, and I hadn't spoken to my mother since I was old enough to take care of myself and move out of her house.

The closest thing I had to a parent now was Mara's parents, who I'd grown close to over the years.

Realizing things could be far worse, I always tried to remind myself that I had plenty to be grateful for. I had three people who loved my daughter and me. Some people didn't even have that.

WISH

I stopped myself at Mara's front door, turned back to focus my attention on her, and said, "Love you."

"Love you."

At that, with Luna's body held close to mine, I walked out and made my way to the car. After buckling her in, I got behind the wheel and drove us home.

For the next two and a half hours, I gobbled up every minute I had with Luna. I fed her, played with her, talked to her, and bathed her. I held off on making dinner for myself. I could do that after she was asleep. I didn't want a second I had with her to go to waste.

Before I knew it and well before I was ready, it was Luna's bedtime. If there was one thing I'd managed to accomplish over the last several weeks, it was getting her on a schedule. I had been worried about how starting my new job would affect her routine, but she didn't even seem to be remotely fazed by it.

Then again, she'd been with Mara. My best friend would have followed the schedule I'd given to her to make things as easy as possible on Luna and me. I had to wonder if that was going to be the case when I had to take her to day care tomorrow.

For now, I didn't want to focus on that. I simply wanted to spend the next few minutes bonding with my daughter while I nursed her to sleep.

So, that's what I did.

I loved that time with her. It was incredibly important and special to me, and I was glad that it was the one thing that hadn't been affected over the last two months. I enjoyed it so much that I often found myself sitting there in the glider, continuing to rock her, long after she'd fallen asleep.

That was precisely what happened tonight. In fact, I sat there even longer than normal, feeling myself get emotional.

It started to hit me just how much I missed being with her today. Just like that, the whole day was gone, and I'd missed out on hours of her life. I couldn't bear to think about how many more I'd miss.

Everything about what I felt in that moment was pushing me to want to wake up tomorrow morning, call the post office, and tell them that I quit. I wanted to. I wanted to do that more than anything.

But I couldn't.

Because even though I was missing out on full hours of Luna's life, I knew that my absence from her in that time was crucial to our survival. I couldn't give her the life I wanted her to have without doing something I didn't want to do.

That was what motherhood was all about, though. Sacrifice. Going to work and being away from Luna was a sacrifice I had no choice but to make.

Eventually, I stood from the glider and settled Luna in her crib. I turned on the baby monitor and gave her one last look. Then I walked out of the room and toward the kitchen.

As soon as I was there, I opened the refrigerator door and realized just how exhausted I was. There was no energy for a big, fancy meal. Quite frankly, I didn't see any point in that anyway. Why go through all the hassle of making a big meal like that when I had nobody to share it with anyway?

A sandwich was going to have to cut it tonight. I didn't have the strength or desire left in me for anything else. I did what I did to get to work today, and I gave my daughter everything I had left when I came home.

On that thought, I pulled out some bread, deli meat, lettuce, tomato, and mayo.

A few minutes later, I flopped down on the couch. I had the plate settled in my lap and the monitor resting on the cushion beside me.

Lifting my sandwich to my mouth in one hand, I reached for my purse with the opposite one. I pulled out my phone and did the same thing I'd been doing for weeks now. I tapped on the screen and went to my list of contacts. Then I allowed my finger to hover over one name.

Beck.

Beck Emerson.

With everything I'd been through since the day I met him, there hadn't been a single day that went by when I didn't sit and wonder what life would be like with someone like him. I hadn't stopped thinking about him and how kind he'd been to me.

A man like him, doing what he did for a living, didn't need to give me the time of day. But he removed me from a horrible situation that afternoon and offered me his number.

As much as I would have loved to have called him, I never had the courage.

I had to be honest with myself, too.

My lifestyle didn't exactly scream rock star. I was a new mom who hadn't even managed to keep her husband satisfied.

A man like Beck could chew me up and spit me out, especially when there was clearly no shortage of women for someone like him.

But I liked to live in the fantasy right now. It was the one thing that helped keep me from becoming completely depressed. I mean, Beck Emerson gave me his number. As long as I never called and gave him the opportunity to shut me down, I could always live with the knowledge that I'd gotten that.

I knew I'd never have a shot with him in a million years, but that didn't stop me from living out the fantasy in my mind every night.

By the time I finished my food, I had successfully refrained from allowing my finger to slip and fall onto Beck's name.

I needed a shower and my bed.

So, I gathered up the monitor, carried it into the bathroom, and wasted no time getting in the shower.

Twenty minutes later, after I'd showered and checked on

Luna one last time, I climbed into bed and allowed my mind to wander. It drifted to Beck, and that's when it happened.

It had been months—at least six of them—since I'd had sex. While it would have been nice to have the real thing, I realized I couldn't hold out forever hoping for something that would never happen. I simply needed to take matters into my own hands.

I rolled over, pulled my vibrator out of the bedside table, and slipped it between my legs. Between the extended suspension in sexual satisfaction and the visions of Beck that filled my mind, it didn't take me long.

By the time I closed my eyes and finally drifted, I realized I fell asleep with a smile on my face for the first time in a long time.

Sadly, that happiness and satisfaction didn't last long.

CHAPTER 5

Chasey

"**D**ON'T MAKE ME DRAG YOU OUT OF THERE."

I sighed. "I'm sorry. I'm not up to it tonight, Mara," I told her. "I just picked Luna up from day care, and I'm on my way home now. I have to get her inside and get her fed and bathed."

"Right. And then she'll be going down for the night before you even need to leave," Mara reasoned. "I'll even come over early so you can get yourself ready."

She wasn't going to take no for an answer. For a couple weeks now, Mara had been trying to convince me to go out with her. It had been two months since I started my job at the post office, Luna was five months old, and life hadn't exactly been all sunshine and rainbows.

I trudged through the day most days, hating every second I spent at my job. It wasn't anything against the actual work or even my coworkers. It simply hadn't been part of my plan. From the moment I found out I was pregnant, everything had changed. I was ecstatic, over the moon. I couldn't wait to be a mom.

But everything that I thought about how my life would be

after I gave birth was nothing like it had actually turned out to be.

Suffice it to say that I was taking it hard.

When I didn't respond to Mara, she spoke again. And this time, I couldn't miss the concern in her tone.

"Chasey, babe, I'm so worried about you," she started. "This is only going to be one night. You *deserve* one night out. You've been working your butt off for months now, and you've not done a single thing for yourself since before Luna was born."

"I'm a mom now," I reasoned.

"Yes, you are," she insisted. "And that's all the more reason why you need to make sure you're taking care of yourself. Luna needs you to be the best mom you can be. I've watched you over the last couple of months, and I see how sad you've been."

Mara wasn't exactly wrong about that.

Being the best mom I could be was all that mattered to me. But I'd have been lying if I said I wasn't feeling the least bit overwhelmed. My daughter was five months old, and her father hadn't seen her since he walked out months ago. It broke my heart whenever I thought about how badly I'd failed Luna.

So, I was sad and heartbroken.

Because not only was I not able to stay home with her, but I also couldn't make the man who should love her more than anything else in the world actually care about her.

It was devastating to know I'd chosen so poorly.

"I don't know," I mumbled.

"You… are… going… out… tonight," Mara ordered. "I'm not going to let you back out of this. Plus, I already talked to my mom, and she's so excited to come over to your place to stay with Luna."

"Where are we going to go?" I asked, not sure I had the stamina for much of anything.

"There's a relatively new bar in Finch called Granite," she answered. "I thought we'd go and check it out."

"I can't drink, Mara. I'm still breastfeeding," I reminded her as I pulled my car to a stop outside my apartment.

"That's okay," she assured me. "We'll call you the designated driver tonight. Just make sure you wear something sexy."

I wanted to laugh. If there was one thing I didn't feel, it was sexy. Something about learning your husband was cheating on you weeks after you gave birth did that to you.

"I'm not sure I've got anything that'll fit," I told her, opening my door.

"I'll come over early," she declared. "We'll figure it out."

Yep. There was no getting out of this. And considering how hard Mara had been pushing for me to go out with her over the last few weeks, I decided it was best to just do what she wanted me to do, so I could go back to being content with where my life ended up.

"I just got home. I need to get Luna out of the car."

"Okay. See you soon."

I disconnected the call with Mara, opened the back door, and got my smiling girl out of her seat. If there was anything in this world that could lift my mood, it was Luna. As much as I loved that, I didn't want to put that burden on her. It wasn't my daughter's job to make me happy. I needed to find a way to do that myself. I just wasn't quite sure how I was going to do it.

For the next two hours, I put all of my time, energy, and focus into my daughter. This was how it had been for me ever since I started working at the post office. I'd pick Luna up from day care on the days Mara didn't come here to watch her for me, and I'd devote everything I had left in me to her.

Of course, I dealt with serious mom guilt and constantly questioned whether I was giving her enough. I always wondered if she knew just how much I loved her.

Before I could get too far down that rabbit hole of feeling shame and remorse for how things had turned out, Mara showed up.

No sooner did I open the door when she waltzed in, looking utterly fabulous, and snatched Luna right out of my arms.

"Be careful," I warned her. "You don't want her to spit up on your dress."

Mara ignored me, looked at Luna, and said, "You won't spit up on your Auntie Mara, will you, Luni?"

Luna responded with a toothless grin. I loved knowing how much they adored each other, and I especially loved Mara's nickname for my girl.

Not wasting another moment, Mara pushed past me and declared, "Let's find you something to wear. My mom is going to be here within the hour."

I closed and locked the front door and followed behind her.

A few minutes later, Mara had shoved four different dresses into my hands. She sat down on the bed and said, "Luna and I want you to model for us."

"I can't wear any of these," I exclaimed as I held them out in front of my body.

Mara's face scrunched up. "Why not?"

Shooting her a look of disbelief, I shared, "One, I've gained some weight since the last time I wore them. Two, I'm a mom now. Three, two of these dresses show some serious cleavage. And four, I'm a mom now."

I watched as Mara took in a deep breath and prepared to launch into a lecture while Luna's tiny fist held on tightly to one of her toys in the middle of my bed.

"You are beautiful, Chasey," she began. "Yes, you've had a baby. But you didn't die. And now that you're breastfeeding, you've got gorgeous cleavage. Honestly, I'm seriously jealous of your boobs right now. Between them and your legs, which I've always been envious of, I'm not sure why you think you can't put on one of these dresses. If they don't fit, we'll move on. But I think you're going to be surprised at how great they look once you get them on."

I sighed. It was better to do this and get it over with. Worst case, I would throw on a pair of jeans and a T-shirt and call it a day.

One dress in, and I was already feeling defeated. I couldn't even zip it up. I managed to get the second dress on, but I hated how I felt in it.

"No way," I declared. "I look awful."

"You do not look awful, but I agree that this is not the one," Mara replied.

If there was one thing I could say about my best friend, it was that I knew she wouldn't lie to me. She wouldn't tell me that I looked hideous, but she'd encourage me to find something else if she thought I was wearing something unflattering.

That, in my opinion, was the mark of a true friend. She'd never tear you down, but she'd make sure you didn't make a fool of yourself either.

I loved her.

When I put on the third dress, I found myself looking in the mirror just a bit longer. It fit, and I didn't feel horrible in it.

"I like this one," Mara remarked.

"I don't hate it," I returned.

She laughed and said, "That's a start. Try the last one."

As quickly as I could, I pulled off the dress that was currently in the running to be the one, and slipped the next one over my head. Actually, it was more like I had tugged it on and less like I slipped it on. Once I'd adjusted the dress in all the spots it needed adjusting, I looked in the mirror, and my eyes widened.

"Holy crap," I marveled.

"That one. Don't even think about putting the other one back on," Mara ordered.

It was a long-sleeved black dress that stopped just above mid-thigh. For years, the fabric that had covered my breasts in the plunging V-neckline was always a bit loose. Now, not so much. My breasts completely filled it out. Just beneath my breasts to the hem of the dress was ruched. The style of the dress had done wonders for hiding the pouch that still remained from my pregnancy. And my booty had filled out the back side of the dress substantially better than it used to.

"I'm not sure I can wear this," I told Mara.

"Are you kidding me? You look incredible."

"Yes, okay, but—"

Mara held her hand up and cut me off. "Don't you dare tell me that you're a mom and can't wear that," she demanded. "You are wearing that dress tonight. You look amazing in it, and I know you feel good in it. Gosh, Chasey, Luna gave you curves that I'd kill for."

I tipped my head to the side and allowed my gaze to shift to my baby. I couldn't stop the smile from forming on my face. My daughter had given me this body, and I looked damn good in this dress.

"Okay," I agreed. "I'll wear it."

Mara flopped back on the bed and cheered, "Did you hear that, Luni? Mommy is going to have all the boys looking at her tonight."

"Stop," I demanded. "I am not going anywhere to look for a boy tonight."

"You're right. We need to find you a *man*," she corrected herself.

I cocked an eyebrow. "I don't want one of those either," I told her. "Besides, I'm not exactly the prime candidate for someone who's looking anyway. Newly single mom? That doesn't exactly scream a great time for any guy."

Mara sat up and nodded. "Yeah. That's why any of them who thought like that would be a waste of your time," she noted. "But that shouldn't dissuade you from getting out there, feeling good about yourself, and having some fun."

At that, I decided not to argue.

Mara was right. I was going to go out tonight and try my

best to have a good time. The two of us hadn't gone out like this in so long, so if nothing else, I'd definitely have some fun. And maybe she had a point. I needed to do something like this every now and then so I could be an even better mom to Luna.

On that thought, I pulled the dress off. I needed to get my hair and makeup done before I had to nurse Luna to sleep. My plan was to get myself completely ready, minus the dress, put my daughter down for the night, and then get the dress back on before Mara and I took off.

Not quite an hour later, we were doing just that. Of course, that wasn't until after I'd gone over every possible thing I could think of with Mara's mom, Ruth.

Though there was still a small part of me that felt wrong about leaving Luna, I found reassurance in the fact that Ruth was watching over her. I knew my girl was in good hands. And because she was sleeping, I didn't feel like I was missing out on whole hours of her life like I did when I went to work.

Since I wasn't going to be drinking tonight, I drove. Mara told me where to go, and it wasn't much later when I started feeling a bit uneasy.

When we got out of the car and I just stood there, Mara asked, "What's wrong?"

"Why are there so many people here? Has it been that long since I've been out?" I countered.

Mara bit her lip and looked away. Instantly, I knew there was something she wasn't telling me.

"What is going on?" I asked, feeling my body grow tense.

She shook her head. "Nothing. It's probably just a bit busier here than you'd expect because they occasionally have live bands play. There's one playing tonight," she reasoned.

"Oh," I replied as I moved toward her and we started to walk toward the front door.

As soon as we got inside, she went on, "Of course, this isn't just any band playing here tonight."

"What?"

Mara stopped, turned toward me, and gave me a look that told me she was worried about how I was going to react to whatever she was about to tell me. She hesitated briefly before she shared, "My Violent Heart is playing here tonight. Beck is going to be here."

"What?!" I gasped.

Mara knew about Beck because she was my best friend. When I told her about what happened the day at the hotel when I caught Aaron, I couldn't leave out the part about Beck and the rest of his band walking in on the fight between Aaron and me. I also hadn't held back from sharing that Beck had given me his number and told me to call him if I needed anything.

For weeks, Mara begged me to reach out to him. Obviously, I refused to ever follow up on giving him a call.

"This is going to be a good thing," she insisted.

"Please tell me you don't honestly believe that," I begged her. "Mara, it's going to be ruined now."

"What is?"

"The fantasy."

Her brows pulled together. "What fantasy?"

I closed my eyes and let out a deep sigh. "The one where I convinced myself that Beck was actually interested in me and gave me his number genuinely hoping I'd call him," I answered.

"That isn't a fantasy, Chasey," she said. "That's what really happened."

I shook my head. She didn't understand. If she had witnessed what happened that day in the hotel, she would have realized that Beck was just doing something to turn around the shitty day of a woman scorned.

If he saw me now, he wouldn't even remember me. And then I'd need to accept the harsh reality of how that made me feel. The fantasy was way better than what my new reality was going to be, even if it meant that I allowed my finger to hover over his name in my phone for years to come.

"We should go," I suggested. "I don't think I can do this."

"You can," she insisted as she took me by the hand and dragged me across the room.

Once we were there, I tried to find a way to calm myself down. There were so many people here. It's not like I was going to stand out.

But I was going to have to see him.

I was going to have to see him and watch him perform on stage. I would probably see how women would throw themselves at him and how he'd gobble that all up. And the whole time, I'd do nothing but wish.

Wish that I could have had a shot with him.

As I pointed my gaze up to the front of the bar where things were clearly being set up in preparation for the band to play, Mara called, "Chasey?"

I looked back at her and replied, "Yeah?"

"I think you should prepare yourself," she said.

"For what?"

Her eyes slid to the side and behind me. "Incoming."

My eyes widened in fear, and I spun around. Barely a moment later, my gaze landed on him.

Beck was walking toward me, and he had a huge grin on his face.

I stood there wondering if it was too late to believe that a wish could come true.

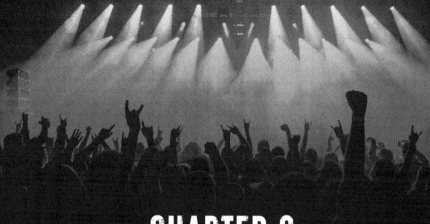

CHAPTER 6

Chasey

"**H**i, Chasey."

I blinked my eyes in surprise. He remembered me. How was that even possible?

Obviously, in my world, the likelihood of me ever forgetting I had an interaction with him was slim. But Beck remembered *me*? I couldn't begin to grasp the concept. He had to have encountered hundreds of people, if not thousands, and yet he hadn't forgotten my name.

I was blown away.

"Um, hey," I rasped.

"How's Luna doing? She's got to be what... five or six months old now?"

The shock didn't end. He remembered me. He remembered *my daughter*. Her own father hadn't bothered to see her, but this man met her once when she was five weeks old and he hadn't forgotten anything about her.

I wanted to cry.

I didn't do that, though.

Instead, I smiled and said, "She's just over five months old now, and she's doing really great. Thank you for asking, Beck."

He hadn't stopped smiling since I'd made eye contact with him when he was strolling across the bar toward me. How he hadn't been mobbed on the way over was beyond me. Maybe people could tell he was simply a man who was on a mission. Now that I'd given him an answer he seemed to like, his smile widened.

"I'm glad to hear that," he returned. "And you're doing okay?"

Beck wasn't coming right out with it, but there was no denying what he was getting at. If he remembered my name and Luna's name, he definitely couldn't have forgotten about what he witnessed that day at the hotel. He wanted to know if I was doing okay.

Any normal person would have nodded, smiled, and said they were fine. I never claimed to be normal.

I stood there and tried to figure out how to answer that question honestly. Unfortunately, taking that time meant that Mara stepped forward and answered for me.

"She's surviving," Mara declared. "It's been tough lately, but I think things will turn around soon. I mean, she's officially divorced now, so that's one step in the right direction."

Beck's eyes shifted between Mara and me until I snapped out of it and lamented, "I'm so sorry. Beck, this is my best friend, Mara. Mara, this is Beck."

He extended his hand to her and said, "It's nice to meet you."

"Likewise," she replied as she placed her hand in his.

Beck returned his attention to me. Something washed over his face, something I couldn't read. Then he said, "I'm glad to hear you got yourself out of that situation. I've been thinking about you and wondered how you were managing."

My lips parted in shock.

"Yo, Beck," someone shouted from behind him.

Beck twisted his neck to look in the opposite direction. I

didn't want to look away from him, but I managed to see that Cash Morris, the lead singer of the band, was standing there. "It's time," he told him as he jerked his head toward the front of the room.

Beck dipped his chin in understanding before he looked back at me.

"I have to go up there now," he started. "I'd really love to talk to you after the performance. Can you stick around?"

What was I going to say? No?

Absolutely not.

Of course, I was going to stay.

I nodded and replied, "Sure."

Beck grinned and said, "Great. I'll see you after."

He turned and took two steps away before he stopped, looked back at me, and allowed his eyes to run the length of me. When they came up to my face again, he shared, "You look incredible, Chasey."

Before I had the chance to respond, Beck walked away.

I stood there, motionless, as I watched him get lost in the crowd as he made his way to the stage. A moment later, Mara's voice whispered in my ear, "I am so glad we came here tonight. I knew he wouldn't forget you."

"I can't believe it," I murmured.

"Believe it, babe. The fantasy just got a whole lot better," she said.

She wasn't wrong about that. There was so much for me to fantasize about now. I mean, he not only had given me his number weeks ago, but now I could add that he'd only met me once and remembered my name. I could add that he had seen me for the first time in months, asked how both my daughter and I were doing *and* told me he had thought about me for months. And finally, I could add that he thought I looked incredible.

Wow.

"I feel like I should buy you a really nice present," I mumbled.

Mara laughed. "I'll settle for a drink tonight and all the juicy details after Beck has his way with you."

At that declaration, I turned fully to face her and insisted, "That's not going to happen."

"Why not?"

"I highly doubt he's interested in me like that," I explained.

Mara's gaze shifted between my face and the stage where I knew My Violent Heart would be playing at any moment.

"You're joking, right?" she asked when she returned her attention to me.

I looked up toward the stage and countered, "What could he possibly see in me that would be of any interest to him?"

Mara cocked an eyebrow at me.

Before she could answer, I added, "Besides, I'm not exactly in a position to be dating."

"You're single," she reminded me. "That's the only position you need to be in to be dating."

I didn't get a chance to respond because the crowd erupted in applause and cheers as My Violent Heart took the stage. I'd always enjoyed their music, but I'd never managed to see them perform live. This was certainly a once-in-a-life-time experience.

While I was sure everyone had their eyes pinned on the vocalists, either Cash or Holland, I didn't. My attention was on one man, and one man alone.

Beck Emerson.

He was breathtaking.

Dark hair, dark eyes, chiseled jawline, and a gorgeous body. He was only wearing a pair of jeans and black T-shirt, but he made them look better than any man could. His arms were strong and muscular while his waist was narrow. Beck was like something from a movie screen.

And he was living, rent-free, in the fantasies I'd been having in my head for weeks.

As the music filled the bar, and the sound of Cash's voice was all around, the only thing that mattered to me was watching Beck do his thing. He was incredible. I watched his hands as they moved over the keyboard for some songs and the synthesizer for others. He did it effortlessly. He did it like it was second nature to him, no different than breathing.

On more than one occasion, Beck's eyes found mine, and he smiled. My body shuddered every time he did that, and I started feeling stirrings of something between my legs that I hadn't felt in a very long time. I found myself wanting to know what he looked like beneath those jeans and that T-shirt.

"I think I'm in trouble," I told Mara as I leaned to my side without taking my eyes off Beck.

"Oh, Chasey, I knew that the minute he walked up and said your name," she replied.

For the first time since the band started playing, I looked over at my best friend. She was focused on me and was positively beaming.

"You're the best best friend a girl could ever ask for," I declared.

"I love you, too."

We both started laughing and my eyes fell on the stage again. Beck was looking at me, and when our eyes locked, he winked at me.

That's when I knew I hadn't been exaggerating.

I was definitely in big trouble.

WISH

Beck

Months had passed.

Months.

I was convinced I'd never see her again.

And now she was here. It felt like my lucky day.

Typically, at the end of a tour, I was ready to wind down and take a break. But weeks ago, when we'd returned to New Hampshire for the second time so Cash could try to work things out with Demi, he'd set us up to come back again when our tour concluded.

I didn't really have any expectations coming into tonight other than knowing that it was the final performance for us for the year. It was the beginning of November, and the tour was officially over. We were all taking the next few months off to relax and recharge over the holidays.

The whole band was planning to head back home to Pennsylvania. That was my plan, too. But now I wasn't so sure I'd be leaving New Hampshire immediately.

I'd accepted the fact that Chasey wasn't going to call. I'd accepted the fact that I wasn't going to see her again. Now that I'd gotten the surprise of my life and saw her here—in that dress, no less—there was not a chance in hell I was going to walk away without putting in a bit more effort.

Her friend had said it. Chasey was divorced now. While I didn't exactly know where she stood as far as getting into another relationship went, I at least knew that I wasn't going to waste the opportunity to get to know her.

And since I didn't have to continue on with a tour, I was pretty sure I'd be extending my stay in New Hampshire for a couple of days.

Throughout the band's entire performance, I was stealing glances at her.

God, she was beautiful.

Considering I thought that the first time I saw her, a time when she hadn't cracked a smile once, she was off the charts tonight. We had been in the middle of a song at one point in the evening when I looked over at her and saw her laughing.

Her face was lit up, and she looked positively radiant. Given the distance and the crowd, I couldn't see the rest of her, but it didn't matter. Chasey standing there in that dress was a vision that was burned in my brain. I'd never forget it.

Long, gorgeous legs, beautiful curves, and a smile that ignited something inside me. I wanted her. I wanted her badly.

But because I knew she'd been through something difficult recently, I didn't think I'd be able to just get what I wanted without putting in some effort. Then again, I didn't exactly just want a one-night stand with her either.

Something about Chasey drew me to her. I couldn't explain it; I just knew I felt it.

So, now that we'd just finished playing our last song for the night, I needed to find a way to get through the fans and over to her. I didn't want to risk having her leave. No way. No way would I be able to go back now and accept that she wasn't going to call or that I wouldn't see her again.

I needed to solidify something with her before I missed my chance.

After signing a few autographs, I managed to sneak away from the crowd of fans surrounding the raised stage at the front of the bar and moved toward the back, where Chasey remained with her friend.

As soon as I walked up, Mara announced, "I'm running to the ladies' room before I grab one more drink. I figure it's worth taking advantage of having a designated driver tonight."

Once she took off, I looked at Chasey and asked, "Do you mind if I sit with you?"

She shook her head. "Not at all."

I sat down opposite of her and asked, "Designated driver?"

"That's me."

"Are you just being safe, or do you not really drink?" I wondered.

"Both, I guess. It's not that I don't enjoy a drink every now and then, but I'm breastfeeding Luna still, so…" She trailed off.

More proof that she was a good mother.

I nodded and asked, "What did you think of the show tonight?"

"It was great. This was my first time seeing My Violent Heart play live," she answered. "I didn't think you all played at such small venues, though."

She was making conversation. I liked that a lot.

"We typically don't," I told her. "But Cash met Demi, and this is her cousin's bar."

Chasey's head tipped to the side as though she were trying to figure something out.

"What's that look for?" I asked.

"I feel like I know the name Demi."

"Oh, yeah, she's Cash's girlfriend," I explained. "She used to work at the hotel I met you at."

About a half a second later, realization dawned in her face. It was all starting to come together now. "Now I remember her," she declared. Following a brief pause, she asked, "So, where is the next stop on the tour?"

"This is it."

"Really?"

I nodded. "Yeah, and I'm actually really glad about that right now."

"Won't you miss it?"

Shaking my head, I explained, "We've been touring for the last few months and have played hundreds of shows. We're all ready for a bit of a break to spend time with family and friends through the holidays before we get back to the music."

Chasey's eyes searched my face, and she remained silent for

a long time. I waited patiently, giving her the time she needed to process whatever was on her mind.

When she finally spoke, I started to panic.

"Well, I should probably find Mara and get going," she started as she began shifting in her seat. "Mara's mom is at my place with Luna, and morning will come fast."

"Wait," I begged, sounding just a touch too desperate. Chasey stopped her movements and stared at me. I continued, "I'm planning to spend a few days here in New Hampshire before I head back home to Pennsylvania. I'd really love to see you again."

She blinked in surprise and asked, "Really?"

"Yes."

Once again, Chasey got silent. She dropped her gaze to the table between us as her eyes darted back and forth. I would have loved to know what was going through her mind at that moment.

I saw the worried look on her face when she returned her attention to me. "I'm really sorry, Beck," she lamented. "The weekdays aren't great for me because I work. I try to make up for missing out on time with Luna on the weekends."

Did she think I would be turned off by her being a hardworking mom?

"I'd love to see Luna again," I shared.

Chasey didn't hide her surprise. "You would?"

"Of course," I confirmed. "And I'm free all weekend long, so you tell me what's best for you and her."

For a long time, Chasey simply stared at me. Her expression held so much emotion. She was definitely in a bit of shock, but there was something else there. Something much softer, sweeter. I couldn't quite work out what it was.

"Where... where would you want to go?" she rasped.

I shrugged. "To be honest, I don't really know the area," I confessed. "But I'll go anywhere that's good for the two of you.

We could go out for lunch, or I can take you both to an early dinner in case you need to get back home to get Luna to bed early."

The silence stretched between us again before Chasey murmured, "Luna and I could do an early dinner tomorrow."

I wanted to jump for joy.

"Great," I said as I reached into my pocket. I pulled out my phone and asked, "How about you give me your number, and I'll reach out to you sometime late tomorrow morning? We can work out the details then."

"Okay."

With that, I held my phone out to Chasey. She took it, tapped on the screen, and handed it back to me. I saved her number, stood, and held my hand out to her.

She hesitated briefly, but eventually placed her hand in mine and stood. I hated the hesitation I was seeing in her, but I had a feeling I knew where it was coming from. I was just going to have to prove to Chasey that her being a new mom—a newly single one, at that—wasn't going to scare me away.

"You think about where you'd like to go, and when I call tomorrow, we can discuss it," I started. "The only recommendation I'll give is that you choose a place that might be a bit more discreet. It's not uncommon for people to walk right up to me in a public setting. I don't want to put that on you, and I especially don't want to put that on your daughter."

"Okay, I'll try to figure something out," she said softly.

"Looks like Mara is at the bar," I informed her.

Chasey looked in the direction of the bar, saw her friend staring at us, and looked back at me.

"She's a good friend," I teased.

Chasey laughed softly and returned, "Don't tell her that. She'll let it go to her head."

I smiled at her and ended, "It was really, really nice to see you again, Chasey. Thanks for staying until the end."

She returned the smile and said, "Thank you for being so sweet. I'll talk to you tomorrow, Beck."

"You will," I promised, giving her hand a squeeze before I let it go.

With that, Chasey turned and walked away to find her friend. I watched her go, loving everything about her in that dress.

CHAPTER 7

Chasey

I COULD NEVER LIVE THE LIFE OF A ROCK STAR.

It was late Saturday morning, and I was curled up in my bed trying to sleep while Luna took her morning nap.

Last night wore me out. And while it wasn't exactly late for a Friday night for someone like Beck, or even for Mara, it had been entirely too late for me.

Even though my best friend had tried to make me feel better about the fact that being a mom didn't mean I couldn't have a good time, there was one thing she failed to take into consideration.

Children wake up early.

Luna woke up early.

Perhaps I wouldn't have been feeling so exhausted today if I had managed to get in last night and go right to sleep. But I couldn't. Because I continued to have all of my interactions with Beck replay over and over in my mind.

I couldn't turn it off.

So much about him had surprised me, and I was still reeling from it all. Most of all, I had a feeling I was struggling to doze off now because I knew my phone might ring at any moment so we could work out the details of where to go later for an early dinner.

Early dinner.

I still hadn't wrapped my head around the fact that Beck had suggested an early dinner for the sake of Luna. If I didn't know any better, I would have thought he had a kid of his own.

Right now, if it weren't for the fact that I felt so exhausted, I would have started to believe that perhaps the fantasy that had been playing out in my head for weeks was suddenly about to become real life.

Part of that terrified me.

Because the truth was that Beck would quickly realize that I wasn't the kind of woman meant for him. I had responsibilities that went far beyond making a living. I had someone who depended on me. I had to raise a human.

The life of a rock star was not meant for a mom like me.

I'd never get so lucky to have a man like Beck settle down for me. And while that stung just a little, it didn't mean that I couldn't do something for myself that made me feel good.

Exhausted or not, I was going to go out with him later today. Luna and I were going to have a good time with Beck. Even if all that came of it was an early dinner one night with Beck before he returned to Pennsylvania and it never amounted to more than that, I was going to enjoy it for all that it was.

On that thought, I closed my eyes and started to drift.

It felt like mere minutes had passed when my eyes shot open again. My phone was vibrating in the bed beside me.

I reached out, saw Beck's name on the display, and answered, "Hello?"

"Chasey?" he replied.

"Yeah," I confirmed.

"Is everything okay? It sounds like I woke you up," he noted.

I rolled from my back to my side before I sat up and swung my legs over the side of the bed. Bringing my free hand up to the side of my face, I closed my eyes and pressed my fingertips into my eyelids to wake myself up a bit.

"I'm sorry," I apologized. "I... well, I'm not used to the late nights, and Luna was up early this morning. She went down for her morning nap, and I decided that it was better to try to catch up on some sleep instead of doing laundry."

"I'm sorry I interrupted your sleep," he lamented. "I imagine that's a bit difficult to come by these days."

"It is, but it's okay," I assured him. "It's better that I'm up now, or I'm going to get all out of whack and off my schedule."

There was a brief pause before Beck asked, "Are you and Luna still up for going to dinner with me later?"

Absolutely, I was. But I had to wonder if it was starting to hit him that this is what my life was, and that it wasn't going to be easy.

"We're still up for it," I insisted. "Unless, of course, it no longer works for you."

"It works for me," he assured me. "So, would you be okay with me coming to your place to pick you up, or is it too soon for that?"

Too soon?

What did he mean by that?

"Pardon?" I replied.

Beck chuckled. "I'd like to be a gentleman and pick you up, but I realize you've got a baby," he started. "If you're not okay with me coming to your place to pick you up, I'm happy to meet you wherever you'd like to have dinner today."

I'll admit that what I'd gone through with Aaron had shaken my faith in others a bit, but I certainly wasn't concerned about my safety when it came to Beck. He was who he was. I didn't think he was the kind of guy who'd do something terrible to a woman and her newborn and risk losing his career.

Quite frankly, even if he hadn't been a member of the hottest rock band in the world, I didn't think I'd be worried. Beck didn't strike me as the serial killer type. Not, of course, that I really knew what the serial killer type was anyway. But still, I had no problem with Beck meeting me at my place.

"You can come here if you want, but to avoid swapping Luna's car seat, we should probably take my car," I suggested.

"That works for me. Do you have a place picked out that you'd like to go?"

"Well, if you want good food at a place that'll be low-key on a Saturday, then I think we should go to Pearl's Family Restaurant," I offered.

"If that's what you want, that's where we'll go," he said. "If I'm there by four thirty, will that work?"

"That should be good for us because Luna usually wakes up from her afternoon nap anytime between three and three thirty," I confirmed as I hopped off the bed and started gathering up the laundry.

"Alright. So, once we disconnect, can you text me your address?"

"I can do that."

There was an extended pause before Beck said softly, "I'm looking forward to seeing you tonight without the crowd, Chasey."

I smiled as I felt my heart rate kick up a couple notches. "Me too, Beck."

"I'm glad. Okay, I'll let you get back to your nap," he said.

I wished. "Too late. I've already started gathering up the laundry," I shared.

"Moms are superheroes," he returned.

I let out a laugh. "Yeah, the problem is that I haven't yet learned what they do to restore their energy reserves."

I could hear the amusement in his voice when he declared, "I'm sure it's still early for you yet. You'll figure it out soon."

"We'll have to see about that," I returned.

"Alright, Chasey. I'll see you soon."

"Okay, Beck. Talk to you later."

With that, we said goodbye and disconnected. No sooner had I done that and gotten a load of laundry in the wash when Luna woke up. I changed her, and we played for a long time. Of course, I told her all about what was happening later in the day, and though she didn't respond nor would she be eating any of the food, I kept telling myself that she was just as excited about going out for dinner as I was. With the exception of last night, I hadn't gone out since long before I was divorced. In fact, the last time I'd gone out to dinner was when I was still pregnant with Luna.

This was going to be a really nice treat. And I intended on fully enjoying it. Obviously, I didn't think that was going to be too difficult to do, considering I'd be spending that time with Beck Emerson.

I mean, how lucky was I?

After we played together for a while and even got in a fair bit of tummy time, I nursed Luna. It didn't take her long to fall asleep. I knew I'd have at least a solid two hours to take care of everything I needed to before she woke up.

So, I finished up the laundry, made sure Luna's diaper bag was all packed for later, cleaned the kitchen and the bathroom, and took a shower. Then I fixed my hair just in time for Luna to wake up. Once I changed her, I took her out to the family room to play and cuddle for a bit. She wasn't being fussy, and I thought I'd take advantage of that. If I could wait until closer to four o'clock to feed her, I wanted to do that. This would be Luna's first trip to a restaurant, and I didn't know how it was going to go.

The rest of the afternoon passed quickly, and before I knew it, there was a knock at my door.

With Luna held firmly in one arm, I extended the other and opened the door. The instant he saw us, Beck smiled. He also held out a bouquet of flowers.

"Oh, that is so sweet of you," I said as I reached for the flowers. I couldn't remember the last time I'd gotten flowers from anybody. "Come on in."

Beck stepped inside and asked, "Is this the little lady? She's gotten so big since the last time I saw her."

"Yep. This is my girl," I confirmed. "Can you say hi to Beck?"

Luna did not say hi. But she did give Beck a toothless grin.

"She's beautiful," he said.

"Thank you."

"She looks just like you," he added.

My eyes left Luna and returned to Beck. I couldn't know if he was just making the observation, or if that was his way of telling me he thought I was beautiful. He didn't offer any clarification, but he was wearing an expression that made me believe it was the latter.

I lifted the flowers to my nose and inhaled. They smelled lovely.

"We're ready to go, but I'd like to put these in some water before we leave if that's okay," I told him.

"Absolutely," Beck replied. "Would you like me to hold Luna for you while you do that?"

My eyes darted back and forth between my daughter and Beck. "Are you… you don't mind?" I stammered.

"Why would I?" he asked.

I nervously bit my lip. "I don't know. I guess… well, you just don't seem like the type of guy that goes around holding babies."

Beck chuckled.

I was mesmerized at the sight.

"I don't typically," he said. "But that's mostly because I'm not really around a lot of babies. I promise I'm completely capable."

Smiling, I replied, "Okay. She's all yours."

Beck held out his hands as I twisted my body slightly to bring Luna closer to him. I wasn't sure how she was going to react, but Luna had absolutely no problem going to him. For a few moments, I stood there and watched to make sure she wasn't going to start crying that some person she didn't know was holding her.

Of course, that was how it started.

But it didn't take long for me to start to notice so much more about what was happening. Luna's little body fit perfectly into Beck's arms. While most of her weight was supported by his single arm, he protectively held his large hand against her back.

I wanted to burst into tears at the sight of it.

She was never going to have that from her father. While I knew I never had it either as a kid and had managed to turn out fine, that didn't mean I didn't want more for my little girl.

"I'm—" I stopped to clear my throat. "You can come inside while I take care of these flowers."

Beck followed behind me as I moved toward the kitchen. He stopped in the doorway to the kitchen since it wasn't really big enough for all three of us.

I didn't have anything fancy to put the flowers in, so I found the tallest and widest drinking glass I had and used that. It was slightly embarrassing that I didn't even have a vase. The next chance I got, I was going to be sure to pick one up. They weren't terribly expensive or anything; it was just that I preferred to spend my money on things Luna and I needed.

Once I had the flowers in the glass, I turned around and found Beck cradling the back of Luna's head as he stared absentmindedly into the kitchen.

That's when it hit me.

Oh God.

Beck was probably disgusted by our accommodations. I kept our place clean and tidy, but right now, I couldn't afford anything swanky. Right now, it was about survival. Right now, it was about doing what had to be done to make sure my daughter had everything she needed. A fancy home with a big kitchen, lots of bedrooms, and flower vases didn't fit into the budget.

I cleared my throat, which caused Beck to snap out of it. He directed his attention to me, and I said softly, "I'm just going to grab her bag, and we can go."

Whatever thoughts Beck had about our living situation must have faded away. He simply said, "Okay."

I allowed my eyes to linger on him a bit longer. I couldn't help myself. He was holding my girl, she was utterly content, and I felt so much longing.

With no other choice, I shook off the melancholy feelings and moved out of the kitchen to get Luna's diaper bag.

Before I knew it, we were seated at a booth at Pearl's and had given our dinner selections to the waitress.

I was holding Luna in my arms as she babbled incoherently. For a few moments, Beck and I watched and listened to her.

But when I looked up at Beck, his eyes connected with mine.

"Luna seems like the happiest baby in the world," he declared.

That felt good to hear. Maybe I was doing a half decent job raising her. "I'd like to take all the credit, but she's really just been a great baby," I said.

"Well, whatever it is, you should be proud."

"Thank you for saying that," I told him.

Beck gave me a nod and shared, "I'm really glad you came to Granite to see us play last night."

"Can I be honest with you?" I asked.

He seemed a bit caught off guard by my question, but he still replied, "Sure."

"I didn't know you all were going to be playing there last night," I confessed. "Mara dragged me out against my will."

Beck's eyes widened. "You didn't know you were going to see us?"

He said the word us as though referring to the band, but

I had to wonder if he was really referring to himself. Did he think I purposely went there in the hopes that I would run into him again?

I shook my head. "No. In fact, last night was the first time I've been out since before Luna was born. I just… well, life has been busy. But Mara had been asking me to go out with her for a few weeks, and I kept putting it off. Last night, I gave in. She knew what she was doing though because she waited until we got there to tell me that My Violent Heart was going to be playing."

Something washed over him, but he didn't say anything. I was too impatient and too curious not to know what that look meant.

"What is that look for?" I asked.

"Did she know?" he countered.

"Know what?"

Beck hesitated a moment before he clarified, "That I met you months ago."

Now it was my turn to pause. Beck had just worked out the fact that I'd shared what happened with Mara. If he knew how I had been when I shared the story with Mara, I'd die of mortification. So, I did my best to act nonchalant.

I nodded casually and explained, "Yes. I mean, she's my best friend, so she was the first person I confided in about what happened that day. I couldn't exactly tell her the story without telling her how I managed to get myself out of there."

Beck lifted his chin in understanding.

That's when I added, "Thank you for that, by the way. I… well, I was pretty out of sorts that day, and I don't recall if I ever really thanked you for stepping in. It was really kind of you to do that."

He lifted his arms up in surrender and insisted, "Hey, no thanks needed. I was more than happy to help, and I'm glad you seem to be doing well."

I wouldn't exactly say I was doing well, but I was certainly doing much better than I had been that day.

"Yeah, we're doing alright," I told him. "It's all work and play for us. Or, work for me and play for Luna."

"Where do you work?" Beck asked.

"Oh, it's nothing exciting like you," I started. "I work at the local post office as a mail clerk."

"Cool."

"It's not cool," I said with a smile on my face. "It's boring."

Beck shot me an apologetic look, but he didn't respond because our meals had arrived.

After we thanked the waitress and she took off, I felt compelled to steer the conversation in another direction. I just wanted to be slightly discreet about it. So, I simply shared, "This is Luna's first time at a restaurant."

Beck's head snapped up. "Really?" he asked, a look of shock and surprise on his face.

I nodded. "Yep."

"Oh, well, you have to document this with a picture," he said.

Even though she wasn't eating any of the food, I still thought that was a great idea. I reached for my purse so I could grab my phone, and that's when I noticed it was missing.

Where was my purse?

As soon as I thought about it, I realized it wasn't missing. I had completely forgotten it at home.

Oh no.

"Is everything okay?" Beck asked.

With wide eyes and a feeling of mortification washing over me, I rasped, "I don't have my phone with me."

"Oh. That's no problem," he insisted as he reached his hand beneath the table. A moment later, he pulled out his phone and started tapping on the screen. "I'll just take a pic of the two of you and text it to you so you'll have it."

I didn't respond.

I couldn't.

A lump was forming in my throat while my arm tugged Luna a little tighter to my body.

"Chasey?" Beck called.

My eyes went from the corded column of Beck's throat to his face. "Hmm?" I responded.

"Is something wrong?"

Despite not wanting it to happen, tears filled my eyes. Beck saw and grew even more concerned.

"Christ, babe, talk to me," he urged gently.

"I don't have my phone because I forgot my purse," I rasped.

"Okay? Are you expecting an important call?" he wondered.

An important call? The only person who called me regularly was Mara. Of course, Mara's calls were important to me, but that wasn't what this was about. How did he not understand?

I shook my head.

"So, what's the problem?"

"I forgot my purse, Beck," I told him. "My purse has my wallet in it."

He jerked his chin to the side and assessed me a moment. "Chasey, sweetheart, I hope you're not upset right now because you're concerned about paying for your dinner," he said with a bit of a warning in his tone.

"I… well, I… yeah," I stammered.

"Stop," he ordered. "I asked you to come out with me today. If I didn't think it'd send you over the edge and make you burst into tears right now, I'd tell you I'm slightly offended that you think I'd take you out and expect you to foot the bill."

I bit my lip in an effort not to have a total meltdown. When I thought I had it under control, I apologized. "I'm sorry. I didn't mean to insinuate anything by it, but I don't want you to think that I'm using you or anything like that."

"I never thought that," he assured me. "And you not bringing your purse is the least of the reasons why."

What did he mean by that?

Before I could ask him, he declared, "This is Luna's first visit to a restaurant. You don't want to remember it as one where you were upset about something that you do not need to be upset about. I'm going to take your picture, and then we're going to enjoy the rest of our date. Okay?"

I nodded and agreed, "Okay."

Beck held up his phone and said, "Look here and smile."

What else could I do? Beck called this a date, he wasn't the least bit bothered by the fact that Luna was here with us.

I entered my fantasy world again and smiled at Beck. When I assumed he had taken a picture, I lifted my girl in my arms, turned my head to her, and pressed my lips to her chubby cheek.

What I didn't know was that Beck had snapped a photo of that, too.

CHAPTER 8

Beck

"WHERE ARE YOU?"

I sighed and sat down on the edge of the bed in my hotel suite. I should have expected the slightly irritated tone of my sister's voice the moment I saw her name come up on my phone.

"I'm still in New Hampshire," I told her.

It was early Sunday afternoon, and I had just gotten myself ready to leave. When Sadie's call came through, though, I decided it would be best to talk to her now so she didn't worry.

Clearly, I'd made the right choice because there was no doubt she was worried. Or, perhaps right now, she was perturbed. But if I went too long without reaching out to her, that frustration would turn to worry, and I didn't want that.

"Why didn't you come home?" she asked. "Everyone else is back."

"How do you know that?"

There was a brief pause before she answered, "Oh, well, I was out yesterday and saw Walker. He told me you guys played your last show in New Hampshire on Friday. Then I talked to Holland earlier this morning. We texted back and forth a few times, and we decided to get together this coming week. You always reach out to me when you get home, and since I hadn't heard from you, I thought you were blowing me off."

Sadie and I had always been close. She wasn't wrong. Whenever I was on tour, I'd reach out to her occasionally just to stay in touch. But when I came home, I always touched base immediately to set up a time to catch up with her.

My sister was such an important person in my life, and I never wanted her to feel like I'd kicked her to the side.

"I'm sorry, Sadie," I apologized. "I've been caught up in something here, and it completely slipped my mind."

"What's going on?" she asked.

Gone was the frustration in her tone. It had been replaced by genuine concern and worry.

"I met someone," I blurted.

"What?"

I took in a deep breath and blew it out. I hadn't shared anything about Chasey's existence with Sadie, so this was going to come as a bit of a shock.

"Long story short," I started. "When we came here a couple months ago to play a few shows, I walked into the hotel we were going to be staying at and met this woman. Her name is Chasey. We talked for a few minutes that day, and I gave her my number. Unfortunately, she never called me. But with Cash meeting Demi and setting up one final performance for us at her cousin's bar here, I ended up running into the woman again on Friday night. I took her out to dinner yesterday."

"That's great news, Beck," Sadie declared. "How did it go?"

It had been great.

Everything about this trip back here had been great from the minute my eyes landed on her wearing that dress. I hadn't been able to get that vision of her out of my head for days now.

"Well, I was about to head out to go to her place just as you called me," I answered.

WISH

There was a lengthy pause before Sadie asked, "Wait? Are you telling me you didn't bring her back to your hotel room last night?"

I let out a laugh. Apparently, my sister knew how things went in this industry.

But that wasn't how it was with Chasey. Oddly enough, I found myself wanting to just get to know her, so I didn't mind the time I was putting in with her right now.

"No, I didn't," I admitted.

"Oh my God," she whispered. "You like her."

"What?"

"You like her," Sadie repeated. "You gave this woman your number, and she never called. But by some odd stroke of luck, you get this second chance, and she agrees to go to dinner with you. So, you don't come home to Pennsylvania, and instead, you extend your stay in New Hampshire. Presumably, dinner went well because you were just about to head to her place since she made you go back to the hotel after dinner."

I shook my head at the same time I rolled my eyes. I loved my sister, but she was crazy. "Where, in all of that, do you get some feeling that there's this profound thing happening?"

"You're putting in a lot of effort for this girl," she noted. "If you didn't like her, you wouldn't waste your time."

There was no point in denying it because if I had my way, things with Chasey and I would eventually get serious.

"Okay, okay. I like her," I admitted.

I could practically hear the smile on my sister's face when she declared, "I knew it. So, tell me about Chasey."

"We're just now getting to know each other, but she's a newly-divorced single mom of the most adorable five-month-old little girl," I shared.

"How newly divorced?" Sadie pressed.

"I don't know the exact date, but when I met her about

four months ago, she had just learned her husband was cheating on her," I offered.

The silence stretched between us before Sadie finally spoke. "Oh, wow, Beck. Is she… are you sure she's ready to get involved with someone else this soon?"

I honestly didn't know. That was one of the things I was hoping to be able to talk to her about tonight. I probably would have dug a little deeper with her yesterday, but once Chasey got emotional about forgetting her purse at her place, I decided to take a step back. Mentioning her divorce while we were out in public and Luna was there just didn't seem like a wise idea.

"We're just getting to know one another right now," I insisted. "But I have every intention of taking this slow because I realize that whatever happens with her will also affect her daughter."

There was another pause, although this one was brief, before Sadie said softly, "You're a good man, Beck. Just promise me you'll be careful."

I understood Sadie's concern. If the roles were reversed I would be the same about her. Actually, that's not true. I'd probably be a lot worse.

"I promise I'll be careful," I told her. "And when I get back I'll reach out to you so we can hang."

"Alright. I'll let you go then. Talk to you later, Beck."

"Love you, Sadie."

"Love you, too. And good luck."

I smiled and ended, "Thanks."

After I disconnected the call with my sister, I sat there a moment and let my conversation with her sink in. Then I stood, grabbed the keys to the car I'd rented, and left my suite.

On the drive to Chasey's place, I couldn't help but feel grateful and a bit of relief at the fact that she had invited me over today. I hadn't been quite sure how to approach the subject with her, but on the way back to her place she directed the conversation there.

"So, how long are you going to be in New Hampshire?" she asked.

I thought it was still too soon to tell her that I was simply staying in New Hampshire for her and that if she told me to stay indefinitely for her that I'd do it. Instead, I answered, "I'll be here for a few more days."

"Oh," she murmured. "Okay."

When she didn't say anything else, I realized I was going to need to tell her where I stood. "I would like to see you again before I leave and head back to Pennsylvania," I shared.

"Really?"

I took my eyes off the road briefly to look over at her. She had been okay with me driving her car back to her place. When I glanced in her direction, I saw the surprise on her face.

It seemed I had a lot of work to do.

"Yes, Chasey. Really."

"Well, I'd say I'm pretty useless during the week," she started. "Between waking up early to make sure I can get both Luna and myself ready, taking her to day care, working all day, and only having a little bit of time to spend with her when I get home, I'm afraid I'd probably just be miserable company."

"So, weekends are best," I noted.

"Weekends would be best," she confirmed. "Luna and I don't have any plans for tomorrow if you're free."

"Are you sure?" I asked.

Chasey didn't hesitate to respond, "Absolutely. Luna seems to really like you, too. If you want to come over, I could make dinner so we wouldn't need to eat super early."

I hated to think about giving her more work to do, but I'd already seen how she reacted at dinner when she realized she didn't have her wallet. Chasey had to know that I was more than capable of buying her dinner, and it surprised me that she got so upset. For that reason, I thought it was best to take her up on her offer.

"I don't want to make you do any extra work," I told her.

"It won't be any trouble," she assured me. "I promise."

I thought a moment before I said, "Okay. You can make dinner if you let me stop and grab something special for dessert."

Once again, I glanced over to the passenger seat. This time, I found Chasey beaming at me. The sight of her looking at me like that made something in my chest tighten.

"It's a deal," she declared.

And now that I was back in the rental driving without her by my side, all I could do is recall that joyful look on her face. I wanted more of that, and there was one way I thought I could make it happen.

So, earlier this morning, I called Cash. I asked him if he could ask Demi where the best place in this town would be for me to get dessert. He had wondered why I was asking, and I didn't hesitate to share. Now that I knew Chasey and I were getting to know one another, I was okay with letting him know what I was up to.

Demi made her recommendation, and I immediately went out to a local bakery—the one Demi had dubbed the best in town—to pick up an assortment of desserts. I made one additional stop while I was out, and now I couldn't wait to get to Chasey's place.

A few minutes later, I had arrived and was knocking on her door.

The moment Chasey opened it, and I saw her beautiful face, I felt that same tightening in my chest.

"Hey," she greeted me with Luna planted on her hip.

"Hey," I returned as I stepped inside and closed the door behind me. I shifted my gaze to Luna and said, "Hi, pretty girl."

She babbled something at me and was happy as a clam.

"We've been practicing sitting up on our own," Chasey

shared as she walked into the living room, where a blanket was opened up on the floor.

She set Luna down and stayed close. Luna's arms flew out to her sides and she wobbled back and forth on her bottom while Chasey kept her hands ready to catch her daughter in case she toppled.

I set the bags I'd carried in down on the floor and joined the two of them as I declared, "That's awesome work. She's doing incredible."

"Isn't she?" Chasey beamed. "I'm so proud of her."

"Considering all this hard work she's been doing, I think it's only fitting that she gets a present," I said.

Confusion washed over Chasey as she put her hands on either side of Luna's body to steady her. "What?"

I smiled and shrugged. "I hope you don't mind, but I went shopping today and got something for her."

"You did?"

Nodding, I reached out for the bag and held it up.

"Beck, that's so sweet of you to do," Chasey rasped. "You really didn't need to get her anything."

"I know. But I started thinking about the fact that you were going to be making dinner tonight, and I thought this would give me something fun to do with her," I explained while reaching inside the bag.

A moment later, I pulled the gift out of the bag. I threw the bag inside the other bag that was carrying the desserts and held the toy up.

Chasey started laughing. "You bought Luna her first piano."

"She can never start music too early," I noted as I started opening the box it was in. I didn't know who thought children's toys needed to be locked down tighter than a vault, but I wholeheartedly believed that somebody needed to redesign toy packaging. "Besides, this is meant for someone right around her age."

I eventually freed the piano, which had six keys that were

each very large and a different color. When I set it down on the blanket facing Luna and pressed one of the keys, her eyes immediately went to it. I pressed another key. She watched intently. I pressed a couple more keys next, and she stayed riveted to it.

Wanting to give her the opportunity to try it out, I moved closer and placed it in front of her. Then I took one of her tiny hands and helped her touch her finger to the key. She laughed. We did it again, and she laughed more.

It was the most incredible experience of my life. Somehow, watching this little girl be completely fascinated with a colorful toy that played musical sounds was the best thing I'd witnessed in a very long time.

I heard a sniffle, looked up, and saw Chasey was wiping away tears.

"Sweetheart, why are you crying?" I asked gently.

"Can I blame it on hormones?" she countered, sniffling again.

I didn't answer and simply continued to stare at her, hoping she'd give me a real answer. Luckily, she must have realized what I was waiting for and shared, "I love my daughter more than I could ever tell you. I just wish I would have made better choices. There's so much she deserves that she'll never have."

"It's just a twenty-five dollar toy," I reasoned.

Shaking her head, Chasey insisted, "No, Beck. It's so much more than that."

I had a feeling there was a lot more behind that sentiment. I wanted to know what it was, but I didn't think it was a good idea to push it now while Luna was still awake. Two days in a row now, Chasey had broken down into tears over me doing the simplest things for her. I had to wonder if she'd ever been able to really unload whatever heaviness was in her heart.

I might have decided to hold off on pushing for more now, but I definitely intended to figure it out later.

In order to lighten the mood, I allowed the silence to stretch between Chasey and me for a moment while only the sound of Luna hitting the keys on the piano filled the room. Then I declared, "I think she's a natural."

Chasey burst out laughing, and I did the same right alongside her.

For the next little while, Chasey and I both put our focus and attention on Luna. I was surprised at just how much I enjoyed it. I loved being around them. After some time had passed, Chasey said, "I did some prep work earlier for dinner, but I haven't put anything together yet. Would you mind hanging with Luna for a bit while I go get everything together?"

"Not at all," I told her. "You don't need any help with the food, do you?"

She shook her head. "If you keep an eye on her, that'll be a huge help."

"Anything you need, Chasey."

With that, she stood and started to move toward the kitchen but suddenly stopped. "Does that other bag have dessert in it?" she asked.

"Oh, yeah," I answered, looking up from where I was sitting with Luna on the floor.

"Is there anything inside that needs to be refrigerated?"

Shaking my head, I replied, "Nope."

Chasey dipped her chin in acknowledgment and responded, "Okay. I'll be back in a few. And I apologize in advance. I don't have any beer or wine or any alcohol. There's really been no point since I can't drink any of it."

"That's okay," I assured her. "Whatever you've got will be fine."

Chasey gave me one last sweet look before she took off toward the kitchen. Then, it was just Luna and me. And it didn't take long for me to realize that even though I had simply been trying to lighten the mood a few minutes before with Chasey, I hadn't been lying either.

I was convinced Luna knew exactly what she was doing when it came to playing the piano. With any luck, I'd still be around when she was old enough to really understand, and I'd be able to teach her a thing or two.

Surprisingly, that thought didn't have me feeling the least bit worried or ready to run in the opposite direction.

I could admit it.

I was completely and totally consumed and caught up in the curiosity and wonder of a five-month-old little girl and the beauty, strength, and courage of her mother.

CHAPTER 9

Chasey

AS I LOOKED DOWN AND WATCHED LUNA'S EYES GET HEAVY WITH sleep, I decided that I didn't care if this was a fantasy. I loved it, and I was staying here as long as I could.

It was Luna's bedtime, and I'd just come into her room to nurse her to sleep and put her down for the night. As she nursed, I couldn't stop thinking about how wonderful the last two days had been.

Beck was simply the best guy ever.

Obviously, I had small moments where I wondered if I was making that declaration too soon because it wasn't as though I hadn't already made some foolish choices in my life. Those choices led to horrible situations, which made me realize that perhaps I couldn't exactly rely on my judgment, especially considering it had only been two days.

But I couldn't ignore how seeing Beck with Luna affected me.

As I cooked dinner earlier tonight, there were a few moments when I stepped out of the kitchen to check on the two of them. In more than one of those instances, I ended up breathless.

Watching a man who wasn't my husband or my daughter's father treat her so well made something squeeze in my chest.

I felt such longing.

Longing and desire.

No matter that he hadn't recognized me standing there. Beck still talked to Luna like she was his best friend. And though it wasn't a real one, he talked to her all about keyboards and music while using the one in front of her to demonstrate his points.

My heart melted.

Then again, it had been doing that within seconds of him arriving and sitting down on the floor with us earlier. Knowing that he thought about Luna sometime between him leaving here yesterday and arriving here today warmed my heart. The fact that he took it a step further and got her a gift was simply too sweet to ignore.

It wasn't about the money he spent.

It was simply the fact that he cared enough to want to do something like that.

So, it wasn't hard for me to feel like it was okay to live in this fantasy world for just a bit longer. If nothing else, Luna deserved it.

But I knew it would be dangerous to her and to me if I allowed myself to linger there too long.

Beck would be going home soon, and maybe that was the best thing for all of us. Because life would get back to normal, Luna and I would do our own thing, and I'd always have the sweetest, kindest memories of him in my heart and in my mind.

After the way things had been for me over the last few months, this weekend with Beck and Luna had been really nice. And since he was still here, I was going to do my best to enjoy the rest of the time I had with him before he left.

Of course, I would have to find a way to keep myself from

tackling him to the ground to make him stay. I enjoyed this too much, and I never wanted it to end.

Unfortunately, I wasn't going to get my way. So, I'd take what I could—whatever Beck offered me tonight—and I'd hold it close to my heart. Being the man he was, treating Luna and me the way he had this weekend, I knew I'd never forget an ounce of it.

And I'd always wish things had been different.

Once Luna had fallen asleep, I stood from the glider and put her in her crib. Then I turned on the monitor, grabbed the display for it from my bedroom, and made my way back to the living room, where I knew I'd find Beck waiting.

We had eaten dinner together but decided to wait until after Luna had gone down for the night to eat dessert. When I excused myself to give Luna her bath and nurse her to sleep, Beck had urged me to take my time and said he'd get the desserts ready.

As I entered the room, Beck looked up and asked, "Is she sleeping?"

I nodded and held up the monitor. "You can see her right here," I told him as I sat down on the couch beside him.

"Oh, wow. I've heard about these, but I've never seen one in person," he said.

"Yeah, they have all kinds now. Some are really fancy, but this one gets the job done," I explained. "Anyway, thank you for waiting so patiently while I took care of her. We've got a routine down, and I'm terrified to deviate too much from it. Everything I read before giving birth said that having babies in a routine makes for much happier kids and parents."

Beck chuckled and assured me, "It's no problem at all. Though, I will say that I've been out here with the scent of these fresh-baked goods filling my nose. I'm surprised you didn't walk out to find me drooling all over myself."

It was now my turn to laugh. "Well, don't let me stop you," I began. "My mouth is watering just looking at these. So, did you ask the people at the hotel where to go or was it simply luck that you found the town's best bakery?"

"Neither."

When I shot him a confused look, he explained, "I called Cash and had him ask Demi. She said this was the place to go."

I tried to ignore the fact that he'd called his bandmate to ask about this. My mind was racing with a million thoughts, but the biggest one was whether or not he had explained to Cash why he wanted to know about the bakeries in Finch. But instead of asking him about any of that, I said, "Ah, that makes sense. The good thing is, we now have all this dessert to enjoy."

And there was a ton of it.

Donuts, cakes, and muffins, to name a few.

"Well, it was the least I could do since you made dinner," he reasoned. "Thank you for that, by the way. It was really good."

As I sunk my teeth into a glazed cinnamon roll, I closed my eyes and moaned. I chewed, swallowed, and opened my eyes again. "I'm the one that should be thanking you," I told him.

"Is it that good?" he wondered.

"What? Oh, um, yes. This is delicious, but that's not what I meant," I informed him.

"Why would you be thanking me?" he pressed.

I swallowed another bite of my cinnamon roll before I answered, "It was nice to finally have someone to cook for again."

Beck's features softened, but there was still a bit of curiosity lingering there. I understood why when he asked, "Don't you normally cook for yourself?"

I didn't know what it was, but something came over me. I suddenly had this overwhelming urge to share more than was probably smart to share with Beck.

Maybe it was him taking Luna and me to dinner yesterday.

Maybe it was him saying he wanted to see us again before he left to go home.

Maybe it was him showing up with a toy for my daughter.

WISH

Or maybe it was me still living in the fantasy and believing that what happened here with him tonight wouldn't necessarily matter moving forward because he'd be gone and life would go back to being as it was.

Yeah, that definitely had to be it. There was nothing holding me back from sharing because I knew that when I woke up tomorrow, it'd all be over.

So, I shared, "All I ever wanted was to be a stay-at-home mom that took care of her house, her husband, and her babies. My life had other plans for me, and I obviously learned that we don't always get what we want. Now that I spend my weekdays working to support Luna and me, all I want to do when I get home is find a way to make up for all the guilt I feel about the time I miss spending with her and raising her. So, to ease my guilt, I push off doing anything for myself, like making dinner, until after she's asleep. And by that point, I'm usually so exhausted that I just throw together whatever is in the fridge."

"You're not eating?" Beck asked. The concern in his voice was almost too much to bear.

"I am," I assured him. "It's just that I don't make anything fancy. I usually just make myself a sandwich or something easy like that."

"What about next weekend?" Beck said.

His question took me by surprise. I didn't understand what he was asking me about since I'd been talking about food.

"I don't understand the question," I admitted.

"Well," he started, as he finished chewing a bite of his chocolate frosted donut. After he swallowed, he said, "Maybe I'm being presumptuous about what you do in your free time, but if you enjoy eating meals like you made tonight, why don't you prepare some next weekend when Luna is with her dad so that you'll have them for the week?"

I stared at Beck like he was crazy.

He saw it, knew it, and asked, "Why are you looking at me

like I've got three heads? Actually, maybe you're looking at me like I've got five of them."

I didn't respond and just continued to stare at him.

This went on a long time.

Finally, Beck broke the silence and called, "Chasey?"

"Yeah?"

"Is everything okay?" he asked. "I'm sorry about what I said. I shouldn't be sitting here telling you how to spend your free time."

"There is none," I blurted.

"What?"

"Free time," I clarified. "There is no free time."

Beck stared back at me. He hesitated to respond, but eventually said, "I guess I can see that. There's probably so many things you can't get done while Luna is here, so they probably take priority when she's not."

I shook my head.

"No?"

I shook my head again. "No, Beck. And there's no reason for you to apologize. The thing is, you're a good guy. That means you would make the obvious assumption that a father would stick around for his child. Not to be harsh, but there's really no other good way to put it. The truth is, ever since that day at the hotel, Luna's father hasn't seen her. In fact, you've seen her more this weekend than he's seen her since then."

Beck's eyes widened. "I'm so sorry, Chasey. I... I didn't know," he apologized.

I could tell he was genuinely horrified at the assumption he'd made about Aaron's presence in Luna's life.

"It's okay," I assured him. "Honestly, it's better this way. I'm not sure I could bear to have whole days go by without seeing her."

Beck looked away from me and took in the space. When he returned his attention to me, he said, "Forgive me if I'm overstepping here. If that's the case, just say so. But does he at least provide for Luna financially?"

"He's supposed to pay child support, but he doesn't," I replied.

"Have you gone back to court about it?"

I shook my head. "No. And I don't want to," I shared.

There was a long pause before he said, "Do you mind me asking why that is?"

I didn't mind him asking. In fact, as much as I hadn't exactly thought that this was where my conversation and evening with Beck was going to go, it was nice to be able to talk to someone about it. Of course, I'd talked with Mara already. And even though she'd given me her opinion in the beginning, she supported my decision in how I chose to handle it all. Since then, she hadn't brought it up.

"I don't want to force him to take care of his daughter," I began. "I realize it's his responsibility just as much as it's mine, but I have no desire to go through all of that. I'd rather spend my time here with Luna instead of in court fighting with her father. It was already painful enough having to come to terms with my new life. I don't want to go through any more of that. Not only that, but if I push for the support, he'll probably push to spend time with her. And he'll be doing it out of spite."

I paused a moment. I wanted to make sure Beck fully understood why I'd made this choice. "I know you're probably thinking that it's wrong or selfish of me, but I don't want her being somewhere with someone who hasn't had a mind to see her for more than five months of her life now. I lived with someone who spited me, and I want better for her."

Beck lowered his plate to the table and said, "You lived with someone who spited you?"

I nodded.

"Who?"

I swallowed hard past the lump in my throat. "My mother," I rasped. "She's hated me from the beginning."

"What about your father?"

After letting out a grunt, I shared, "He's the reason my mother hated me. Apparently, they loved each other enough to make me, but once I was born, he was gone. She made sure I knew that I ruined her life."

"Christ, Chasey, I'm so sorry," Beck lamented. His words told me how much sympathy he had for me, and his voice indicated how much anger he felt on my behalf.

"It's okay. I'm okay," I assured him. "But my life has taught me a lot about the kind of person I want to be. It's taught me everything about the kind of mother I want to be. And maybe it hasn't all worked out the way I had hoped, but for now, my daughter is happy and healthy and blissfully unaware of any of the guilt or struggles I feel. That's all I can ask for."

The silence stretched between us for a few moments, and I had no choice but to wonder if I'd killed the entire vibe for the evening.

I mean, Beck hadn't made me feel that way, but I had to be realistic. What guy, especially a guy like him, wanted to hear a woman rattle on and on about the problems in her life with her ex-husband and her piss-poor excuse for a mother?

"Chasey, can I ask you a question?"

I looked over at him, cocked an eyebrow, and retorted, "What in all that just happened would make you think that you couldn't ask me one?"

"I'm just… I'm trying to be gentle here," he said. The minute the words were out of his mouth was the minute I realized it was true. His voice was so soft and tender, and he spoke to me with such care and concern.

"What's your question?" I asked.

He hesitated briefly but ultimately said, "Why didn't you call me?"

"Why didn't I call you?" I repeated.

He nodded. "I gave you my number that day at the hotel, and I told you to call me if there was anything I could do to help," he reminded me.

God, if he only knew how many times I wanted to call him.

I licked my lips and rationalized, "I thought you were just being nice. And that doesn't mean I don't think you would have answered if I called. I don't know. I guess I couldn't understand why you would want to be bothered with any of this. It was a nightmare."

"I had no doubt that it would be, which is why I wanted to help," he explained.

"But what could you have done, Beck?" I questioned him. "I was here going through a divorce while struggling to take care of my daughter. You were on tour with your band. Our lives couldn't be more different."

"I'm just a normal guy," he insisted.

No, he wasn't.

He was unlike any guy I'd ever met.

"You're a famous rock star, and I'm—"

"The most beautiful woman I've ever met," Beck declared, interrupting me.

Now he was just being ridiculous. I didn't think I was hideous by any means. But this was Beck Emerson. He had traveled the world, and there was no doubt he'd seen thousands of beautiful women.

"Stop," I ordered.

"I'm serious, Chasey."

"Okay, well, even if that's the truth—"

"It is," he interrupted me again.

"Right. What I'm saying is that if that's the truth, it still doesn't change the fact that you live a very unconventional life, and mine is nothing special," I reasoned.

Beck shot me a strange look.

I didn't know where this conversation was going to go, but the uncertain vibe in the room caused me to resort to begging.

"Can we please talk about something else?" I pleaded. "Is the band planning another tour soon?"

At that, I held my breath as I waited for Beck's response. It took him a moment, but he ultimately nodded his head. Then he told me about the band's plans for the future. There were talks of another tour, but nothing had been decided on just yet. Beck and I spent a bit more time talking about his life on the road. Though I was definitely more of a homebody now, I thought it sounded incredible. I couldn't imagine what it was like being able to travel all over the world like he did.

As the evening wound down, things got slightly awkward. Or, at least, they did for me. Part of me had been hoping there would be something more... physical with Beck. Sadly, he never gave me any indication that he wanted to take things there.

Any hope I had of something like that happening came to a grinding halt when he finally stood and said, "Well, I had a really great time with you tonight, Chasey. Thank you for letting me come over to see you and Luna before I leave New Hampshire."

Not wanting to show my disappointment, I looked away as I stood, hoping to breathe beyond the stinging I felt at the tip of my nose.

When I got myself upright, I looked at him and said, "Thank you for this weekend, Beck. We had a really great time with you. I hope you have a safe trip back to Pennsylvania."

"Thanks."

We started to move to the front door, and once we made it there, Beck turned and looked back at me. "Would you mind if I reached out to you when I got back home?" he asked. "I'd love to stay connected and hear all about how you and Luna are doing."

That surprised me.

It also felt like a precursor to torture.

Would I have to live with Beck calling every now and then

just to see how life was going for me only to know that nothing would ever come of it?

"Really?" I asked.

"Yes."

"Sure," I answered, even though my brain was screaming at me to tell him the very opposite. "If you have time and want to talk, I'd love to hear from you."

He smiled at me and responded, "Good."

Then, he held his arms out to the sides. I couldn't stop myself from moving in and allowing him to hug me. I hadn't had the comfort of a masculine embrace for a long time.

And, damn, did it feel good to be inside Beck's arms.

I hugged him back and discreetly inhaled his scent. When I pulled my face back from his chest, Beck loosened the hold of one of his arms. He lifted that hand to the side of my face and pushed a lock of hair back behind my ear before he gently stroked his thumb over my cheek.

That one touch was all it took. One tender touch from him ignited my skin, and it was all I could do not to react.

"Take care of yourself, Chasey," he whispered.

I nodded and rasped, "I will."

He smiled one last time, let me go, and opened the door.

After he walked out, he looked back and promised, "I'll call soon."

"Goodbye, Beck."

A moment later, he was gone.

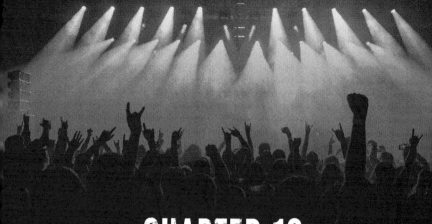

CHAPTER 10

Chasey

JUST AS I HAD SUSPECTED, LIFE WAS BACK TO NORMAL.

It hadn't even been a full twenty-four hours since I last saw Beck, but I was already feeling the loss of him. I hadn't felt that way Sunday morning after he'd taken Luna and I out to dinner on Saturday evening, so I knew what I was feeling now was all because last night's goodbye was final.

Of course, Beck had said he wanted to keep in touch with me, but even if he did remember to call me, I wasn't convinced it was going to be anywhere near the same as being in his presence.

This had been the very definition of a Monday. I'd had one of the best weekends I'd had in months, and I was now back to reality. My alarm went off early this morning. I had no choice but to get up, get myself ready, get Luna ready, and wait for Mara to arrive.

Mara had been running a few minutes behind, so I didn't have a chance to really tell her much of anything about the weekend. But because I wanted her feeling crazy all day long about it, I did share one bit of information with her before I left.

"I'll be back at the usual time," I started before I kissed Luna on the cheek. Mara had been holding her at the time. I began moving toward the door when I stopped, turned, and said, "Oh, and by the way, there's a new toy piano on the couch in the living room. It's Luna's. Beck got it for her and gave it to her as a gift yesterday."

I watched for a brief moment as the surprise and excitement hit Mara's face. I could tell she was about to ask for more details but I grinned, turned, and said, "I'll check in on my break."

While I had checked in with Mara on my lunch break, we hadn't discussed anything pertaining to Beck. I knew she wanted to know all the juicy details about my weekend with him, but she wanted to be able to talk uninterrupted. There was no way I'd be able to tell her everything while I was on my break.

So, she told me all about her day with Luna to that point.

And now, I was on my way back home, but it wasn't until after I'd put in a long first day back on the grind since seeing Beck for the first time in months.

The day had been tough. Following my break and phone call with Mara, I got back to work, but it wasn't easy. As had been the case through most of the morning, I often found myself getting distracted by my thoughts of the weekend Luna and I had with Beck. That would have been bad enough at home, all things considered.

But given the fact that it was early November, and the holidays were approaching, I really couldn't be distracted. I never would have thought that a small-town post office could be so busy, but apparently I was wrong. There were too many packages, too many customers, and too much mail to sort through for me to be spending my days being sidetracked by a man I'd never see again.

I had to figure out how I was going to pull it together because I couldn't continue to do this every day. I'd be fired if I continued to be unfocused, and then I'd really be in trouble.

It was my hope that Mara would have some advice for me.

The minute I walked through the front door, I let out a sigh of relief. It was always such a good feeling to be home.

I kicked off my shoes and found Mara and Luna in the living room playing together. While there were a bunch of different toys strewn across the floor, it was the piano that Beck had given her that was currently occupying my daughter.

"She loves this thing," Mara declared. "All day long, if she wasn't eating or sleeping, she was playing with this."

"She was just as fascinated by it yesterday, too," I marveled. "Luna, baby girl, Mommy is home."

Luna ignored me and banged her fists on the piano.

Beck had created a monster. My little girl didn't even care that I was in the room.

"Look, she's not going to be distracted by whatever you have to say to her right now because she's busy," Mara began. "But I'm completely ready to hear everything about your weekend. And don't leave out a single detail."

I sent a coy smile her way before I shared, "It was a nice weekend."

"Don't you dare think you're going to play that game with me," she said. "I want to know what happened."

After taking in a deep breath, I blew it out and dove in. I told Mara all about the weekend I had with Beck. I shared everything from the flowers he brought me on Saturday before he took us out to dinner to the desserts we shared on Sunday evening after I put Luna down for the night. I also told her about the conversation he and I had last night about Aaron, the divorce, and the fact that my ex-husband didn't have the slightest interest in his daughter.

When I finally finished telling her everything, she asked, "And?"

"And?" I repeated.

"And was that all?" she questioned me.

I thought back over everything I'd just shared with her.

I'd been replaying the entire weekend over and over in my mind since Beck left last night, so I was certain I hadn't missed anything.

"Yes, that was all," I assured her.

"Are you positive?" she pressed.

I nodded. "Of course I am. What do you think I'm forgetting?"

Something changed in her expression, and she shrugged. "I don't know. I mean, I know you said he left here each night and went back to the hotel, but was there any kissing or anything else?"

That's what she'd been getting at?

If it wasn't so devastating, I might have started laughing at her question.

Shaking my head, I answered, "No, there was no kissing or anything else like that."

Mara narrowed her eyes on me.

"What is that look for?" I wondered.

"I'm trying to work out how you feel about the fact that there was no kissing," she explained.

I wondered if she'd come up with an answer to it because I didn't exactly think I had figured it out just yet. On one hand, I definitely wished it would have happened. After all, this was Beck Emerson. I'd have to be crazy not to want to kiss him. But that alone was the very reason I also felt grateful that it hadn't happened.

Something told me that Beck would be no slouch in that department. And considering how long it had been since I'd received any sort of affection like that, it was safe to say that he'd be so good at it and I would just want more of something I couldn't have.

"I think it's best that nothing happened," I finally admitted.

"Really?" Mara asked.

"Really," I confirmed.

For several moments, my best friend didn't respond. She simply stared at me, looking a little shocked and a lot befuddled. Eventually, she spoke. "How is that possible?"

"He doesn't live here," I said.

"Okay? And?"

"And so what would have been the point?" I countered. "Mara, I'm relatively certain I'm never going to see the man again. You know me. I'm not exactly the kind of woman who spends her weekends making out with random guys."

Mara held her hand up and ordered, "Okay, wait a minute. I never said you were the kind of woman who did that. *But* Beck is not just some random guy. He's *Beck Em-er-son*. You'd have to be crazy not to want to kiss him."

I shrugged my shoulders. "I mean, I'm not going to say that it wouldn't have been nice," I began. "I'm sure it would have been wonderful. But if it had happened, then what? I would still be stuck here doing the same thing I've been doing for the last how many months, and he would have left. Yeah, the fantasy might have gotten a little nicer and slightly more enjoyable, but in the end, I'd be the one having to cope with not having that ever again. It's better this way."

She shot me a look of indifference as Luna really began to bang on the keys of her piano. It had gotten so out of control that we both started to laugh.

"So, that's it?" she asked when we both settled down. "He gives you the best weekend you've had in months, possibly longer, and nothing? He just goes home, and you go back to life as it was?"

I nodded.

"What was the point in that?"

I couldn't say I didn't understand her frustration or her question. Unfortunately, the answer I was going to give her wasn't going to make her feel any less frustrated.

"I think it was too much," I explained.

"What?"

"Mara, I told him everything," I started. Even though I didn't want to admit it, I continued, "The likelihood is that Beck probably heard my whole story and realized it was far too much drama to get involved with beyond being friendly."

She shook her head. "No way."

"What do you mean?"

"Chasey, he walked into the hotel the day you caught Aaron," she reminded me. "It doesn't get any more dramatic than that. This isn't about him not wanting to be involved in your drama. And it definitely isn't about him not liking the way you look a whole lot. I heard what he said to you when we were out at Granite on Friday night, and I saw the way he looked at you. I've got to be missing something."

Once again, I couldn't say I didn't feel a lot of the same sentiments that Mara was feeling. The problem was that I didn't really want to admit that I was just as confused. Because it had been hard enough for me to accept that Beck had had me in his arms last night and never made a move.

He had hugged me close, tucked a lock of hair behind my ear, and gently stroked the apple of my cheek. He did all of that while also speaking to me in a way that made me feel like there was so much more meaning and promise behind his words.

If it had just been the hug and the words, I might have overlooked it. But I couldn't ignore the way his touch felt on my skin. And to know I felt something that powerful and he didn't was disappointing.

I couldn't fault Beck for not having that same overwhelming desire to kiss me as I did for him. He had still given me the best weekend I'd had in months. So, I refused to say anything bad about him to Mara.

Instead, I reasoned, "He's just a really nice guy. I feel very lucky that he even gave me the time and attention that he did this weekend. Because if nothing else, it showed me that there are good men out there."

"I just don't get it," Mara murmured as she looked down at Luna, who was still content with her piano. "I really didn't think he'd just go back home without wanting more with you."

I appreciated Mara's words because they indicated just how much she wanted this for me, how much she thought I deserved something special.

"Well, it's not like he said he'd never talk to me again," I told her.

Mara's head snapped up. "What do you mean?" she asked, her whole body on alert.

I smiled and shared, "He did ask if it was alright for him to reach out to me when he got home. He said he wanted to stay connected so he could check in on Luna and me."

"Chasey!" Mara cried out. "That's the kind of thing you lead with!"

"What's the big deal?" I asked, shrugging my shoulders.

Her face lit up. "It means that I wasn't wrong and that he's into you," she declared.

"I don't think that's it," I argued. "He was just being nice. He's a rock star with a busy life, one very different from mine. He does not need to be spending his time checking in on a single mom and her baby."

"Maybe he wants to," she countered. "Maybe he knows just how incredible you are, and he wants to be a part of whatever craziness your life is."

I rolled my eyes. "I highly doubt that," I said. "And I'm not exactly convinced he's actually going to call. I think he was simply trying to make sure he didn't leave here with it feeling awkward… or more awkward than it already was."

"Awkward?"

I bit my lip and looked at Luna. Maybe I should have kept that part to myself.

"Chasey?" Mara called.

"Yeah?"

"What happened?"

I swallowed and rasped, "He hugged me and stroked his thumb tenderly over my cheek."

Her eyes nearly fell out of her head. She stared at me for a few long seconds before she announced, "Oh, he likes you."

I loved that she felt that way, and part of me wished that was the case. But I didn't want to get my hopes up for something that seemed utterly impossible. Not only did we not even live close to one another, but Beck and I lived very different lives. We had even discussed it. Or, I had basically told him how it was, and he didn't refute it.

So, as much as I might have wanted what Mara was saying to be the truth, I knew it wasn't realistic. I was more than pre-pared to deal with what was going to come my way over the next few days, which would likely be me trying to forget all that happened with Beck. I'd probably have a few difficult days of muddling through the distraction he provided, but eventually, without any additional communication, it would all be like it never happened. The only thing that would remain, proving I hadn't made this all up in my head, would be the toy piano he gave to my daughter.

Despite feeling the way I did, I didn't want to crush Mara's hopes about it all. So, I replied, "I guess we'll see what happens. Maybe he'll call."

She beamed at me. "He will. And I can't wait for it to happen."

At that, I decided there was one thing I needed. A cuddle from my girl.

I reached out and said, "Luna."

For the first time since I walked in, she tore her attention away from Beck's piano and acknowledged me.

"Hi, baby girl," I said to her.

Her face lit up, and it was all I could do to not burst into tears at how happy she made me. Moving forward, no matter what happened or didn't happen with Beck, I knew I'd be fine as long as I had this girl with me.

I picked Luna up in my arms and smothered her with kisses. She giggled, and the sound of her laughter was like music to my ears.

Yeah.

I might have had a wish for something more in my life, something extraordinary with a man like Beck, but if Luna was all that I got, I'd still consider myself the luckiest woman in the world.

CHAPTER 11

Beck

MY ARMS WERE WRAPPED AROUND THE WOMAN WHO WAS MY hero.

My mom.

I was back in Pennsylvania, and suffice it to say, my mom had missed me. She was holding on to me like she hadn't seen me in years, even though it really hadn't been anywhere close to being that long.

In fact, we'd stopped here toward the tail end of the tour to play a couple of shows, and I'd made it a point to visit with her.

But I guess this was how it was always going to be with my mom. No matter how old I was or how short the time between each of our visits had been, she would always hug me like she hadn't seen me in decades.

When she finally started to loosen her hold on me, she didn't hesitate to step back and start scolding me. "It's about time you got over here to visit your mother," she chastised me.

I knew she was just teasing me, but I also wanted her to know that I hadn't really delayed the visit.

"I just got in yesterday afternoon," I told her. "You're the first visit I've had with anyone since I got back."

It was now late Wednesday morning, only a few days since I left Chasey's place. After a lot of deliberation on Monday, I decided it was best for me to come home.

But it wasn't easy.

A big part of me had wanted to stay and spend more time with Chasey and Luna. I loved being around them, and I hadn't stopped thinking about them since I left their place on Sunday night—the same night I had to muster up all the self-control and willpower not to kiss Chasey when we were standing just inside her door saying goodbye to one another.

That just might have been the hardest thing I'd ever done. But it was necessary. Or, at least, I thought it was necessary. After everything that I'd learned earlier in the evening, I knew this wasn't the kind of thing I could rush with her.

The amount of trauma Chasey was recovering from was unbelievable. Catching her ex-husband in the act of cheating would have easily been enough to deal with, but she also had to cope with what her childhood had been like for her.

Though I couldn't say for sure just how much all of it was still affecting her, I definitely knew she wasn't over it. Chasey had gotten emotional a couple of times over the weekend, so there had to be some heartache lingering.

More than anything, I wished she would have called me when I was still on tour and she was going through her divorce. I hated thinking about how badly she had struggled. I hated knowing she had to give up doing what she loved the most, which was staying home to take care of her daughter. And I hated seeing that she was still struggling.

I knew it the minute I walked into her kitchen on Saturday while I held Luna in my arms. I watched Chasey put those flowers I'd gotten for her into a drinking glass. It didn't matter to me, and Chasey didn't seem to care; she loved the flowers all the same. But I thought she deserved to have a vase to put them in. I wanted to kick myself for not getting one and having them already put in one for her.

Regardless, Chasey didn't even seem remotely concerned about the glass. In fact, she just didn't seem to care much about material things in general. From what I could see, she didn't have any lavish things, and she definitely wasn't splurging on herself. Luna was her whole world.

And I had this unexplainable and overwhelming urge to take care of the both of them.

So, despite how badly I wanted to kiss her, I held myself back. I wanted to give her time and take this slow. I was willing to do whatever it took to make sure we had a fair shot at this.

That was precisely the reason I came home. I figured it would be a bit easier on both of us if we were able to get to know one another a little better over the phone.

Truthfully, it might have just been easier on me. I couldn't exactly say how Chasey would have felt about it. She seemed perfectly content and pulled together when she was around me. She shared openly and freely while also managing to take care of her daughter and didn't seem the least bit affected by being around me.

It was certainly possible that she would have been okay having me around while we got to know one another better. I was the one who needed the distance. Not because I didn't like being around her, but because I liked it too much. It was a herculean feat to stop myself from acting on my impulses.

Feeling all that I was feeling, I wanted to make sure I was doing it right. So, the reason for this visit with my mom was twofold. I missed her, knew she missed me, and this had sort of become a ritual. But I also wanted her advice.

"What do you mean you just got back yesterday?" my mom asked as we walked deeper into the house. "Your sister told me she met up with Holland the other day."

"Yeah, well, everyone else came back a few days before I did," I shared. "I stayed in New Hampshire for a little longer."

"Wait a minute," she remarked as I sat down at the island in her kitchen. Years ago, I'd purchased this house for my mom. After everything she'd done and sacrificed for Sadie and me, I wanted to give her something to show my appreciation. "I didn't think your last show was in New Hampshire."

"It wasn't supposed to be, but Cash met a girl when we had played there back in the summer," I started. "Her name is Demi. Anyway, it took him quite a bit of time to convince her to give him a shot, but she eventually did. In the midst of all of that, he'd asked all of us if we'd be willing to play a show at the end of the tour at her cousin's bar. We all agreed."

My mom's brows shot up. "So, is Cash still dating this Demi?" she asked.

I nodded. "I think she's the one for him," I shared. "He's in so deep with her, and she actually moved back here with him."

There was a long pause while my mom digested the news. "I never would have thought," she murmured.

"Thought what?" I asked.

"That of all of you Cash would be the first to settle down," she said.

I let out a laugh. "You aren't the only one," I noted. "It came as a shock to the rest of us, too. But they're both happy, so I'm happy for them."

"My heart can't handle this," she rasped, her emotions getting the best of her.

That reaction caught me off guard. "What's wrong?"

Shaking her head, my mom explained, "Nothing. I just… if Cash has found someone, maybe it's only a matter of time for the rest of you."

Now I understood.

If there was one thing I knew, it was that my mom adored everyone in the band. We'd all been friends for so long that in some ways, it was like we'd all become family. So, to know that Cash had found someone that was making him happy, it only made sense that my mom would have that kind of reaction.

After pulling out a bunch of food for me to snack on since that's what moms did, she asked, "So, I still don't understand."

"Understand what?" I asked.

"Well, if Demi was the one moving here with Cash, it would seem that he'd be the one staying back in New Hampshire to help her pack up her things," she started. "Why is it that you were the one to stay? What were you doing there?"

For several long moments, I didn't respond. I had wanted to get my mom's advice, but I wasn't sure how to bring this up to her. Once she knew that I was seriously interested in someone, she was going to lose her mind.

"Would you have wanted someone?" I questioned her.

Confusion marred her features. "Wanted someone? What do you mean?"

Hoping I wasn't about to open a can of worms that would make her upset, I clarified, "When Sadie and I were little. Would you have wanted someone there with you to help out? I know we had Gram, but I'm talking about you having a partner."

Her expression went from confused to curious. "What's this about, Beck?"

I held her gaze a few seconds before I asked, "Do you remember that day back in the summer when I called you and told you about the new mom who had caught her husband cheating?"

"Yes."

"That was when we were in New Hampshire," I reminded her. "It was the same trip where Cash met Demi. Anyway, I had given that woman my number, but over the months that followed, I never heard from her. When we went back to play there on Friday, I saw her again."

My mom's eyes widened, and I could see the hopeful look in them.

Wanting to give her something that'd make her happy, I shared, "I stayed in New Hampshire for a few extra days because I wanted to spend some time with Chasey."

"Chasey?"

I nodded.

She took that in, thought a moment, and pressed, "What happened?"

"We spent the weekend together," I told her. "It was great, and I really like her. Plus, her daughter, Luna, is the most adorable kid I've ever seen."

"That's great news," she declared. "Why do I feel like you're struggling with something?"

"She's been through a lot," I started. "I like her a lot, but I don't want to push for something she may not want when she's already dealing with enough stress. That's why I was wondering what you would have wanted."

"Beck, my experience is not going to be the same as someone else's," she said. "I wouldn't change anything about my life. I love it, I love you, and I love Sadie."

Nodding my understanding, I replied, "I get that. Nobody would ever doubt how much you love and care about us. That's not what I'm getting at, though. And I know you were completely capable of raising us on your own. I'm just wondering if you would have wanted someone around. Not just to help ease the burden of raising children on your own but to care for you, too."

"Well, of course, that would have been nice," she finally declared. "Raising kids isn't easy, and that's the truth whether you're a single parent or happily married. It's the hardest job in the world. And while I managed to do okay on my own, there's no doubt I would have loved to feel like I wasn't alone."

I always knew that my mom was beyond amazing for

everything she'd done to give Sadie and me the life she did. Recognizing that she worked hard for us wasn't difficult to do. But until now, I don't think I ever took the time to really consider how it must have been for her on a personal level. As a kid, I never thought about my mom not having a husband or partner to go through all the struggles with or having someone to vent to after a long day.

Coming to that understanding now was affecting me a bit more than I would have liked. "Thanks, Mom," I said, feeling the tightness in my throat.

"For what?"

"You gave up so much of your own happiness for us," I answered.

She smiled and insisted, "I'd do it all over again in a heartbeat, Beck."

There it was again. That little reminder that moms were superheroes.

I held on to my appreciation and love for everything my mother sacrificed for her children and allowed that to settle somewhere deep inside me. Once it did, my thoughts drifted to Chasey. Her selflessness when it came to her daughter was inspiring, and I knew she'd give up everything she had to in order to make sure Luna had it all. And it was then that it hit me.

I didn't want Chasey to have to give up anything. I wanted her to have it all. And it had nothing to do with anything that I could buy for her. It had everything to do with wanting her to have that companionship, a partner, someone she could rely on to be there for *her* when she needed it.

"You look like you've just had some massive revelation," my mom said, cutting into my thoughts.

I chuckled. "I think I have a phone call I need to make tonight."

Her face lit up. "I'm glad to hear that. In the meantime, why don't you tell me all about this woman and her little girl before you tell me how the rest of the tour went?"

At that, my mom settled in for all the details. We spent the next few hours talking about Chasey, Luna, and the tour. I wasn't sure I'd ever seen my mother so happy before.

"Beck?"

The sound of that voice was like music to my ears.

At the same time, I was slightly concerned that there was such surprise littered in the tone of that voice.

"You sound surprised, Chasey," I returned.

There was a moment of hesitation before she replied, "I just... well, I wasn't expecting your call."

"I told you I wanted to stay in touch," I reminded her.

"I know, but... well, never mind."

"What?"

Another pause before she insisted, "It's nothing. So, are you back in Pennsylvania now?"

"I am."

"That's good. Did you have a safe trip?"

I wanted to laugh. I was a grown man who'd been taking care of himself for years. I hadn't had anyone, not even my mother, ask me about how my trips to and from places had been.

Maybe Chasey was just trying to make conversation. Perhaps she was nervous.

Instead of laughing, I answered, "It was fine. How are you and Luna doing?"

The sound of Chasey's soft laughter came through the line. "We're good," she responded. "I just put her down for the night."

"I was hoping I got the time right," I told her. "I didn't want to interrupt your bedtime routine with her."

"Well, you did great. I was going to go out to the living room to clean up, but then I realized there wasn't much to put away anyway," she said.

"Oh?"

The silence stretched between us a moment. "My daughter has not stopped banging her hands on that piano you got her," Chasey eventually declared.

I grinned.

For some reason, I loved knowing that Luna was enjoying that piano. Of course, I hoped it wasn't driving Chasey crazy.

"I'm sorry if it's made you lose your mind," I lamented. " I should have thought about that before I got it."

"It's okay, Beck. I love that she has it. It's her favorite toy," she shared.

"Maybe she'll be in her own band one day. You probably know that I'm already partial to the keyboard, but if you think she might prefer the drums or a guitar, I'm happy to supply her with those as well," I offered.

"I think she's okay for now," Chasey insisted. "She's more than happy with just the keyboard."

While I was sure that was the case, it still didn't stop me from wanting to get her all of it. I kept telling myself it was because I believed it was best to foster that love for music early, but I think there was part of me, deep down, that knew my need to do that was about something else entirely.

"If that changes, you'll let me know?" I asked.

"I'll let you know," she promised.

"So, how have you been?" I wondered.

I heard Chasey take in a deep breath and release it before she answered, "I'm alright. Tired. Get up and go to work before I come home and take care of the baby. Just going through the motions every day, you know?"

I didn't.

I honestly didn't, and I hated that I couldn't relate to what she was feeling.

Every day felt like an adventure for me, so I couldn't even begin to imagine what she was experiencing each day. Even when I was on tour and knew that I was going to be playing the same show over and over, it still felt thrilling. I loved what I was doing.

That's when I recalled what Chasey had said to me when I was there. All she wanted was to be a stay-at-home mom who took care of her children and her husband. She was going through the motions now because she wasn't doing what would bring her joy.

I didn't know if it was the right thing to say, but I thought it might help. So, I said, "It's worth it, you know?"

"What is?"

"Everything you're doing right now to take care of Luna," I clarified. "She might be too young to understand it now, but she'll eventually figure it out. What you're doing for her is something she'll live her whole life wanting to make sure you know she appreciates."

If I thought Chasey had hesitated to speak before, I would have been wrong. Once I'd delivered my little speech, she didn't respond. The silence waged on, and I waited.

It went on for so long, I'd managed to convince myself that I overstepped. Just as I was about to apologize, I heard a sniffle.

Shit.

I didn't want to make her cry.

"Chasey…" I trailed off. At that moment, I wanted nothing more than to be there with her to dry her tears and hold her in my arms.

"I'm sorry. I think I'm still dealing with my hormones being all out of whack," she declared, clearly searching for any excuse not to admit what she actually thought about what I had to say.

"There's no need to apologize. I probably got a little too deep there," I reasoned.

"Yeah," she agreed. "But it was really nice to hear. I hope you're right."

"I am."

"That makes me feel good," she said.

I was back to grinning. "I aim to please."

Another soft laugh came through the line. It was sweet and delicate. I wanted more of it.

"So, when did you get back home?" she asked.

"Tuesday afternoon," I replied.

"And now what?"

"Now what?" I returned.

"Yes. The tour is over and you're home. What are you going to do with all your free time?" she wondered.

I wanted to tell her that I planned to come right back to New Hampshire because I missed her so much. Instead, I said, "Well, I visited my mom earlier today. But moving forward, I'm going to take each day as it comes and do whatever inspires me. The holidays are coming, so there's at least going to be a My Violent Heart pre-Thanksgiving party."

"That sounds like fun. What happens at one of those?"

It was.

I smiled at the fact that Chasey seemed interested in getting to know a bit more about me. If telling her about what I had going on for the next few weeks was going to keep her on the phone with me, I'd tell her anything she wanted to know.

For nearly an hour, I stayed on the phone with Chasey, sharing some things about my life. She seemed to appreciate it, even once claiming that it was nice to be the one listening instead of the one doing all the talking.

I wanted to hear her voice more, but I'd give her mine for a while. Especially if it was giving her something she needed that went far beyond simple conversation.

CHAPTER 12

Beck

"THANKS FOR BEING MY DATE TONIGHT."

"You're welcome, Beck."

My sister and I were making our way from my truck parked in the driveway up the front walkway of Cash's house, the house he now shared with Demi.

It was the Saturday before Thanksgiving, and we were heading into the My Violent Heart pre-Thanksgiving party.

For the most part, we hadn't really seen one another as a group since our final performance in New Hampshire at the end of our tour. So, this was going to be a nice reunion for all of us.

"Though, just to be completely honest with you, I was already planning to come anyway," Sadie shared. When I glanced over at her and gave her a questioning look, she added, "Holland already invited me like a week and a half ago."

Lifting my chin in understanding, I replied, "That was cool of her to do, but you should know that you always have an invite to things like this because of me. Truthfully, everyone in the band loves you anyway, so you don't ever really need to wait for the invite. It should just be a given."

There was a lengthy pause before my sister said, "I'm really glad you feel that way, Beck."

We made it to the front door, rang the bell, and waited. A moment later, the door swung open, and Cash greeted us.

"Hey, guys. Come on in," he urged as he stepped back to let us in.

Once we were inside, Cash directed his attention to my sister. "How's it going, Sadie?" he asked as he gave her a hug.

"Great," she answered. "Thanks for having me here tonight."

"Ah, you know you're always welcome," he insisted.

Just then, Demi strolled up and Cash took a moment to introduce them. No sooner had he done that when Holland shouted, "Beck and Sadie are here!"

Holland rushed toward us as the rest of the group followed. After pulling Sadie into an embrace, Holland threw her arms around me and said, "Hey, Beck. Happy Thanksgiving."

"Happy Thanksgiving, Holland," I returned as I hugged her back.

For the next minute or so, Walker, Killian, Roscoe, and Walker's brother, Raiden, who was our road manager, all came up to greet Sadie before they said hello to me and we all moved deeper into the house.

"So, it's surprising you didn't bring someone other than your sister as a date," Killian said. Then he quickly directed his attention to Sadie and insisted, "No offense to you, darling."

"None taken," she returned. "Beck's got his head in the clouds these days, so you might not see him with a date for the foreseeable future."

"Are you still holding out hope for that single mom, Beck?" Roscoe asked.

"I don't need to hold out hope," I retorted. "We've been talking to each other regularly ever since we played that last show."

"Aw, that's great news," Holland chimed in. "I still cringe

thinking about what we walked into that day back in the summer. That poor woman. What's her name again?"

"Chasey," I answered.

"So, are you two officially together?" Demi asked.

I shook my head. "No. No, it's not like that yet," I answered honestly. "We're just taking some time to get to know one another."

I didn't understand why no sooner had I walked in the door when I was suddenly being bombarded with questions about my relationship with Chasey. It wasn't that I was bothered by talking about her, but I hadn't even had a chance to get a drink yet.

"I think that's a good thing," Walker declared. "She's a single mom, and she's newly divorced. It's probably not a wise idea to jump right in anyway."

Out of all of us, Walker was probably the most sensible. Well, him and Holland. Where Cash, Killian, Roscoe, and I had always been the ones to party a little harder, Walker and Holland always turned in early or, at the very least, stayed relatively low-key.

It wasn't until sometime over the last couple of months when Cash pointed out how they always were that Killian, Roscoe, and I started to wonder if perhaps there was something going on between the two of them. We'd decided that unless and until they shared the news, we wouldn't say anything about it. It didn't make sense to us why they'd hide it; however, I guess it was possible they just wanted time to navigate through it without having to worry about any outside pressure from us. For the rest of us, we all pretty much planned to stay out of it unless it started to affect the rest of the band.

So, hearing those words from Walker, knowing he typically took a sensible and levelheaded approach to just about everything, made me feel like I had made a wise choice in deciding to take things slow.

"Thanks, man," I said.

At that, Cash declared, "Now that we've got that settled,

there's tons of food waiting in the kitchen. Please eat because it's not all staying here."

Cash didn't need to make a second request because we all started to move to the kitchen.

Not long after everyone had gotten some food to eat, smaller groups of conversations had popped up. Holland, Walker, Raid, and Sadie were having their own while Killian, Roscoe, and I had been having another. I had just gone out into the kitchen to get myself a beer and found Cash and Demi there. She was sitting on the counter, and he was standing in front of her.

I wasn't sure I'd ever seen a guy fall so hard for a girl, and I certainly never would have expected it would happen with Cash. Not this quickly, anyway.

I let out a laugh, convinced I'd interrupted something, and apologized, "Sorry."

"It's okay," Demi insisted. "We were just talking."

My eyes slid to Cash, and I could tell from the look on his face that they were not just talking.

I quickly grabbed a beer and said, "Oh, well, I'll just let you get back to it."

"No!" Demi cried out.

I froze on the spot and stared at her. "What's wrong?"

"I wanted to ask you about Chasey," she said.

I couldn't imagine what else anyone here could possibly need to ask me about Chasey. Other than private conversations the two of us had had with each other, which I had no intention of sharing, they knew all there was to know about Chasey.

Even still, I asked, "What about her?"

"Well… I was just wondering what her plans are for the holiday," Demi said.

"Her plans?" I responded.

Nodding, Demi repeated, "Her plans."

I shrugged. "Well, we hadn't really discussed it," I said. "I know she has the day off."

"Oh," Demi murmured as she looked away.

That response told me that she had been thinking I'd have a different answer to her question. I had no idea what that was, but I intended to find out.

"Why do you seem disappointed by that answer?" I asked.

Demi's eyes went to Cash before they came to me. "There's no real reason," she began. "I just... well, I don't know. I mean, this is her daughter's first Thanksgiving, right? I just wondered if she was spending it with her family or close friends. Being a new mom who has just gone through a divorce, I can't imagine it's going to be easy."

The minute the words were out of her mouth, I felt a burn hit my lungs. My stomach dropped as my throat got tight.

Chasey didn't have family she'd be spending the holiday with; I knew at least that much. I knew she was close with Mara, but that was about all. And I wasn't sure if they'd made plans to get together to celebrate.

"That doesn't look good," Cash declared, interrupting my silent panic.

"It's... it's fine," I insisted.

But it wasn't. It definitely wasn't even close to being fine. As a kid, I could recall the holidays for us. We had my mom's parents around, so we didn't necessarily feel like we were alone.

I had a feeling Chasey would feel like she was alone.

"Beck?" Cash called.

"Yeah?"

"What's going on?"

I shook my head. I didn't want to sit and spout Chasey's personal business to people she didn't know. But Cash had been my best friend since kindergarten, so I didn't want to lie to him either.

"I'm good," I assured him. "I just realized I've got something I need to take care of tomorrow."

The look that came over him told me he understood my mindset.

120

"If there's anything we can do," Demi offered.

I dipped my chin. "Thanks."

With that, I walked out of the kitchen and returned to the rest of the crew. I must have done a decent job of covering up what was happening inside my head because nobody questioned me when I walked back in.

I was grateful for that, but my relief stopped there.

I'd need to take the next few days to confirm what plans Chasey had for the holiday, and then I was going to need to come up with a plan of my own.

I refused to allow her and Luna to be alone.

Chasey

I didn't expect it was going to be this hard.

It was the day before Thanksgiving, and I'd just picked Luna up from day care. When I left my place this morning, I told myself that I'd get Luna and make a quick stop at the grocery store before taking her home.

I gotten to the store, pulled into the parking lot, and sat there.

What am I doing? I thought.

As I watched the droves of people pouring in and out of the store, their faces brimming with happiness, I felt nothing but wave after wave of sadness wash over me.

We'd never have that again.

Never.

Of course, I didn't doubt that we'd have happy days ahead. Perhaps I was being a bit dramatic. It was entirely possible that as Luna got older, she and I would make the holidays something special for the two of us. We could cook, bake, and decorate together.

But not now.

She was too small, and I was too sad to even think about all the wonderful possibilities that were ahead for us.

Just like that, it all hit me in my car, in a parking lot, on the day before Thanksgiving.

I was alone.

Feeling the weight of that harsh reality settle in me, I blinked back the tears threatening to fall, turned the car back on, and drove away.

It was only when I was back home that I started to feel the slightest bit of gratitude. At least I'd thought ahead. A few weeks ago, I had spoken with my boss. Luna's day care was closed through the holiday weekend, and Mara had to work. Since I had nobody to watch Luna, I was granted Friday off.

So, if nothing else, I'd have the next four days off with my girl, and somehow, I knew we'd find a way to make the best of it.

For the next couple of hours, I did my best to ignore the overwhelming feeling of sadness and focus all my attention on Luna.

I also spent some time thinking about the good that I'd experienced over the last few weeks. Things hadn't been horrible, and I did really have something else to be thankful for.

Beck.

Though I didn't think he'd ever know it, he'd been something of a lifesaver for me. I hadn't ever expected that he'd call me like he said he would. He reached out that first Wednesday after he left, and he contacted me several times since then. We spoke often, we texted occasionally, and I always felt happier after I talked with him.

Initially, I'd waited around for him to call, but eventually, I reached out to him. Of course, I only ever initiated contact via text message. I never wanted to interrupt whatever he had going on in his life, so I always figured it was best to just send him a text so he could respond whenever it was convenient for him.

The first text I'd sent him was one of Luna sitting up on

her own with the piano he'd gotten her sitting in front of her. I had been talking to her like a crazy lady to get her to smile for a picture, and when she did, it was perfect.

I knew that because she was my daughter, and I'd always think she was perfect.

But I also knew it because Beck had said those exact words. *She's perfect.*

I often went back through our text messages to reread that one. I loved that he thought that of her.

I'd managed to keep my spirits up throughout the remainder of the evening while I was busy with Luna. Unfortunately, after I got my daughter down for the night, I couldn't help but feel the misery taking over again.

I wanted to tell myself it was because I felt sad about the holiday. I tried convincing myself that it would pass. But I knew that wasn't the case.

The truth was, I hadn't heard from Beck in days.

He called on Sunday and told me about the party he'd had with his bandmates the day before. We talked a bit about the holiday and about Luna. It was an ordinary conversation, just like we always had.

But something must have happened.

Because Beck never let this many days go by without reaching out.

That was what all this heartache and sadness was about for me.

Maybe it was that I finally started to realize that whatever fake scenario or fantasy I'd made up in my mind about what I meant to Beck was just that.

Fake.

He'd never indicated that what we had was anything other than us being friendly acquaintances, but I told myself differently. I wanted to believe that I was special, even if I knew deep down that we'd never be anything more than we were.

I wanted to believe it was the business of the holidays. But something was nagging at me, telling me that wasn't the case.

Maybe he'd met someone and would no longer have any interest in how Luna and I were doing anymore.

The urge to call him was strong. I wanted to reach out and, if nothing else, have that closure. I just wanted to know for sure that I'd never hear from him again. It'd be easier to start moving on and accepting my reality.

But I couldn't bring myself to do it.

Not yet, anyway. Maybe after the holiday.

On that thought, I moved to the bathroom and got in the shower. I didn't take long in there, though. There was a big part of me that had been hoping that maybe Beck would call tonight. When he did reach out, it was almost always in the evenings after I put Luna down.

That was another thing. He knew my schedule—as boring as it was—and adjusted whatever he had going on to accommodate that.

I wasn't too proud to admit that the minute I got back to my bedroom, I was still wrapped in a towel when I checked the phone.

No calls.

No texts.

My mood only deteriorated from there. As I threw on a pair of panties and a sleep shirt that just barely covered my ass knowing I'd pump before going to bed so I wouldn't need to wear my nursing bra, I could only think about how much I wished I'd known it was going to be like this.

I wished I had known just how lonely I'd start to feel.

So much of what I felt before I'd gone out with Mara weeks ago to Granite when I saw Beck again for the first time was resurfacing.

I'd have to take the night to feel my emotions and sit with

them because in the morning, holiday or not, I had to be a mom again.

No matter what I felt in my heart, I'd only ever give Luna the very best of me. I'd never allow her to feel my sadness or see my heartache. I'd show her love, joy, and compassion. She would always know that regardless of what happened in her life, she'd always have someone standing in her corner.

I took in a deep breath and let it out.

Since I had nowhere to be tomorrow, I decided I'd try to watch a movie. Morning would come early, but I had too many thoughts in my mind right now. There's no way I'd fall asleep anyway.

Grabbing the monitor, I made my way to the kitchen. Dinner and a movie. It would be a late dinner, but it was better than nothing. As I stood there looking in the refrigerator, I made a decision. I'd wake up tomorrow morning, bright-eyed and bushy-tailed for my girl, and I'd send a text to Beck.

I'd reach out and wish him a wonderful Thanksgiving holiday with his family and friends. After that, I'd be done. I'd be grateful for what he gave me while he gave it, and I'd do my best to heal my heart and move on.

Just then, a gentle knock came at the door.

Mara.

I couldn't imagine why she wouldn't have called first.

Not thinking twice about it, I closed the fridge and walked to the front door. A moment later, I opened the door and gasped.

Beck was standing there.

All I wanted to do was burst into tears.

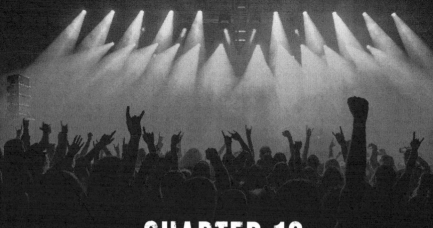

CHAPTER 13

Chasey

"**B**ECK! WHAT ARE YOU DOING HERE?"

After allowing his heated gaze to drift down my body, over my legs, and back up to my face again, Beck held up two grocery bags and answered, "I thought we could celebrate Thanksgiving together."

My eyes widened in surprise and shock as undeniable joy and warmth spread through my body. At his words, at the promise in them, I couldn't hold myself back. I launched myself forward, threw my arms over Beck's shoulders, and kissed him.

Mere seconds passed before I heard the familiar thud of grocery bags landing on the floor, and barely a moment later, I felt Beck's strong arms wrap around my body.

It took no time, none at all, for me to become completely wrapped up in kissing him. I was lost in the feel of his solid body pressed tight to mine. I was utterly spellbound by the touch of his lips against mine. And I was entirely addicted to the taste and sensation of his velvety tongue as it explored my mouth.

Desire pulsed in my veins as the touch, the feel, and the scent of Beck consumed me. I wondered if this man knew what he did to me.

And just like that, it hit me that I'd practically attacked him.

Instantly, I tore my mouth from his and brought my hand up to cover my lips. "I'm so sorry," I mumbled beneath my palm. Closing my eyes tight, feeling mortified, I repeated, "Oh, God, I'm so sorry."

My eyes were darting back and forth across the floor, frantically trying to locate something. Anything that could distract me from the horror I felt. I couldn't even bring myself to look at Beck. I was humiliated.

"Chasey?"

"What?" I returned, still not looking at him.

"Sweetheart, look at me," he urged gently.

I didn't look at him. At least, not immediately. How could I ever look him in the eyes again? I was still so horrified by what I'd done that I didn't notice Beck move close. The next thing I knew, I felt the gentle touch of his thumb and forefinger at my chin. He placed a bit of pressure there and tipped my head back.

When my eyes locked with his, I thought I would burst into tears. But I didn't get a chance to do that because Beck said, "There's nothing to apologize for."

"But I... you... I just attacked you," I stammered.

Beck let out a soft chuckle. "Chasey, if you're calling what you just did an attack, I'm curious what you call it when you're doing something you think is nice."

I shook my head as much as I could move it with him still holding on to the tip of my chin and insisted, "I just lost control for a minute. It's been an emotional day, and I didn't mean to do that."

Beck's brows shot up, silently questioning me.

I didn't answer; I'd already done enough damage.

"Was it not good?" he finally asked.

"What? No. I mean, yes. It was fine. You were fine. I just shouldn't have done that," I told him.

There was a small smile tugging at the corners of his mouth. "Why not?"

I swallowed hard. "Um… we're just acquaintances. We're not dating or anything like that," I explained.

For the first time since he'd taken it between his fingers, Beck let go of my chin. He did that so he could cup the side of my face and stroke his thumb over my cheek.

"Why do you think I'm here, Chasey?"

Why was he here?

I mean, I knew he said he wanted us to celebrate Thanksgiving together, but I had a feeling that wasn't the answer he was looking for.

"You're a nice guy, and you wanted to see Luna?" I guessed.

"That's all true," he confirmed. "But that's not all."

"Why are you here, Beck?" I rasped.

He smiled and answered, "I'm here because I missed you. I'm here because I missed Luna. And I'm here because I've really wanted to kiss you for a long time now." There was a brief pause before he added, "But you beat me to that part, and I'm not the least bit upset about it."

He missed me. He missed Luna. And he had wanted to kiss me for a long time now.

I chewed on the inside corner of my mouth for a moment, allowing that information to penetrate. Then I asked, "Would you like to come in?"

Beck grinned at me. "I'd love to come in."

I stepped back and allowed him to come completely inside. He closed the door before he bent down and picked up the grocery bags.

"We should probably get this stuff in the refrigerator," he suggested.

The next thing I knew, I was squeezed into my kitchen with Beck while he unpacked the bags. I stood there and stared in amazement as he pulled out turkey, potatoes, stuffing, vegetables, and pie.

Though I'd felt the urge several times throughout the day and had managed to stave them off, I finally reached the point where I could no longer hold them back. Tears silently rolled down my cheeks.

Beck had been caught up in unloading the bags, but when he looked up at me and saw the tears, he set the pie down and held out his arms.

"Come here, babe," he urged.

I didn't hesitate to move to him.

Beck folded me into his arms and asked, "Do you want to tell me why you're crying?"

With my cheek pressed to his chest and my arms around his waist, I replied, "I can't believe you're here. One minute I'm standing in front of the refrigerator trying to figure out what to have for dinner while feeling so sad, and the next thing I know you're just here."

"You didn't have dinner yet?" he asked.

I tipped my head back to look up at him. "No."

"You're sad?"

"Yes. Well, I was."

He searched my face for a few minutes before he declared, "Okay. Let's feed you first. Then we'll talk about why you were sad."

"Did you eat?" I asked.

"I got food on the drive," he said.

My whole body went solid. "The drive?" I repeated. "You drove here?"

Beck nodded. "Yeah. I've been on enough planes lately and felt like taking the drive," he shared.

He drove here. Beck drove here all the way from Pennsylvania to have Thanksgiving with me.

"How long was the drive?" I wondered.

"About six hours."

"Wow," I marveled.

I hadn't meant to say that out loud, but I was so blown away by the news. He'd driven six hours to visit with Luna and me.

I didn't know where the courage came from, but at his admission, I said, "I guess it's a good thing I kissed you when you got here. It might have made the drive worth it."

He smiled at me and dipped his chin. Then he responded, "Yes, it was. But if I'm honest, it was worth it the minute you opened the door and I saw you standing there in this little shirt."

I bit my lip.

I had forgotten about my barely-there shirt.

Beck's eyes dropped to my lip momentarily before he shared, "I don't know if it's your thing, but I make one heck of a grilled cheese sandwich."

Cocking an eyebrow, I asked, "You want to make me dinner?"

"There's a whole lot more than just dinner I want to do for you," he confirmed.

My lips parted. "I like grilled cheese," I rasped.

Beck grinned, pressed a kiss to my forehead, and urged, "Let's get to it then."

Ten minutes later, the groceries had been put away, and Beck and I were sitting on the couch in the living room while I ate a grilled cheese sandwich.

While I ate, Beck asked about Luna. I appreciated him keeping the conversation a bit lighter so I could actually eat. I knew if we had immediately ventured into a discussion about why I was sad, I probably wouldn't have been able to get through the sandwich.

By the time I'd filled him in on all things Luna, I had finished eating and set my plate down. For a few brief moments, the silence stretched between us. Surprisingly, I was the one to speak first.

"I'm really glad you're here, Beck," I told him.

"I am, too," he replied. "Do you want to tell me why you were sad before I got here?"

My eyes lingered on his handsome face for a bit, and he didn't seem to mind that I was taking my time to respond.

"I went to the store today," I started. "I had planned to purchase a few things to make a Thanksgiving dinner for one with a baby. But I couldn't get out of the car. I don't know why it took me this long. Today, I realized I'm officially alone."

Beck's features softened as his head tipped to the side.

Seeing that look on his face did something to me. "Have you really missed us?"

"More than I could probably ever tell you," he replied.

"Are you staying here tonight?"

"Here in New Hampshire?" he countered.

I smiled and clarified, "Here in my bed."

Beck held my gaze for a couple moments, the look in his eyes intense. "Is that what you want?" he asked.

"Yes," I answered honestly.

I couldn't explain what came over me. I didn't know why I was suddenly so keen on being reckless. Maybe it was because with Beck, it didn't feel reckless.

It felt good.

It felt necessary.

I stood from the couch, grabbed Luna's monitor, and extended my hand to him. Once Beck stood beside me, his hand linked with mine, I led us to my bedroom.

The next thing I knew, I was walking backward, inching us closer to the bed. My eyes never left Beck's handsome face. When we stopped beside the bed, Beck took the monitor from my hand and placed it on the nightstand. Then he took both of my hands in his and stroked his thumbs over the backs of them.

When I could no longer take the anticipation and the budding desire between us, I begged on a whisper, "Please, Beck."

He didn't need any other words or instruction.

Without an ounce of hesitation, Beck raised one hand to the side of my face, his thumb on my cheek and his fingertips pressed into my hair. As his other arm wrapped around my waist, his lips just barely touched mine. He brushed them back and forth across my lips before he claimed my mouth in a bruising kiss.

All I could do was hold on to him, my nails gripping his shirt tightly at his sides.

Beck Emerson was kissing me.

And if I had my way, we were going to have sex, too.

Beck's hand at the side of my face drove back into my hair as he angled his head and deepened the kiss. His arm loosened on my waist but only so his hand could drift down over my ass. He squeezed me there while pressing his hips forward into mine.

The evidence of his excitement was pressing hard into me, and I loved knowing that I'd done that to him.

I needed more.

I desperately wanted more.

My hands kept their firm hold on Beck's shirt, and I started to drag it up his body. When I could go no farther, he begrudgingly tore his mouth away from mine and lifted it over his head.

The moment it was gone, I stared.

I stared at his flawless body. It was impeccable.

Absolutely perfection.

Broad shoulders, a solid chest, muscled arms, and defined abs were all that made up Beck's torso. Though I'd seen it in pictures before, I now had the opportunity to see his tattoos. He had some on his right arm and shoulder, but it was the one on his left pec, shoulder, and upper arm that stole my attention. It wasn't even so much about the design of the tattoo as it was about the way it seemed to be perfectly molded to his body, like it was designed for his body and his body alone.

WISH

Staring at the utter perfection that was Beck, I marveled, "Wow, you're flawless."

The moment the words left my mouth, I immediately started having second thoughts. God, I wanted him so bad. But I didn't know if I could do this anymore.

I'd had a baby, and pregnancy changed my body in ways I knew it'd never be the same as it was before. The backs of my arms were no longer slender and defined. My ass had gotten a bit bigger, which could arguably be a good thing depending on Beck's preference. But my belly still had that rounded pouch beneath my navel that had protected and sheltered my daughter as she grew inside of me.

Suddenly, with my eyes continuing to roam over Beck's exquisite body, I was regretting that grilled cheese sandwich.

"Babe, get it out of your head right now," Beck's firm voice demanded.

"What?" I breathed a bit absentmindedly as I tipped my chin up to look at him.

"You're beautiful," he insisted.

"But I'm not—"

"You're beautiful," he repeated.

"Yes, but Beck, I think you should know that I'm—"

This time I was cut off by him pressing his finger against my lips to silence me. "You are beautiful, Chasey," he maintained. "That's all there is to it. Nothing else. Do you understand?"

I didn't know if Beck actually wanted me to answer considering he still had his finger pressed against my lips, but I figured it was best to try to communicate my understanding. So, I slowly nodded.

Once he received my confirmation, Beck urged, "Lie on the bed, sweetheart."

I climbed into the bed and sat in the middle of it facing him. He shifted back and forth on his feet as he kicked off his shoes, but he didn't take his eyes off me. As he reached down to remove his socks, he instructed, "On your back, babe."

I hesitated briefly, but eventually lowered myself to my back. As soon as I was there, I closed my eyes and heard the sound of metal.

His belt.

A moment later, that metal clinked on the floor, indicating he'd removed his pants. Just as I opened my eyes again to look at him, Beck's hands touched my ankles. They slowly slid up my calves and over my thighs until they slipped under my shirt and grasped the material of my underwear at my hips. He dragged my panties down my legs and tossed them aside.

Before I could even react, Beck buried his face between my legs.

And he was feasting.

It only took one swipe of his tongue for my back to arch off the bed, but it was the relentless torture of him licking, sucking, and devouring me that had me clamping my legs around him and holding him close.

I never knew torture could feel so good.

Beck groaned every time I squeezed my legs tighter, and I thought it was the most incredible sound.

His tongue.

His tongue. His lips. His mouth.

I couldn't even begin to understand how incredibly talented he was at this.

While one of Beck's hands remained firmly on my hip, the other slid underneath my shirt to my breast. He squeezed it before rubbing his thumb over my nipple.

That was it.

That was all I needed to put me right on the edge.

"Beck," I called out a warning.

Beck ate ravenously.

"I'm going to come," I warned him more clearly.

Cautioning him of what was coming did little to distract him from his greedy endeavor. Beck licked faster, sucked harder, and plunged his tongue deeper.

In the next instant, I felt like my entire body was exploding. Stars dotted the backs of my eyelids as I grabbed a fistful of Beck's hair in my hand and rode the wave of pleasure.

It was glorious.

It was intense.

It was beyond anything I even knew existed.

Beck kept his mouth on me and worked me through to the end. And once I came down, it seemed he was in no mood to remove his mouth.

He simply adjusted its location.

Moving up from between my legs, Beck licked and trailed kisses along my upper thigh to my hip. He pushed my shirt up my body and began moving his mouth toward my stomach. I started to tense, and he felt it.

He lifted his head and stared me right in the eyes.

Beck didn't need to say a word. With just that one look, I knew what he was communicating.

You're beautiful.

My frame relaxed beneath him, and Beck returned to worshiping my body.

When his mouth made it to my breasts, he sucked them into his mouth and lavished them with nearly the same attention he'd given to my vagina. And in the midst of that, I thought things were going to take a turn. I still hadn't pumped, I was extremely turned on, and I was still a breastfeeding mother. Beck must have tasted breastmilk because he stopped and looked up at me.

"Sorry," I lamented sheepishly.

"Sweetheart, that's beautiful. Why are you apologizing?" he asked.

I lifted my shoulders toward my ears. "It's not exactly sexy, and I feel like I'm killing the mood."

"My cock feels about ready to explode, babe," he informed me. "I'm not the least bit turned off by this."

"You're not?"

He shook his head. "Do we need to stop so you can take care of this, or are you cool with continuing?"

My eyes widened. "You'd continue even if I might experience a bit of leakage."

Beck dipped his chin. "That's why we have showers and washing machines, isn't it?"

I smiled at him, loving that he wasn't making me feel bad about this. Then I confirmed, "I'm very happy to continue with what we were doing."

He grinned at me, dipped his mouth toward my breasts again, and flicked his tongue over my nipple. Breastmilk forgotten, my eyes closed and I just enjoyed what Beck was doing.

Once he had his fill of teasing me and I was quickly approaching dangerous territory again, Beck shifted his body higher and tore my shirt over my head.

Completely naked underneath him, I relished the feel of his heated, smooth skin against mine. Unable to hold myself back, I lifted my head from the mattress and kissed him, the taste of my orgasm lingering on his tongue.

The weight of his body, half covering mine, felt unlike anything I could have imagined. Though I knew it had been a long time, I hadn't realized just how much I missed physical intimacy. And with Beck, it was better than I'd ever experienced.

"I want to feel you," I said softly after pulling my mouth from his.

Beck smiled against my lips. "Yeah," he agreed. "Me too."

With not another moment of delay, he reached for his jeans, pulled out his wallet, and grabbed a condom. Beck handed me the packet while he pushed his black boxer briefs down his legs.

I tried to focus on opening the condom, but my eyes were

riveted to him. To his beautiful body. To his gorgeous cock. It was long, thick, and seriously hard.

I heard a chuckle as the condom packet was plucked out of my hand. "I can't give you what you want if you're just going to sit there drooling, babe," he said.

Somehow, before I could even respond, Beck rolled on the condom and positioned his body over mine. He didn't waste any time either.

Gripping his penis in one hand and my hip in the other, Beck positioned himself and drove inside, making me cry out in pleasure.

Buried deep, his solid chest pressed against mine and his lips just barely touching mine, he asked, "Are you okay?"

"I'm perfect," I assured him.

With those words, Beck moved. He pulled his hips back and surged forward again. It was slow and steady for all of two thrusts as Beck restrained himself.

It was nice. Great, in fact. But the minute he let go of some of his control, it was fantastic. Beyond incredible.

My mind could barely keep up with how good Beck was making my body feel. And the touching.

My goodness, the touching.

How he managed to get his hands everywhere he did while he continued to drill into me was a mystery. It was incomprehensible.

The level of skill required to do what Beck did so effortlessly was the kind of thing that could win awards. It was the kind of thing a woman like me would never dream of experiencing.

And yet, here I was. In my glory, spreading my legs for Beck and loving every single second of it.

A second orgasm was building. And it was doing it at lightning speed.

I didn't know how that was possible.

That *never* happened.

I was a once and done kind of girl. I had assumed Beck had already gotten my orgasm out of the way and was going to get what he needed.

But it seemed the man had other plans. Of course, I wasn't complaining. I simply wondered how he was accomplishing it.

Wanting to take all that I could, not knowing the state of play between us after his trip here, I went after all I could get.

With my body buzzing higher and higher, the ache between my legs growing stronger with each stroke of his cock, I couldn't keep my hands off him. I wanted it all. Every inch of him.

And though I'd likely be useless after this hit me, I had every intention of getting my mouth on every delicious part of his body before the holiday was over.

"Beck," I panted. "Fuck, Beck, I'm going to come again."

Beck drove in harder. He went deeper. He moved faster.

Seconds later, I was digging my nails into his back and crying out in satisfaction.

"That's it, baby. Give it to me," Beck grunted.

I had no choice but to give it to him. It was consuming me. It was pleasure like I'd never experienced before.

And just as I started to come down from it, Beck buried himself deep and groaned, "Fuck, Chasey. Fuck, you're beautiful."

I watched with avid fascination as every inch of his body tensed and flexed while the force of his orgasm tore through him.

God, he was beautiful.

After his climax hit, Beck collapsed on top of me. He gave me a substantial amount of his weight, and I took it.

I wanted everything, so I was willing to take that, too.

And I liked it. Though he was heavy on me, I liked having his weight there.

After some time passed and we both regained some control of our breathing, Beck lifted his head, looked down at me, and asked, "Are you alright?"

"Yes."

His eyes searched my face. "If I run to the bathroom to toss this condom, are you still going to be awake when I get back?" he pressed.

I smiled at him and promised, "I'll still be awake."

"Want me to grab you a washcloth to clean up with?"

My eyes widened. "You don't mind?"

Beck tipped his head to the side. "Babe, you just gave me all of that. Why would I mind getting you something so you can see to yourself, especially considering in doing so, I'm hoping that I get myself another shot at going back in there?"

I wanted to laugh and tell him that I'd let him back in there without him doing something to see to me. Instead, I said, "A washcloth would be appreciated."

He kissed my cheek and declared, "I'll be right back."

With that, he pulled out, got out of the bed, and strode in the direction of the bathroom. I watched the rounded globes of his ass until they disappeared behind the door.

Then I lay back and reminded myself that despite everything I'd gone through over the last couple of months, I still had a lot to be thankful for this year.

Luna was number one.

But Beck wasn't far behind.

CHAPTER 14

Beck

MY MIND WAS MUDDLED WITH SO MANY DIFFERENT THOUGHTS and emotions.

Being naked with Chasey in her bed, it was hard not to feel a lot.

Shock was consuming me, and it had been since Chasey threw her arms around me and kissed me at her front door. It was certainly not the welcome I had expected, but I definitely wasn't complaining about it.

And now that we'd had everything we just had, it was safe to say I was feeling very fortunate. Getting to know her a bit better over the last couple of weeks, I had hoped to come here for the holiday and maybe take things to another level. I thought I might be able to get her to kiss me before the holiday was over.

Apparently, I'd been taking it slow for no reason.

As lucky as that made me feel, I also felt a bit aggravated with myself. This one little thing that I'd done had meant the world to Chasey. I hated knowing that she was sad. To learn that she had driven to the store and left without getting anything because she couldn't bear the thought of being alone was almost more than I could handle.

I regretted not doing something about the way I felt about her sooner. It was all I could do to focus on the relief I felt knowing that the moment I arrived, she was no longer sad.

Now that I'd returned from the bathroom after disposing of the used condom, I decided it was best to focus on the positive.

I was on my side, my head propped up in my hand, looking down at Chasey, who was lying on her back.

"Are you sure you're alright?" I asked her as I stroked my thumb over the soft skin on her bare hip. "I got a bit out of control there."

A soft laugh escaped her as she brought her shining eyes to mine. "Beck, I've just had my first two orgasms that weren't self-induced in over a year, and I had both of them on the same night, which is a first for me. So, I think it's safe to say I'm alright."

My brows shot up in surprise at her declaration. "Wait a minute," I said. "I'm not sure I understand what you just shared."

"What are you confused about?" she asked.

"It's been over a year?" I questioned her.

She nodded.

Okay. I mean, I guess I could understand that. She was newly divorced, and I recalled her saying that she'd been put on pelvic rest toward the end of her pregnancy. I didn't know exactly what that meant, but if I had to guess based on the argument she'd had in the hotel with her ex-husband, she hadn't been allowed to have sex. Plus, she was essentially raising Luna all on her own.

Maybe it shouldn't have come as such a shock to me that it had been so long for her. Even though I knew she was saying she felt good, part of me wanted to skip the conversation now and dive back in for another round so I could help her make up for lost time.

But my mind was still stuck on something else that she said.

"What did you mean when you said it was a first for you to have two orgasms in the same night?" I asked.

"Isn't that self-explanatory?" she countered.

I stared at her in disbelief.

She couldn't actually mean that she'd *never* experienced that before. And while the idea of anyone else making her come was one I did not like to think about, I had to admit it blew my mind.

When I took too long trying to comprehend what she was saying, Chasey reasoned, "I mean, if that seems strange to you, I guess it's possible that it's because it's been so long. I just… well, um, never mind."

"No. Tell me. What were you going to say?" I urged.

Her voice became incredibly soft as she shared, "I just thought it was because it was you."

I grinned at her. "I like that," I told her. "But you deserve some of the credit here."

"Me?"

I nodded. "Babe, you make it easy for me because you're so damn sexy."

I barely got the words out before Chasey turned bashful, rolled toward me, and shoved her face in my chest. My hand that had been on her hip was now on her ass. I squeezed her there and asked, "Why is this making you hide right now?"

Chasey didn't answer, and a moment later, I heard her sniffle.

"Chasey?" I called while I started to stroke my hand up and down her back. "Talk to me, sweetheart."

She took another couple seconds to pull herself together before she drew her face away from my chest, tipped her head back, and looked up at me.

"You make me feel good about myself," she rasped.

"You should feel good about yourself," I reasoned.

"Yes, but I haven't felt sexy since about five minutes after I learned I was pregnant with Luna," she shared.

That surprised me.

I would have thought that Chasey, being the kind of mother she was, would have loved everything about what brought her Luna.

As I tried to wrap my head around what she'd shared, she continued, "I wanted to be one of those women who felt like she was glowing throughout her pregnancy. But I'd been sick early on which didn't help at all. When my body really started to change in the second trimester and the sickness started to wane, I thought I'd feel radiant. I didn't. And my ex-husband never indicated that he loved seeing those changes. By the time the third trimester rolled around, I felt so undesirable. To top it off, I was put on pelvic rest, couldn't have sex, and started having suspicions about my ex-husband's faithfulness. Or, lack of it."

In the blink of an eye, I'd gone from feeling surprised to feeling angry.

What kind of a man gets his wife pregnant and doesn't go out of his way to make sure she feels like she's the most beautiful woman in the world? Furthermore, what kind of a man doesn't do whatever he's got to do to make sure his wife is satisfied sexually, at least up until the point that she received doctor's orders otherwise?

Worst of all, how could a man make a baby with a woman, a woman he married, and not think that every single thing about her changing body was anything but a miracle?

I didn't ever claim to be perfect. I'd had a lot of fun over the years.

I just couldn't seem to wrap my head around any of what Chasey's ex-husband had done to her.

"I'm sorry that you went through all that you did," I lamented. "I hate that you feel any insecurity about your body or the way you look, and I hope you know that I'm being completely honest with you about how I see you. I'll never forget walking into the hotel months ago and seeing you from the back. Your legs and your ass were perfect, even if it was only five weeks after delivering Luna."

A small smile spread across her face. "I wish I would have known that a long time ago," she said. "Maybe I wouldn't have stopped myself."

"Stopped yourself?"

"From calling you," she clarified.

My body went solid. "You... you were going to call me?" I stammered.

Chasey nodded. "Yes. Well, I thought about it to the point I pulled your name up in my list of contacts several times," she started. "But I don't think I ever would have tapped on the screen."

She couldn't be serious.

"Why not?" I asked.

The silence stretched between us for a long time before she answered, "I thought you were just being nice that day at the hotel."

"What?"

"I didn't think you actually wanted me to call you," she began again. "I assumed you were just doing something to make a woman who'd just suffered the ultimate betrayal five weeks after having a baby feel better about herself."

I swallowed hard.

All that time.

All that time I'd been worried about her and how she was doing, and she wanted to call but didn't because she didn't think I was serious when I offered her my number.

"Chasey, I was trying to make you feel better," I insisted. "But that doesn't mean I didn't want you to call."

"It just seemed impossible."

My brows knit together. "What did?"

"The idea that you'd actually want anything to do with me," she replied. When I gave her a look that told her I hoped she was joking, she added, "Look, Beck, I get it now, that's not the kind of guy you are, but at the time, I didn't know that. I mean, you're a rock star. I'm just me. I'm a new mom who has a routine and schedule that's so strict because it's the only thing that keeps me sane. Why would you ever settle for that?"

I had to stop myself from immediately responding because I was afraid of what I might say if I didn't take the time to calm myself down.

When I thought I had it under control, I said, "Babe, the fact that you think that anyone, rock star or not, would be settling if they landed you is just plain ludicrous. I might not have known all that I do now about the kind of woman you are when I first met you, but you did. You knew who you were, and I can't imagine why you'd think you aren't worthy of me or anyone else."

"My husband cheated on me," Chasey rasped. "I might not have caught him in the act while I was pregnant, but I have no doubt it was happening then. I already felt crappy about my body. What he did didn't exactly help matters."

Lifting my hand to the side of her face, I brushed a lock of her hair back. "You are so much more than just your body, Chasey. You're hardworking, selfless, and humble. You're caring and sweet. And if you want to talk about your looks, believe me when I say that you are gorgeous. Trust me, if I didn't like what I saw, if I didn't like the woman you are, I wouldn't have driven six hours to be here with you."

Nodding her head slowly, Chasey noted, "That is a long drive."

"It is," I confirmed. "And even if I wasn't going to get what I just got from you, even if it was going to take longer for you to be ready for what we just had, I'd still make the drive to see you and Luna until that time came."

Chasey traced her fingertips slowly over the skin on my chest. I loved the feel of her touch on my body. This was nice, soft, and delicate. I loved it just as much as I did when she was clawing her nails into my back when I was buried inside her.

For a long time, she continued to move her fingers over my skin without saying anything. But eventually, she called, "Beck?"

"Yeah, babe?"

"Can you roll to your back?" she asked.

I didn't ask her why because in that moment, hearing her voice like that, I'd do anything for her.

So, I rolled to my back.

Once I was there, she swung a leg over my body so she was straddling me. Then she began kissing my chest. One of my hands gently drove into her hair and cupped the back of her head while the other was pressed firmly into the middle of her back.

Chasey's tongue came out and licked a path along my pec toward my nipple. As soon as she got there, I felt her teeth nibble on it before she licked it again. The fact that it was Chasey doing this to me was enough to get me excited. But when she did what she was doing *and* reached her hand down to my cock and curled her fingers around it, there was no holding myself back.

I let out a groan.

"Somebody likes that," Chasey teased with laughter in her tone.

She tightened her grip and stroked while continuing to run her tongue all along my torso. It seemed Chasey was reserved and shy when I was telling her what I thought about her, but deep down she was a little minx with a wild side.

Though she took her time getting there, eventually, I looked down and saw Chasey's body nestled between my thighs. Her fingers were still curled around my dick, and she was smiling up at me with a glint in her eyes.

When she moistened her lips with her tongue, I thought I'd lose my mind. She knew what she was doing, and she didn't seem to care that she was driving me crazy. She seemed completely interested in prolonging the teasing session.

She could.

I'd take it.

I'd take anything from her.

Chasey lowered her mouth to my cock, parted her lips, and allowed her tongue to glide up the underside all the way from the base to the tip. She looked up at me, smiled, and did it again.

Once she made it to the tip again, she swirled her tongue around it before taking me in her mouth.

Feeling that, I clenched my hands into fists. Chasey took me deeper before pulling back. She quickly worked up a rhythm, and she did not slack. She moved fast. She moved slow. She took me deep. She'd play at the tip.

She licked.

She sucked.

She moaned the entire time.

Before I was ready for it to be over, I started to feel myself heading to the point of no return. Every muscle in my body was tensing preparing for what was coming.

But as much as I wanted it, I wanted her to have more.

I reached down, lifted her away, and she let out a cry of surprise. I dragged her up my body and kissed her before I said, "You are incredible."

"I wasn't finished," she declared.

"You are for now," I informed her, reaching out for my wallet.

In record time, I rolled on another condom and demanded, "Climb on, babe."

Chasey climbed on. Then she positioned herself over me before she slammed herself down. Her head flew back while I grabbed one of her tits and squeezed.

"Fuck," I bit out. "Fuck, you feel amazing."

"Beck," she panted.

Seeing her on my cock, bouncing up and down, I knew I wasn't going to last much longer. Needing to make sure she got there, I reached my free hand out, found her clit, and began circling.

Chasey groaned and stopped bouncing. Instead, she began moving her hips, undulating them from back to front several times before circling them.

"Oh, you feel so good," she blew out.

"Babe, you've got to get there," I urged, desperately working my hand on her clit.

Chasey ignored me and continued to roll her hips. I went at her harder. Her moans got louder.

"Chasey," I called out. "Are you close?"

"Oh, God," she whimpered.

If I wasn't so caught up in what was happening, I might have said a silent prayer of thanks.

Her movements began to dwindle, and her breathing grew shallow.

"Beck, baby, I'm going to come," she warned me.

I planted my feet into the mattress, gripped her hips in my hand, and thrust my cock into her fast and hard.

She fell forward onto her palms, her gorgeous tits in my face. I lifted my head, captured one of her nipples in my mouth, and began to lick and suck as I took her there.

Not more than a few seconds later, Chasey was coming apart on top of me. The moment I knew she was there, I let go of the hold I had on my own orgasm.

The pace of our movements slowed as we allowed the pleasure to consume us until they eventually stopped. And for several long minutes, neither of us said anything. I simply held on to Chasey while her body remained draped over mine.

"I'm tired," Chasey murmured. "You're wearing me out."

I chuckled. "You started it," I reminded her.

"Yeah, but I didn't expect all that stuff at the end," she explained. "I just thought you'd want to finish in my mouth."

"Babe?" I called.

"Hmm?" she returned, her cheek still pressed to my upper chest, her forehead just grazing the side of my throat.

"I'll never not take care of you," I said.

Chasey lifted her head. "So, you're saying I can't ever see to you without you stopping me?" she asked.

"I didn't say that," I replied. "I'm just saying that I'm not going to take without making sure that you've gotten the same first."

She smiled at the same time she rolled her eyes at me.

I didn't care if she thought I was being ridiculous. I would never, ever take for myself and not see that she was satisfied, too.

Thinking about how her ex might have treated her wasn't something I was prepared to do. All I knew was that if she had expected for me to treat her the way he did, she'd have to re-think that. It was never happening.

A few minutes later, after Chasey rolled off of me so I could dispose of the condom and get her a cloth to clean up and after she pumped, we were curled up in her bed and had turned out the lights.

When I left Pennsylvania to come here for her, I didn't know what to expect. All I knew was that I wanted to spend time with her and Luna. The fact that I was naked in her bed and spending the night was beyond what I could have hoped for.

I thought that would be all I needed to make my night. I mean, I didn't exactly think there was much else that could top that.

But this was Chasey.

I should have known better.

Minutes after we'd rolled to our sides and I'd tucked the back of her body tight to the front of mine, she called, "Beck?"

"Yeah?" I answered.

She hesitated. I held on, waiting for her to share what-ever she wanted to share. When too much time passed with no response from her, I decided to encourage her to speak. But the minute I opened my mouth to talk, she did.

"I'm really glad you're here."

That right there was it.

That meant more to me than everything else we had tonight.

Chasey was glad that I was here with her.

In that moment, all the emotions I'd been experiencing throughout the night had vanished, and I was left with one.

I was one lucky man.

CHAPTER 15

Chasey

MY BODY SAT BOLT UPRIGHT AS A HUGE GASP FILLED THE ROOM.
That gasp came from me.

I looked to my left and saw Beck there. I'd clearly woken him up. Shifting my attention to my right, I noted the time.

It was late.

That's when the sound that I was sure I had heard and was woken by sounded in the room again.

"Everything okay?" Beck said as I tossed the blanket back and scrambled out of the bed.

"Oh my God. I slept in," I declared, feeling frantic.

Luna was awake, and even though she wasn't crying, I hadn't gotten up and done anything I normally would before she started to stir.

"But it's the holiday," Beck reasoned as he sat up. "You don't have to work today, do you?"

I had already dashed across the room and opened my dresser to pull out a fresh pair of panties. I was pulling them up my legs when I replied, "No, I don't. But I still have to take care of Luna."

"She's not crying," Beck noted.

As though on cue, Luna began to cry. I paused my movements, standing there in nothing but a pair of panties as I cocked an eyebrow.

"She's crying now," Beck corrected himself.

"Yep."

Not wasting another second, I found my T-shirt, threw it over my head, and said, "I'll be back."

Sprinting out of my bedroom without waiting for Beck to respond, I hurried to Luna's room. What had I been thinking? I stayed up entirely too late because I was more concerned with having sex than making sure I got a good night's sleep so I could take care of my daughter today.

Beck was going to turn me into a bad mom. Maybe I'd been able to hold myself back when I believed that all he wanted was to be a nice guy. But now that he had made it clear he was interested, he opened the flood gates.

I couldn't have what I had with him and never want it again. No way.

No way I could be okay with giving that up. It was too good.

Unfortunately, I didn't have the chance to figure it out because I made it to Luna's room and needed to be back in mom mode.

I made it to the crib, reached in for her, and as I lifted her into my arms, I said, "Good morning, baby girl. Mommy is so sorry."

I pressed several kisses to her cheek before I asked, "Are you hungry, mama?"

Luna continued to cry.

"Let's get a fresh diaper on, and then Mommy will feed you," I told her.

I didn't know if there was a world record for diaper changing, but at that moment, I had to believe that I might have put myself in the running. It was amazing what I could do when I felt so much guilt.

My poor girl.

Once she was in a dry diaper and I lifted her into my arms again, Luna's cries had eased a bit. I ambled back down the hall to my bedroom and found Beck sitting up in the bed with the monitor in his hands.

Crap.

He'd been listening to me.

I avoided his gaze as I moved to the bed. After I climbed in, I lifted my shirt, adjusted Luna in my arms, and began feeding her.

For several long moments, the only sound in the room was that of my little girl nursing. She was eating so fast, and it made me feel horrible. I'd never seen her nurse so frantically.

"You're a good mom, Chasey."

"She's so hungry," I murmured, not looking up at him. Unbearable guilt consumed me.

"I think that's normal for babies," he reasoned.

At that, I lifted my gaze to his. Tears were filling my eyes, and at the sight of the first one rolling down my cheek, Beck's features softened.

He reached out, wiped it away, and said, "You shouldn't be crying."

"I put my own needs above my daughter's," I argued.

"Luna was asleep last night. You didn't neglect her, and she's eating now," Beck pointed out. "I'm not really in a position to tell you what to do, but I think it's important that you do the things you need to do to take care of yourself so that you are able to be the best mom you can be. You didn't do anything wrong."

I understood what he was saying, but I couldn't exactly turn off my emotions. I mean, I knew that parents had sex. Hell, there were married couples all over the world that were raising children. They wouldn't have had two, three, four, or even more kids if they didn't find the time to give in to those natural urges and make more babies.

"You're right," I said softly. "I just... I feel bad."

"I understand," he returned. "Is there anything I can do for you right now? Do you need anything?"

I shook my head. "We could talk," I suggested.

"Okay. What do you want to talk about?" he asked.

Leave it to me to suggest something and not have the slightest idea on what to say. It wasn't like I was very good at this. For months, I'd become accustomed to nursing Luna in silence. If it weren't for Beck wanting to make sure I didn't spend the holiday alone, I'd have been doing just that.

On that thought, something hit me.

"Are you close with your family?" I asked.

"Yes."

"So, are they upset that you're not spending the holiday with them?" I pressed. "I couldn't imagine not seeing my child on the holidays."

Beck smiled at me as he reached out and squeezed my thigh. "Relax, babe. It's all good. My mom and my sister both know that I'm here with you today, and they couldn't be happier for me. Once they knew that I was going to be coming here to surprise you, they actually planned for all of us to celebrate the holiday on Tuesday."

"They were happy you were coming here?"

He nodded.

My brows knit together. "It was just the three of you?" I questioned him.

"No," he replied. "My mom has been dating a guy for about two years now, so he joined us as well."

I didn't know that his parents weren't married.

"What about your dad?" I asked.

"You and I have more in common than you might think, Chasey," he began. "Though I had him for a couple of years, my dad walked out on us when I was six and Sadie was two."

Instinctively, my free hand went to Beck's that was resting on my thigh. I squeezed and lamented, "I'm sorry."

Beck shrugged. "It was his loss," he insisted. "He missed out on raising two really cool kids and having a woman in his life who, until now, I thought was the most hardworking woman in the world."

I cocked an eyebrow. "Until now?"

Smiling at me, Beck clarified, "I think it's a single mom thing. You are just as selfless as my mom was. Always working hard and putting the needs of her children before anything she might need."

Beck was raised by a single mom. It suddenly all started to make sense to me. Weeks ago, he'd told me how Luna might be too young to understand it all now, but that when she was older and realized the sacrifices I'd made for her, she'd want to make sure I knew how much she appreciated it. While I didn't doubt what he was saying, I had a feeling he was referring to how he felt for his mom. It felt good to know that my daughter could grow up feeling just as fulfilled in her life, even if her dad wasn't around.

"It's not all single moms," I mumbled.

"Oh, Chasey, I'm sorry," he apologized. "I didn't mean—"

"It's okay, Beck," I assured him. "You had a great mom, and I'm so happy about that. I had a crap mom. It sucks, but it also did a lot to teach me about the kind of mom I wanted to be. So, the fact that you're telling me I'm a good mom means everything to me."

"I promise I'm not making that up," he said. "You really are a wonderful mother. Luna is so lucky to have you."

"Thank you." I beamed at him, and the guilt I had been feeling since I woke up this morning started to dissipate. "So, you have a sister?"

"Yes. Her name is Sadie, we're very close, and I'm super protective of her," he shared.

"What does she do?" I wondered.

"She's an artist," he replied. "She paints a lot, and she's really good at what she does."

My eyes widened. "So, both of you are the creative types," I noted. "That's really cool. I have zero talent for making anything beautiful like that."

"Chasey?" Beck called. There was a warning in his tone that I couldn't even begin to understand.

"Yeah?"

His eyes dropped to where I was holding Luna in my arm while she ate. His hand left my thigh and reached for Luna's little hand, which had been gently scratching the top swell of my breast. Her tiny fingers curled around one of his, and Beck's thumb stroked over the tops of her knuckles.

"You can't honestly sit there while holding this little girl in your arms and tell me that you have zero talent for making anything beautiful," Beck began. "I've never, not in my whole life, seen anything more spectacular than Luna. To know that you made her, that she grew inside your body, is the most beautiful thing I can imagine anyone being able to do."

If I didn't think it would make me look like I was crazy, I would have burst into tears. Nobody had ever said anything so wonderful to me in all my life.

"Beck…" I trailed off, feeling the tightness in my throat grow.

He was the best thing that had happened to me since Luna. I was terrified I'd never survive it when he left.

Beck lifted his gaze from Luna to me. His features were so warm, and the look in his eyes was filled with adoration.

Without saying another word, he leaned closer and kissed me on the lips. When he pulled back, he said, "I'm going to run out to my car and grab my bag with my clothes in it. I thought I was going to be staying in a hotel last night, so I left it out there."

"Okay," I replied.

"When I come back in, I'll make us breakfast," he began

again. "Then it's up to you, but I'd like to get some time with this little lady afterward."

"She'll probably be ready for her piano lessons by then," I told him.

Beck let out a laugh, kissed me again, and then lifted Luna's foot to his lips. He kissed the bottom of her foot before he slid out of the bed and pulled on his jeans.

I sat there long after he walked out of the room staring at the space where he'd been, and I did it wondering how I'd managed to get so lucky. Who would have thought that the day that was arguably one of the worst of my life could have turned out to be the day I met the best man I ever knew?

I didn't manage to come up with an answer to that by the time Luna finished eating, but at least I knew I had a reason to look on the bright side. For now, that was more than enough for me.

It had been the best Thanksgiving ever.

Not once in my whole life had I ever had such an amazing holiday.

Nothing extravagant had happened, and maybe that was why it was so special. It just felt perfect.

Perfect for me.

Perfect for Luna.

I could only hope it was perfect for Beck, too.

After I finished feeding Luna, I met Beck in the kitchen and found that he was in the middle of making breakfast. It felt strange initially to have someone there cooking for me, more strange than it did when he made the grilled cheese sandwich the night before.

Once he had the food on our plates, he set them down on the table in my small dining area and took Luna out of my arms.

"Hi, princess," he greeted her for the first time since she woke up. "Are you feeling better now that you've got a full belly?"

She brought both of her hands to either side of his face and leaned in closer to him.

My heart melted at the sight.

It melted even more when Beck sat down at the table with me and kept Luna tucked tight to his body while he ate with his other hand.

"I can take her," I offered.

"I know, but I'd really like to hold her if you don't mind," he replied.

I didn't mind. Not at all.

In fact, I loved seeing him hold her. Not only that, he talked to her quite a bit throughout breakfast, asking her frequently about what new music she had learned to play while he was gone. Luna was in such a good mood and babbling away. Beck listened intently to every ounce of nonsense that came out of her mouth like it was the most fascinating conversation he'd had in his life.

Seeing the way he was with her, it took everything in me to hold myself back from jumping him right then and there.

And it didn't get any easier as the day went on.

Following breakfast, Beck got down on the ground in the living room and played with her. They talked about music. Or, I told myself that's what they were discussing. Beck had continued his conversation from breakfast with her, and she didn't stop babbling. They played together nearly all morning until it was time for Luna's morning nap.

Part of me was surprised that I hadn't felt upset by the fact that Beck monopolized the time with Luna. Something about seeing the way he was with her just moved me, and I was completely content to sit back and watch their interaction.

I loved it for my daughter, even if I wasn't sure it was something she'd always have.

Once she was down for her morning nap, Beck didn't slack on being attentive. He turned all of his focus and attention to me, sliding his arms around my waist and burying his face in my neck the moment I returned from Luna's room.

"She's so much fun," he declared.

Feeling my heart burst with happiness, I rasped, "Yeah, she is."

"You're so much fun, too," he added.

With my arms thrown over his shoulders as we stood in my living room, I let out a laugh. "Good to know."

"I don't know how to make a turkey," he confessed.

"What?"

"I bought all that stuff at the store yesterday before I got here, but I have no idea what to do with any of it," he began after he pulled his face from my neck and looked down at me. "I hope you do."

I grinned. "I do," I assured him.

"I want to help you make it all, so if you tell me what to do, I'm more than ready to dive in," he offered.

"Really?" I asked, cocking an eyebrow.

"Yes. Did you think I bought it all in hopes that I'd kick my feet up and leave you to do all the work?" he wondered.

I mean, I hadn't exactly thought about it like that, but yeah, I did. Aaron had never really helped me when it came to things like that. I guess I didn't really mind at the time. It had been what I wanted to do anyway—to take care of my husband and my family.

Of course, that sentiment flew out the window when I started suspecting him of cheating. Making meals for a man who wasn't putting in much effort with me in other parts of our relationship led me to feeling a bit of bitterness.

Thankfully, I was no longer feeling that way.

And Beck claimed he was more than ready to help. So, we took advantage of Luna's naptime and worked on getting the food prepared. I might have always felt bad about the size of my kitchen, but today, I liked it.

I enjoyed being in such close proximity to Beck. It not only meant that we were simply working side by side; it also meant that Beck spent a lot of time stealing kisses and doing a lot of touching in between our conversations. He frequently placed the palm of his hand on my ass and rubbed it before he squeezed a handful.

Truth be told, I got a little daring, too. When I saw him concentrating on peeling potatoes, I walked up behind him, pressed my breasts into his back and reached my hands around to the front of his jeans. As I did that, I told him about how I was off from work for the next three days, hoping it built even more tension and made him a little more excited about the days ahead.

Needless to say, we were both relishing in the sexual tension building between us all afternoon. I liked that we held ourselves back from the urge to give in to what we both clearly wanted, even when Luna went down for her nap in the afternoon.

I liked that we were letting it build.

In the end, dinner had been delicious, I was the happiest I'd been in a really long time, and Luna had the best first Thanksgiving. We even snapped a photo to commemorate the occasion.

Just a little while ago, I had taken some time alone with Luna to put her down for the night. After I put her in her crib, I stared at her for several long minutes. I hoped she knew how much I loved her, and how hard I'd always work to make sure she had days like today for the rest of her life.

When I walked out of her room, intent on telling Beck just how much I appreciated what he'd done for us today, he was standing there waiting for me.

"Is everything okay?" I asked.

He smiled and nodded. "Yeah. I just thought that maybe we could grab a shower together," he shared.

A shower with Beck Emerson?

Count me in.

A shiver ran through my body. Beck noticed and chuckled.

Minutes later, we were in the shower together. That had been no less fabulous than what Beck had given me in my bed the night before.

And now, we were curled up together in my bed. I was feeling fantastic, and I'd just recalled all that had happened throughout the day.

I needed to let Beck know just how much it meant to me.

"Beck?" I called after silence had fallen across the room.

"Yeah, babe?"

"Thank you."

"For what, sweetheart?"

I loved when he called me that. "For coming here to New Hampshire and spending Thanksgiving with Luna and me. It was the best day I've had in a very long time. Thank you for not allowing us to be alone today."

Beck's arm tightened around my waist. "You're welcome, Chasey. It was the best day I've had in a very long time, too."

I couldn't imagine how that was possible considering what he did for a living, but I wasn't going to question it. He'd given me that, another piece of wonderful, and I was going to take it.

At that, we both settled in and drifted.

CHAPTER 16

Chasey

"**I** CAN'T BELIEVE I LET YOU TALK ME INTO THIS."

"It's not a big deal," Beck returned. "Besides, it's completely necessary."

I cocked an eyebrow, put a hand on my hip, and insisted, "It's not."

Beck ignored me and returned his attention to Luna. I rolled my eyes and got back to getting ready. That meant I got back to packing Luna's diaper bag.

It was Saturday morning, and we were getting ready to go out shopping. Yesterday, we'd had a wonderful day inside with Luna and each other, and at one point during the day, Beck and I had gotten into a discussion about the holidays.

"When are you planning to put up your decorations?" he asked.

"What decorations?"

Looking around the living room, he answered, "The Christmas decorations."

"Oh. Well, I decided not to keep any of the stuff from when I was married because I knew I'd never take care of a real tree," I shared. "And I really didn't want to keep any reminders with the ornaments we had, so I don't have anything to decorate with."

"Are you planning to get anything?" Beck asked.

I shrugged. "I mean, I'll probably just pick up one of those mini artificial trees so that there's something here for Luna, but it's not like she's going to remember it."

Beck shot me an incredulous look. "You're joking, right?"

I shook my head.

"Babe, you should have your place decorated for Christmas," he said. "This is Luna's first one. It has to be special."

He wasn't wrong about that. I knew it was Luna's first Christmas, and I wanted it to be special for her. But the truth was that I couldn't see myself spending all that money on decorations right now. It was just a waste.

I must have been wearing the internal struggle I was having on my face because Beck interrupted my thoughts and asked "What's going through your mind right now?"

I bit my lip nervously. I hesitated to tell him what I was thinking because I didn't want him to get the wrong impression.

"Chasey?" he called.

"Hmm?"

"What's going on?" he pressed.

I sighed. "I just can't bring myself to spend money on a bunch of things that won't make a difference in our lives," I explained. "I'd rather save that money for more important things Luna will need. She's growing so fast and she's going to need bigger clothes. And diapers are not cheap either. Plus, I want to save money for her so she can have a better start in life than I did. A stuffed snowman or a Santa cookie jar might improve our mood or make things feel festive and cheerful, but those things aren't important."

For a long time, Beck stared at me.

Did he think I was crazy? Was anything I'd just said to him weird?

I didn't know what was going through his mind, and I was too freaked out to ask. So, I waited. And eventually, he declared, "We're going shopping for Christmas decorations tomorrow, and I'm buying. Whatever you want, whatever you need, I'm getting it."

"Beck—"

He put his hand up and cut me off. "Chasey, don't," he requested. "Please let me do this for you."

"Why? It's really unnecessary, and I feel weird about it."

"Cash called me earlier today," he shared.

His response caught me completely off guard. I didn't understand what Cash calling him had to do with what we were discussing.

"Okay?" I returned.

"He wrote a song for Demi, and he wants to get together to work on it this coming week," he began. "He already talked with the rest of the band about it, and they're planning to start on Monday."

"Alright. So, I'm guessing that means you have to leave to go back to Pennsylvania," I surmised.

He nodded but didn't offer anything else.

Still feeling confused, I said, "I don't understand what any of this has to do with me having Christmas decorations."

I wish I had understood what he was getting at because there was a big part of me that really wanted to try and start dealing with the fact that Beck was going to have to leave and go back home. I knew the time would come, but I hadn't wanted it to be so soon. Unfortunately, I couldn't quite focus on that when I was still so perplexed by him telling me about Cash wanting the band to work on a song when we'd been talking about Christmas decorations.

"I have to go back home, and I don't want to do that without knowing that my girls can feel the joy of the holiday season all around them while I'm gone," he shared, his voice low and husky.

His girls.

His girls.

After delivering that bit of news, Beck reached out in front of him, lifted Luna in his arms, and pressed a kiss to her cheek.

My heart felt so full in that moment, I thought it would burst right out of my chest.

We were his girls.

It didn't matter anymore whether I felt awkward or weird or anything else about the situation. There was no way I could deny Beck.

So, I whispered, "Okay. We can go shopping tomorrow."

And now, despite knowing his reason for wanting to do it and loving everything about it, I was packing up Luna's diaper bag and back to feeling unsure about this.

Regardless of my need to debate this further, it seemed Beck was no longer interested in discussing what we'd already discussed yesterday. And because he'd returned his attention to Luna, I started to wonder if he knew that she was my soft spot. Or, more specifically, I wondered if he knew that me seeing him interact with her would make me agree to just about anything he wanted because the truth was that the moment he started playing with her again, I gave up and got back to packing up Luna's bag.

The next thing I knew, we had pulled into the parking lot at the store, and I instantly decided this was a bad idea.

There was no place to park.

Yesterday was Black Friday. That meant it didn't matter where we went. Every place we'd go would be packed with holiday shoppers looking for the best bargains on their gifts for the season.

"This is crazy," I murmured.

"This is going to be fun," Beck assured me.

Ten minutes later, we'd found a spot, gotten a shopping cart, and were walking through the store. Luna had drifted off for a nap while we were in the car, so we kept her in her car seat and placed it in the back of the cart.

Much to my surprise, it took me a matter of a few minutes to let go of all the concerns I had about doing this with Beck.

It was a bit hard not to let it go when he was making it so much fun. Not long after we'd entered the store, he'd found Santa hats. He put one on my head, one on his head, and he picked up one for Luna. We looked at the artificial trees first, and when I had indicated one that was slightly smaller and less expensive, Beck shot me a look of disbelief.

"No," he declared. "We're getting *this* one."

It was decidedly larger than the one I'd suggested and was probably the largest that would fit into my place. Beck pulled out one of the cards to give to an associate indicating which tree we had wanted to purchase.

We then moved along to kitchen décor.

"What are we doing here?" I asked. "We should be looking at ornaments."

"We will," he assured me. "I'm looking for a Santa cookie jar first. Then we need to find some stuffed snowmen."

He was going to purchase the items I'd tossed out as examples yesterday of things that would be nice to have.

"Beck, you're going overboard," I told him.

"No, I'm not," he replied as he continued to push the cart with one hand while he threw his free arm out behind my back so his hand could land on my opposite shoulder.

I looked up at him, saw the joy in his face, and suddenly realized that I needed to get into this as much as he was. He clearly was having the best time, and I didn't want to spend the day upset because I was overthinking all of this.

So, when Beck made it to the section with the cookie jars, I told him which one I liked best. We then found several stuffed snowmen that we'd be able to put all over the living room, the dining area, and even the bedrooms.

When we finally made it to the ornaments, Beck asked, "Do you want some kind of theme for your tree, or do you want it to be a mix of everything?"

I tipped my head to the side, thought about it, and couldn't decide. Then I glanced at the ornaments, saw one that was a drum, and an idea came to me.

My face lit up, excitement flooded my veins, and I declared, "I want it to be a music-themed tree. It can have snowmen or reindeer or Mr. and Mrs. Claus so long as they're holding an instrument or caroling or something like that. I want it to have drums and guitars and Luna's favorite. Pianos. Lots of pianos need to be all over the tree."

Beck's features softened and his expression was warm. "Come here," he urged, his voice husky.

I moved close.

As soon as I was next to him, Beck hugged me tight to his body and whispered in my ear, "I think you're amazing, Chasey."

I couldn't stop myself from sharing, "Not as amazing as you."

Beck pulled back, looked down at me, and smiled. Then he pressed a kiss to my lips. Just when his mouth touched mine, we heard movement by the cart. We separated, looked down, and saw Luna had opened her eyes.

"Hi, baby girl," I said. "Did you have a good nap?"

Luna yawned and fluttered her still sleepy eyes.

Beck put his hand to the middle of my back and instructed, "You take the cart and pick out the ornaments you want. I'm going to take Luna and let her pick out the ones she wants."

It was a wonder I was still standing, breathing, and living. My heart had exploded and melted and beat so fast in all the time that we'd been here, I didn't know how it hadn't stopped functioning.

Beck didn't wait for me to respond. He simply reached down, unbuckled Luna, and lifted her out of her seat.

"Hi, princess," he said as he held her close.

He kissed her cheek, grabbed the Santa hat, and put it on her head. I was convinced she'd rip it off, but I shouldn't have been surprised that she didn't. Luna seemed to love anything that Beck gave her.

Once he had her all ready to go, he pinned his eyes on me and said, "Get whatever you want. I don't care if you find two hundred ornaments. Get them all."

"We might not be able to see the tree if we get that many," I noted.

Beck laughed and turned to walk away. I watched him a few seconds longer as he carried Luna in the opposite direction. Then I focused my attention on the ornaments and started picking out all the ones that had any hint of a musical connection. Before I knew it, I'd filled a good portion of the bottom of the cart that wasn't already filled with Luna's car seat or any of the other items Beck had tossed in with the ornaments.

Just as I was looking at a display behind the ornaments that had Christmas villages, I heard, "What do you think, Mama?"

I lifted my gaze up and to the right. Beck was standing there, and he was still holding Luna in one arm. In the other were two boxes that he seemed to be doing an incredible job of balancing. I took the smaller box off the top and inspected it.

Tears instantly filled my eyes.

It was a pale pink ball ornament that had white musical notes dotting the entire ball as though they were snowflakes falling from the sky. A white drum and guitar had been painted on the front on one side of the text. Wrapping around the entire ball were white piano keys. And on the front were the words *Baby Girl's 1st Christmas*.

It was perfect, and I didn't know how I stopped myself from bursting into tears.

I lifted my stare to Beck's handsome face. "Thank you," I rasped.

He smiled and held the second box out to me. "I thought we could get this for her room," he said.

I took the box and realized he'd picked out a ceramic Christmas tree nightlight. It looked as though it had been hand painted green and tiny colorful lights stuck out from every part of it.

"It's perfect," I told him.

"I'm glad you like it. Did you get everything you want?" he asked.

I glanced down at the items in the shopping cart, then to the two in my hands, and finally up at Luna and Beck. Right there, in that moment, I had absolutely everything I ever wanted.

After placing Luna's ornament and night light into the cart, I moved toward them and slid my arm around the back of Beck's waist and looked up at him.

"I have everything I want," I promised.

I wasn't sure if he would get the real meaning behind my words, but I had a feeling he understood when his expression softened and he leaned down to touch his lips to mine.

Just then, I heard, "Chasey?"

My entire body froze.

Beck noticed and pulled his mouth away. When we looked in the direction the voice had come from, that's when we saw him.

My ex-husband.

No.

No. No. No.

I did not want him ruining this moment or this day.

The moment he saw my face and confirmed it was me, his eyes went to Luna.

That's when I really began to panic.

"Hey, you're Beck Emerson," another voice declared.

That's when I noticed the woman who had been standing beside Aaron. She was the same woman I'd seen him with that day at the hotel.

At her words, Beck's hand squeezed my shoulder. "Yes," he confirmed.

"Wow, I can't believe it," she announced.

She looked like she was about to say something else but Aaron beat her to the punch. "Can I hold her?"

I absolutely did not want him to hold her.

But he was her father.

I swallowed hard, looked up at Beck, and gave him a slight nod.

Beck must have realized I was struggling because he simply stared at me and didn't make a move to give Luna to Aaron.

"It's okay," I rasped, trying my best to sound reassuring and failing miserably.

His gaze lingered on mine a moment more before he let go of my shoulder and handed Luna off to her father. The second she was in Aaron's arms, Luna started to cry.

"Hi, Luna," he said to her.

He tried to console her by bouncing her up and down a bit and swaying from side to side, but she wasn't having any of it. She continued to cry, and they got louder and louder as the seconds ticked by.

"What's wrong with her?" he asked me, a look of disgust on his face.

Was he serious asking a question like that?

"Nothing is wrong with her. She just doesn't know you," I told him.

Aaron continued to try to get her to stop crying, but it wasn't working. I couldn't take it any longer, so I reached for her. Luna practically jumped out of his arms and into mine. Within seconds, she settled herself down.

Aaron's gaze shifted between Beck and me before it drifted

to our cart and back to Beck again. Something strange washed over his face.

I didn't want to leave the door open for him to say anything else, so I declared, "I'm sorry, but we really need to get going."

"Chasey?" Aaron called as Beck and I started to move away. "What?"

"You look good," he said.

I let out a sarcastic laugh. "Yeah. That's what happens when you have someone who treats you the way you're supposed to be treated."

Aaron winced.

He deserved that.

I didn't care. After the humiliation and embarrassment I suffered at his hands, what I said didn't even come close to what he'd done to me. But at the same time, I realized I had no desire to stoop to his level.

"Goodbye, Aaron."

With that, Beck and I walked away, and Luna had stopped crying. Once we had gotten far enough away from Aaron and his girlfriend, Beck stopped walking and turned toward me.

"Are you okay?" he asked.

I nodded. "Yeah. I hate that Luna was upset, but I'm fine. Better than fine, actually."

Beck assessed me a few seconds to confirm that I was being honest. When he realized that I was, he urged, "Come on. I have one more thing I want to get."

The next thing I knew, Beck had put one more item into the cart.

"What's that for?" I asked.

He brought his hand up to the side of my face, stroked his thumb along my cheek, and said, "You deserve to have a vase for your flowers."

He remembered.

Oh, God. He remembered that I'd had to put the flowers he'd given me into a drinking glass.

I looked away.

"Chasey?"

"Yeah?" I murmured.

"You've done what you had to do to be a good mom," he began. "I'm doing what I've got to do to show you that you're a worthy girlfriend."

At the mention of me being his girlfriend, I had no choice but to return my attention to him.

"For real?" I asked.

Tipping his head to the side, a look of disbelief washed over him. "Absolutely," he insisted. "And just so you know, I'm the kind of man who intends to make sure his girlfriend has fresh flowers in this vase all the time, especially when I'm not around."

He was incredible.

This wasn't about flowers or ornaments or Christmas trees.

This was about a man who was beyond anything I could have ever wished for. He just cared. He took care of me in ways I hadn't realized I needed. And something about that felt so unbelievably good.

"Looks like the little lady is getting hungry," he noted.

And it was that, too. He not only knew what I needed and gave it, but he recognized when Luna needed something.

"Yeah," I agreed.

"You packed food for her, right?"

Nodding, I confirmed, "I did."

"Good. Let's go get this stuff paid for so we can get out of here and I can take my girls out for lunch," he declared.

I smiled at him and felt my heart bursting with something else this time.

Love.

I was falling for Beck, and every time he called us his girls, I fell a bit harder.

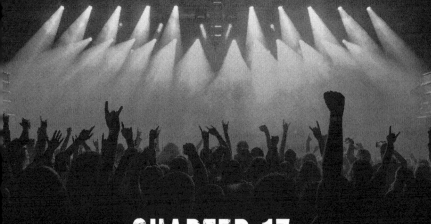

CHAPTER 17

Chasey

A KNOCK CAME AT MY FRONT DOOR.

I wanted nothing more than to open it and see Beck standing on the opposite side, but I knew that wasn't going to be the case.

It was Monday now, and it was time to get back to reality.

As much as I didn't want to do it, I had to say goodbye to Beck early this morning so he could get back on the road and head home to Pennsylvania. I never would have thought it would be so hard.

"I'm going to miss you," I said to him as he pulled me in for a hug.

"I'm going to miss you, too," he returned. "And Luna. But I promise to call frequently, and I'll be back as soon as I can get away again."

"Do you think we'll see you before Christmas?" I asked.

"Babe, if I have my way, I'll be back here by next weekend," he declared. "It'll just depend on what happens in the studio this week."

I tried to smile and be happy, but the truth was that I felt miserable. The last couple of days had been some of the best of my life. I hated that it was ending.

Beck and I spent the last few minutes we had together making out just inside my front door. And well before I was ready for it to happen, he had to go.

"Kiss Luna for me when she wakes up, okay?" he asked before he opened the door.

"I will. Drive safe."

He stepped outside, leaned back in, and gave me one final kiss. Then he was gone. All I wanted to do was cry.

But I couldn't.

Because I had to get myself ready for work.

So, I did that. Then Luna woke up, and after giving her a good morning kiss from me, I gave her one from Beck.

And now, not quite two hours after Beck left, I was walking back to my front door to let Mara come inside.

The minute I opened the door, she grinned and said, "Morning."

"Good morning, Mara. How was your Thanksgiving?" I asked as I stepped back and allowed her to come in.

Knowing she'd close the front door behind her, I walked back into the living room. But when I'd gotten there and she hadn't answered my question, I turned around to make sure everything was okay.

Mara was standing there with her mouth agape as her eyes drifted over nearly every surface of the living room.

"What happened here?" she asked.

I still had about fifteen minutes before I needed to leave for work, and since I was all ready to go, I figured I'd share the details now.

"Beck took Luna and me shopping for Christmas decorations on Saturday," I shared.

For the first time since she'd entered the room, her eyes shot to mine. "I'm sorry. What?"

"Beck showed up here on Wednesday night to surprise me," I started. "He didn't want us to be alone for the holiday."

Mara's eyes widened. "Oh my," she marveled.

Nodding with a big smile on my face, I decided to really shock her. "I kissed him before he even walked through the door," I told her. "And then he made me a grilled cheese sandwich before we had sex. Then we talked and had sex again. And then he spent the night."

Just as I had suspected, Mara was shocked. She stood there with a look of utter amazement and disbelief on her face. I wanted to laugh.

"What? I mean, wow, that's great news. Is he here now?" she questioned me.

I shook my head. "No. He left early this morning," I answered. "He had to go back to get back in the studio with the band."

Mara was still trying to come to terms with the news, so I urged, "I've got a few minutes before I have to leave. Why don't you sit down so I can fill you in on all the details?"

Before she settled herself on the couch, Mara walked over and plucked Luna out of my arms.

"Your mommy really knows how to keep a secret, doesn't she, Luni?" she asked her.

Luna, obviously, did not respond.

Once she'd taken a seat, I'd used the next few minutes to get Mara all caught up on everything that had happened since Wednesday evening. While she remained silent the entire time, only indicating how she was feeling with her facial expressions, by the time I finished, she could no longer hold back.

"I can't believe this," she bubbled. "You're officially dating a rock star!"

I was.

And as much as he was just Beck with Luna and me, I had a hard time separating him from his career.

He was a rock star.

"I know. And I'm utterly terrified about it," I shared.

"What? Why?" she asked. "Chasey, he drove six hours to get here to see you. And instead of being with his family and friends on the holiday, he spent it with you and Luna. I don't think you have to worry about him doing the same thing Aaron did to you."

Shaking my head because she'd misinterpreted my words, I clarified, "I'm not worried about Beck cheating on me. I don't know what it is, but I genuinely don't believe he is that kind of guy."

"Okay. So, what's the problem?"

"He's a rock star, Mara," I reminded her, even though I knew she didn't need one. "He lives a completely different life than I do. My life is filled with diapers and schedules and a mess of toys all over the place. His life is all about travel and excitement and the freedom to do as he pleases. I can't expect that this is going to last forever."

"I don't see why it can't," she argued. "Besides, if he didn't want it, why would he tell you that he wants to come back this weekend?"

I looked away as I shrugged. I didn't have an answer for her. The truth was, Beck made me believe that he was all in with me. He said and did all the right things, and he made me feel better than I had in years.

I just couldn't be sure that this would be a lasting thing for him. I didn't know that I brought nearly as much to the table as he did.

"I think I'm falling in love with him," I rasped.

"Aw, Chasey, I'm so happy for you," Mara replied. "You deserve this. After everything you've been through this year, there's nobody that deserves this more than you."

"But what if I'm setting myself up for disaster?" I worried.

There was a moment of hesitation before Mara said, "I

really think you're overthinking it. I can understand why you'd have nerves considering how things ended with Aaron, but Beck is doing all the right things. I mean, I guess there is that small chance that he could be doing this for some sick, twisted reason. But nothing that you've told me indicates that that's the case. I think you should enjoy what you've got with him now. If things change, we'll deal with the fallout later."

I absolutely did not think Beck had some evil or malicious plan to hurt me. Considering he was raised by a single mother, I had a feeling that he would never intentionally set out to bring heartache to another one.

Things happened, though. He might like the way things are now, and it could easily change.

But maybe I needed to do what Mara said. I needed to enjoy what I had with Beck right now. Whatever happened would happen. I'd already gotten through devastation once before. If I needed to do it again, I could.

So, I agreed, "You're right."

"Of course, I am."

I glanced down at the time. I had to leave.

I got up off the couch, kissed my daughter, and said, "I'll be back later."

"We love you," Mara said.

"Love you both, too."

With that, I walked out the front door. A few minutes later, as I drove myself to work, my mind started to wander.

I did my best to remain focused on all the good that had happened over the last few days, but it was difficult not to allow the pain I felt when Beck left this morning to settle inside me. I had a feeling that as time went on, having to say goodbye was only going to get harder.

I didn't know how many times I'd be able to do that.

Beck

My life had never really been wrought by personal struggle.

I'd witnessed it, especially now when I looked back at the sacrifices my mother had made for Sadie and me, but I personally hadn't ever really dealt with a lot of hardship. If the extent of my suffering throughout my entire life was that I had been a six-year-old boy whose father had walked out, I could honestly say I didn't feel that sting for long.

The truth was that my mom more than made up for his loss, and she and I along with my sister were a very happy family.

The older I got, the more fortunate I became.

I had great friends with similar interests. And while our path to success didn't come without any bumps along the way, it never felt particularly arduous. Maybe that was because we loved what we were doing, or perhaps it was because we were all going through it together. I didn't know. I just knew that being part of My Violent Heart left me feeling like I'd been luckier in my life than most.

But now, for the first time, I was feeling as though my luck had run out. It felt awful to think that because there had been so much good I'd experienced over the last few days with Chasey and Luna.

It was late Monday morning, just before lunch, and I was back in Pennsylvania on my way to the studio. I loved where I lived, and it had always been nice to come home, particularly after being on tour.

Sadly, I didn't have that same feeling now.

I missed Chasey, I missed Luna, and I wanted them here with me.

It had only been a few hours.

Saying goodbye to Chasey this morning hadn't been easy. I hated seeing the tears in her eyes. I hated leaving her and Luna behind.

For roughly six hours this morning as I drove home from New Hampshire, all I thought about was how much I'd enjoyed the last few days, how badly I wanted to turn around, and how much I was going to miss my girls.

That had surprised me.

It didn't take me very long at all to get to a point where I realized that they were mine. I wanted to do anything I could to make sure they were both happy and felt loved.

Yes, loved.

There was no doubt I'd been feeling the attraction to Chasey since the first day I met her. But following that second trip there where I was able to spend some time with her and then the weeks that followed where we spoke regularly on the phone, physical attraction turned into something else. Now that I'd spent just over four uninterrupted days with her, I didn't need any more time.

I was falling for her.

Hard.

What I had with her over the last few days was something I wanted forever. I didn't want to have to go visit again and have to leave them behind once more. Unfortunately, I was worried that it might be too soon for her.

So, I'd suck it up for as long as I could. I'd invite her and Luna to come to Pennsylvania for Christmas; I'd even drive them here myself.

In the meantime, I'd find a way to get myself back there as frequently as possible. And if that was going to happen, I'd have to do what I could to see that this recording session went well this week.

Just as I pulled into the parking lot at the studio, I saw Cash had just gotten out of his car. When he saw me, he stopped and waited for me to park.

"Hey," he greeted me when I got out of my car. "How's it going?"

"Good. Did you and Demi have a nice Thanksgiving?" I asked.

"We did," he confirmed as we started walking toward the front door to the studio. "Thanks for being willing to come in so soon afterward to work on this."

"It's no problem," I assured him.

"I thought I was going to be content to take some time off right after the tour and just enjoy the holiday season," Cash began. "But I've been writing a lot lately, and I've been feeling the overwhelming urge to get working on this one beyond just the words."

I completely understood what he was saying. Sometimes, especially when we were feeling particularly creative, we needed to bite the bullet and get to work.

"Well, I hope this one turns out to be a hit because I just drove six hours to be here," I shared.

We made it to the front door and stopped.

Well, Cash stopped with his hand on the door handle.

"Six hours?" he repeated.

I nodded.

"Hey, guys!"

Twisting my neck to the side, even though I knew the sound of that voice, I saw Holland approaching us.

"Hey, Holls," I greeted her.

"What's going on?" she asked. "You two look like you're in some kind of deep conversation here."

I shook my head. "No. I was just telling Cash that I drove six hours this morning to get here on time," I explained.

"Six hours? Did you get lost?" she asked.

"New Hampshire is six hours away," Cash chimed in.

At that tidbit of information, Holland's eyes widened. "You went up to see her? How'd it go?" she pressed. There was no mistaking the excitement and hopefulness in her voice.

Just then, the front door to the studio opened, and Killian

and Roscoe both walked out. "Are we working outside today? It's freezing, and you're all having a powwow out here," Roscoe said.

"Hey, Beck, how was New Hampshire?" Walker asked as he strolled up. There was a strange look on his face, like something was troubling him.

"How did you know he was in New Hampshire?" Holland asked him.

Walker's eyes shifted from me to Holland and back to me again. "Uh, I'm pretty sure he mentioned something about it at Cash's place before Thanksgiving," Walker answered.

Did I?

I remembered talking to them about where things were with Chasey and me then, but I didn't recall actually telling them that I was going to go visit her.

Deciding it didn't really matter, I answered, "It was really good."

"Wait, you were in New Hampshire?" Killian asked.

"Fuck, it's freezing out here," Roscoe bit out. "Can we at least hear all about Beck's love life inside?"

With that, we all shuffled inside. A minute later, Killian pressed, "So, you went back to see her?"

I nodded. "I went up last Wednesday and just got back this morning," I shared with them.

"How did it go?" Walker asked.

Thinking back on how good it all went, I couldn't stop myself from smiling.

"Oh, this is such great news," Holland declared.

"What news?" Cash questioned her. "He didn't even answer the question."

Holland huffed. "Isn't it obvious? The look on his face says it all. Beck is no longer single."

"Really?" Roscoe asked. "Another one of you is down for the count?"

"Yes, and I'm very happy about it," I replied.

"How's Chasey doing?" Cash asked.

This morning she'd been very sad, but I knew Cash wasn't referring to that. "She's great, and Luna is doing really well, too."

"Luna?" Killian repeated.

"Her daughter."

Understanding washed over him and the rest of the crew.

"So now what?"

That came from Walker.

I shrugged. "What do you mean?"

"Well, are you going to do this long-distance with her?" he wondered.

I really didn't want to, but I didn't think I had much of a choice in the matter. Not yet, anyway. It was still way too soon for me to expect that Chasey would have no problem picking up everything and moving to Pennsylvania with me where she didn't know anybody and hadn't ever lived before.

"It kind of feels a bit selfish of me to expect that she can just come here to live with me after only a few weeks of us getting to know one another," I responded. "Plus, she's got her daughter to think about."

"What about her ex-husband?" Holland asked.

Shaking my head, I shared, "He's not in the picture anymore. Then again, he was gone long before they even got divorced. The asshole isn't even taking care of his daughter."

"Are you serious?"

I nodded my head to confirm.

"Well, I hope it works out for the two of you," Cash said.

"Yeah, me too."

"Alright, but I've got a question," Roscoe jumped in.

"What's that?"

There was an extended pause before he asked, "What's going to happen if we go on tour again? I mean, there were talks about it toward the tail end of the last tour. You seemed to be on board with it then. Will this relationship change your feelings on that?"

I hadn't wanted to think much about touring again. Right now, my focus was on being with Chasey. All I wanted to do was spend time with her, to prove to her that there was a good guy in the world who'd make her every wish come true.

Instead of sharing that, I countered, "Why aren't you giving Cash a bunch of shit?"

"His girl is here with him now," Roscoe noted. "It's a safe bet that she'll be coming with us, but she's a grown woman. I'm not sure I can handle having a kid running around on a tour bus with us if you decide to bring your girl along."

"Roscoe, man, that wasn't cool," Walker warned him.

"Don't be heartless," Cash added.

Roscoe threw his arms up. "What? I'm not trying to be a jerk, but think about it," he declared. Shifting his attention to me, he said, "Beck, I'm being completely realistic. I don't mean any disrespect to her or her kid, but do you honestly think this lifestyle is one that is kid-friendly?"

Chasey had already made mention of how different our lives were on several occasions. She hated that I had to leave this morning, even though she understood it and didn't try to make me feel bad about going.

Was Roscoe right? Was Chasey right?

Maybe I was too consumed with how I felt about her that I was failing to take notice and consider just how difficult this would be for her and for me.

If there was a healthy balance for us, I certainly didn't know what it was.

Realizing I didn't have any answers to give him, I said, "You're getting way ahead of yourself, Roscoe. I'm loyal to this band, and I always will be. But I do expect that if and when I talk with Chasey and make decisions about what's best for us that you'll respect that."

He held my gaze a moment and dipped his chin. "As long as you aren't ready to turn your back on us, you know I've got yours," he assured me.

"Appreciate it," I replied before turning my head to Cash. "So, you want to tell us about this song?"

"Yeah," he answered.

Just like that, any of the tension that had been in the air dissipated, and we got down to business. And though I knew it wouldn't last, diving into some new music took my mind off all the troubling thoughts I'd been having since I got in my car this morning.

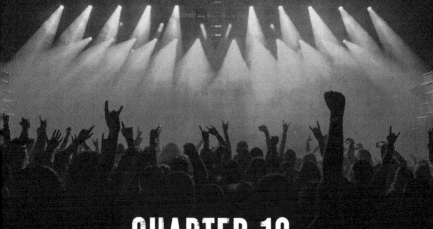

CHAPTER 18

Chasey

AS I NERVOUSLY BIT MY LIP, I HELD THE PHONE TO MY EAR AND listened to it ring.

I hoped Beck would answer.

It was now Wednesday evening, and I'd just gotten Luna down for the night. Since Luna was now sitting in her high chair during meals as she started eating solids, we had dinner together every evening. Given that, once she had gone to sleep, I'd showered and hopped into bed. It was still early, but I was tired, I needed to get up for work tomorrow, and I was hoping to talk to Beck for a little bit.

We hadn't spoken to each other since he left on Monday morning. To be fair, Beck had called me later that morning to let me know that he'd arrived safely in Pennsylvania, but I was at work at the time, so I'd gotten a voice mail message instead of actually being able to speak with him.

I had hoped to hear from him later that evening or even the following night, but Beck never called. I tried not to think too much about it. I knew he was probably busy at the studio, but I would have been lying if I said I wasn't just a little bit upset that we hadn't spoken at all.

Prior to coming for his surprise visit a week ago, Beck made the effort to call me regularly. I gotten accustomed to that, so this was not the norm for him. And considering we were officially together now, it only seemed natural that we'd talk at least as often as we did previously.

I knew that he was busy working, so I had no intentions of monopolizing his time. It just would have been nice to have a quick call from him to know that I was on his mind.

I hadn't stopped thinking about him.

I'd been having days at work that were particularly busy, and I took that as a good thing because it made my days fly by. When I got home, I soaked up my time with Luna. And while I still didn't love the fact that I had to leave my daughter at all, I was finding that the routine was getting a little bit easier to manage. I didn't know if it was the busy holiday season at work making the days feel like they were going by quickly or if it was coming home to my girl and our apartment that was decorated for the Christmas season. It could have been a combination of both along with the knowledge that Beck was in our lives.

The bottom line was that I had something to look forward to.

Only, for the last two days, I'd been left feeling rather disappointed that I hadn't heard anything from Beck since that voice mail he left Monday morning.

Unable to stand it any longer, I decided to call him. Normally, I'd always texted him. But that was before we became what we became to each other about a week ago. For that reason, I felt a bit more at ease with calling him.

Considering the fact that I was now gnawing on my lip while I listened to the phone ring, I didn't know what that said about how terrified I'd been to reach out to him beforehand.

"Hello?" he answered.

"Hey," I greeted him.

"Hi," he returned. "What's going on?"

WISH

"Nothing much," I answered. "I just got Luna down for the night and thought I'd call since we haven't had a chance to talk to each other since you left on Monday."

There was a brief pause while I heard some shuffling. "Hang on just a second," he said.

I hung on, listening to a bit more shuffling and wondering what he was doing.

Eventually, Beck lamented, "Sorry about that."

"It's okay. Is this a bad time?" I asked.

"Kind of," he replied. "We're still at the studio working."

"Oh. I'm sorry," I apologized. "I didn't mean to interrupt."

There was another beat of silence before Beck returned, "It's alright. I can take a quick break. Is everything okay there?"

This felt strange.

Awkward.

Beck was always so attentive and caring. He reached out to me regularly. We spoke frequently. Of course, that was all before he'd had a chance to see what life was like with a single mom. I tried to tell myself that I was overreacting to that. Beck was raised by a single mom. He already knew what life was like.

Or maybe while he was here, he was all about Luna and me. Maybe it wasn't until he got back home and had a dose of freedom again that he realized he didn't want to give it up.

Until he said otherwise, though, I didn't want to assume the worst and make this even more awkward than it already felt.

"Everything is okay," I confirmed. "I just wanted to talk for a little bit because I missed you."

"I'll be right there," Beck said, and I could tell he was talking to someone else that was there.

"I'm sorry, I should let you go," I told him.

"No, it's okay," he assured me. "What's going on there?"

Did he really want to know? I felt like he was incredibly distracted with what he was supposed to be doing. Maybe it wasn't that he didn't want to talk to me, but perhaps he really couldn't

187

focus on a conversation with me when he was making music. I didn't know. It wasn't like I had a single creative bone in my body.

Despite my doubts about whether or not he really wanted to talk to me, I answered, "Work has been really busy for me. It's good because my days are flying by and I feel like I'm getting home to Luna faster, but I can't get over how much the workload has changed since I first started my job. The number of packages that are being shipped out is incredible. I guess that's just par for the course at this time of the year, though."

"Sounds intense," he returned.

That's it. That's all he had to say.

I'd just rattled off all that, and he gave me two words.

I decided on a different tactic.

"Guess what?" I said.

"What?"

"Luna discovered her reflection yesterday," I told him. "I was holding her when I'd walked into the bathroom, and she saw her face in the mirror. I'd done that before, but it wasn't until yesterday that she actually seemed to really see the baby staring back at her. She was so happy seeing herself. I took her back in front of the mirror again today, and her whole face lit up."

There was another extended pause before I heard Beck sigh. "That's really great, Chasey," he said. "Listen, I hate to do this to you, but I've really got to get back in there. I'll reach out to you as soon as I can, okay?"

"Oh. Um, yeah. Sure."

My throat felt like it was closing up, and my belly started clenching.

"I'm sorry, babe," he lamented.

"It's okay," I insisted even though I was devastated.

"We'll talk soon," he said.

I felt so much doubt. "Sure. Whenever is fine. I've got to go," I replied.

With that, I didn't wait for him to respond. I disconnected the call, turned off my phone, and buried my face in my pillow.

This feeling was all too familiar.

I didn't think Beck was anything like Aaron. I didn't think he was a cheater. But I wasn't entirely sure he was a guy who wouldn't become disinterested. The thought that I'd fallen for him when he was no longer interested was crushing.

Suffice it to say, I barely got a wink of sleep that night.

I pulled out my phone as I walked to my car.

It was finally Friday, and I had just gotten out of work.

Looking down at the display, I saw I had a missed call and voice mail message as well as a text. I didn't want to even think about the missed call or voice mail just then, and that was mostly because the text was from Beck.

Beck: Call me when you get out of work.

Instantly, I was a bundle of nerves. My insides began trembling as my teeth began to chatter. It was cold out, but I was certain the reaction I was having had nothing to do with the weather.

I made it to my car, got inside, and turned it on. Convincing myself that I needed to give it a few minutes to warm up anyway, I decided to call Beck right away.

After tapping on his name, I held the phone to my ear. It barely rang a second time when Beck answered, "Hey, babe."

"Hi," I returned.

Despite the ease with which he spoke and the gentleness in his tone, I still felt awkward and uncomfortable.

The truth was that Beck and I hadn't spoken to each other since I'd reached out to him on Wednesday evening. When I got up and turned my phone on Thursday morning, there had been a text message from him. It came in quite a few hours after we had spoken. He simply stated that he'd just left the studio and was heading home for a few hours. He also told me to have a good day at work that day.

I never responded. And other than that text, there hadn't been any additional communication between us.

For the last two days I'd been feeling rather defeated.

Now that I was talking to Beck, I just didn't know what to expect.

"Before I got too far, I wanted to make sure that you were free this weekend," he said.

My body immediately perked up, and I sat a bit taller. "Um, yeah," I replied. "Luna and I don't really have anything crazy planned other than a quick trip to the grocery store after I pick her up from day care in a few minutes."

"Okay, well, I just left home about an hour ago," he started. "Everyone decided we needed to take a break from the music for the weekend, so I was coming to see the two of you and just wanted to make sure you didn't have any plans."

He was coming to visit.

Maybe I'd overreacted.

Perhaps being in the studio really did distract Beck from anything else in his life. Maybe when he was making music he couldn't afford the outside distractions.

I could understand that.

I could accept that.

"We'd love to see you," I told him.

"It might be late when I get there, though," he informed me. "Right now, I'm thinking it'll be a little after ten o'clock tonight. Although, if I hit any rush-hour traffic, it could be later."

"That's okay," I insisted.

"Do you still want me to come there to you, or would you rather I get a hotel tonight and come there in the morning?" he asked.

WISH

I didn't hesitate to demand, "Tonight."

Beck did hesitate before he questioned, "Are you sure?"

"Positive," I assured him. "Just give me a call or even a text when you arrive so that I can let you in."

"Okay. I'll see you in a few hours then," he declared.

I smiled. "Sounds great. I'll see you soon."

"Chasey?" he called.

"Yeah?"

"When I get there," he started. "It would not go unappreciated if you were wearing that little T-shirt you answered the door in the last time I drove up to your place."

He wanted me to wear my T-shirt?

"I can do that," I promised.

"Babe?" he called.

"Yeah?"

"*Only* the T-shirt," he clarified.

Another shiver unrelated to the temperature outside ran through my body.

My voice was husky when I replied, "I'll be waiting."

Beck groaned into the phone.

Yes.

Okay. This was good.

Suddenly, I felt infinitely better about where things were with Beck and me.

After we disconnected, I dropped my head back against the headrest and smiled. I felt such immense relief. One call. One single phone call had turned everything around.

Well, not everything.

It was then I remembered that I had a voice mail message waiting for me. I knew who it was from, and if it was anything like the one that had been left on Wednesday night after I turned off my phone, there was no doubt I wasn't going to like it.

I looked down at my phone again, tapped on the screen a few times, and lifted the phone to my ear.

"Chasey, it's me again. I already left one message and haven't heard back from you. This will be the last call I make. I want to see my daughter."

Fuck.

My head dropped back to the headrest again, but this time, there was no smile on my face.

Aaron had called for the second time. The first message he left was mostly the same, even if it was slightly less threatening. I wasn't quite sure how to take this message. What exactly did he mean to imply by saying this would be the last call he'd make? Was he just going to give up and go away? Or, judging by my luck, was he going to try to go the legal route?

I did not want this.

I did not need this.

Luna *did not* need this.

It felt a mix of both strange and awful to even have that thought. What little girl didn't need her father?

Obviously, I'd managed just fine without mine. But he walked away and didn't want anything to do with me.

Aaron was asking for time with Luna. Was it wrong for me to not want to give it to him? It wasn't because I wanted to purposely keep him away from her out of spite. I just didn't think it was going to be a good thing for Luna. She didn't know him. The interaction they had in the store was evidence enough of that.

Why would I ever be okay with putting her in a situation that was going to be stressful and upsetting to her?

And if I was being entirely honest about it, I didn't know exactly what Aaron's intentions were. He wanted time with Luna. How did he expect that time? Did he want her there overnight? Did he even have a crib for her to sleep in? He didn't know what foods she ate nor did he know the schedule she was on.

Maybe… maybe I could manage to give him a short visit with her. But overnight? I couldn't. I just couldn't bear to not have her sleeping under my roof.

Unfortunately, I had a feeling that if Aaron decided to go the legal route with this, what I wanted for Luna wouldn't matter. He'd have his rights, and I'd have no choice but to abide by whatever the court ordered.

Wasn't that something?

I'd have to hold up my end of things by giving him time with her, but beyond two payments in the beginning, he hadn't paid a stitch of child support since things ended between us.

I took in a deep breath. I wasn't going to deal with this now. It was Friday, I needed to pick up Luna from day care, and Beck was coming to visit for the weekend. There wasn't much I could think of that Aaron could do over the weekend anyway.

Deciding I wasn't going to drive myself crazy about this now, especially not after the week I'd had, I tossed my phone back into my purse and took off.

I'd deal with this mess with Aaron next week. And I absolutely was not going to discuss this with Beck. If I had any lingering concerns about the future of our relationship, I didn't think this mess would help us at all. If anything, it was likely to push Beck further away.

That wasn't a risk I was willing to take.

But I had to wonder what that meant about my confidence. If I assumed he'd rather walk away instead of sticking by my side through the difficult times, wasn't I setting myself up for disaster anyway?

CHAPTER 19

Beck

I PUT MY CAR INTO PARK AND SIGHED.

It felt good to be back here. Back where she was. Back where Luna was.

My drive here to Chasey's house had taken a bit longer this time since I ran into a bit of rush-hour traffic closer to the bigger city. Other than that, the drive hadn't been bad.

Anybody else might have thought I was crazy for making the drive when I could easily fly here and arrive in under two hours. Surprisingly, I was finding that I actually didn't mind the drive. It gave me time to think without any interruptions, and I had the chance to clear my head.

After the week I'd had this week, the quiet time was just what I needed.

I picked up my phone and sent a text to Chasey.

Me: I'm here. I'll be at your door in less than a minute.

I didn't wait for her to respond. It had been entirely too long without seeing her, and I didn't want to delay it any longer. Especially not when I was hoping she would have done what I'd requested when we spoke earlier.

As quickly as I could, I got out of my car, grabbed my bag,

and locked the doors. Just as I had said I would be, I was at Chasey's door in less than a minute.

Not wanting to wake Luna, I tapped the knuckle of my pointer finger on the door. Barely a second later, the door opened.

She was wearing the T-shirt.

I kept my eyes glued to hers as she stepped back while I walked inside. After I closed the door and dropped my bag on the floor beside me, I simply stood there and stared at her.

Yeah, it had definitely been entirely too long without her.

Not even a full week away, and I'd missed her tremendously. I didn't know how I was even refraining from going to her, scooping her in my arms, and kissing her.

Something held me back.

Something in her expression. There was a small smile tugging at her mouth, but there was something else. There was an uneasiness about her.

I had a feeling I knew where it was coming from, and I had every intention of resolving that. But it would have to wait.

I had other plans.

"Is Luna sleeping?" I asked.

Her chin jerked down slightly as she whispered, "Yes."

"Lift up your shirt," I requested.

Chasey blinked in surprise at my demand, but she ultimately bit her lip and brought her hands to the hem of her shirt. Slowly, she began to pull the fabric up her body until it exposed her naked pussy beneath. Then she stopped.

I kicked off my sneakers.

"Keep going."

Chasey hesitated. I knew what that was about, too, but I wanted her to do this. She had no reason to feel insecure about her body. She was beautiful.

Eventually, she lifted the shirt higher and exposed her breasts.

Perfection.

"Take it off, babe," I encouraged her.

A moment later, my beautiful girl was standing in front of me with nothing on. She was exquisite, and I couldn't wait another moment longer to touch her.

Since I didn't want her to feel like she was completely alone, I pulled my jacket down my arms before I tore my shirt over my head.

I watched as the look in Chasey's eyes intensified and she licked her lip. With her gaze on my chest, I stepped forward and closed the distance between us. I stopped myself inches away from her, but slightly off to the side. Then I pressed my palm into her abdomen.

Instantly, she tensed.

"Look at me," I urged quietly.

She lifted her gaze to mine.

I didn't say anything. I simply stared at her, keeping my palm right where it was. She needed to understand that I had zero problems with her body. And while I guess I could understand the insecurity she felt, I needed her to know that she had no reason to feel that way with me.

It took her some time, but she eventually relaxed. Once she did that, I rewarded her. I slid my hand down her body until I stopped between her legs. My fingers gently rubbed her there before I slid my fingers through her wetness and plunged one finger inside her pussy.

Chasey immediately brought a hand to my chest and pressed her fingertips into my skin as she moaned.

I slowly pulled my finger out before burying it inside her again.

"Beck," she cried out softly.

I brought my free hand up to the side of her head. My fingers drove into her hair, caught her at the back of her head, and angled her mouth up to mine. I dropped my head forward, captured her lips, and kissed her as I continued to play between her legs.

She never stopped moaning, and she now had both of her hands on me—one still planted squarely at the center of my chest, the other gripping the back of my arm firmly. I never would have imagined that such soft hands could have such a bruising grip.

Then again, I knew what I was doing to her. And if what she was experiencing now was anything like what I imagined I'd feel if she had her hands on my dick and was stroking me, I could understand why she felt the need to hold on so tightly.

With my tongue exploring the warm recesses of her mouth and my finger plunging into the wetness between her legs, I felt something come over me.

Maybe things would be tough for us as we tried to navigate through the hurdles of this new relationship, but the fact of the matter was that I did not want to be without this woman. She had hooked me from the very first day I saw her, and she didn't even know it. There was no way I could give her up.

Whatever it was going to take to make this work—for her, for Luna, for me, and for my band—I was going to make it happen.

I begrudgingly tore my mouth from hers and pulled my finger from her body. Chasey whimpered.

I did my best to ignore that as I slid an arm around her waist and the opposite hand underneath her ass. Then I lifted her up and moved to the living room.

After planting my ass on one of the cushions, I captured one of her breasts in my mouth and drove two fingers inside her.

Chasey cried out in pleasure. "Beck, baby."

I thought my dick was going to explode in my pants just hearing her like that, full of lust and need and desire.

"Ride my fingers, Chasey," I said when I freed her tit from my mouth. "Get what you need."

She did just that.

Within minutes, her rhythm had gone from fast and steady to frantic and irregular. That, along with her shallow breathing and her nails digging into my skin, told me that she was on the verge.

So, I helped her out.

I pressed my thumb to her clit and began to circle as my fingers moved swiftly in and out of her pussy.

Chasey came apart over me, and I worked her through her orgasm. I barely let her come down before I wrapped an arm around her back, lifted myself from the couch, and dropped her to her back against the cushion.

As I pulled my wallet out of my jeans, I ordered, "Free me, babe."

Chasey immediately leaned forward to unbutton and unzip my pants. In record time, she was pushing my jeans and my underwear down my legs just as I got the condom out of the foil packet.

While I sheathed myself, I said, "Lean back and spread your legs, Chasey."

She did as I asked, and I was convinced I'd never seen a more breathtaking sight in my entire life.

"You're beautiful," I declared, my voice deep and husky, as I leaned forward with one hand guiding my cock to her pussy and the other planted firmly on the back of the couch.

The second I was inside of her, I lost control. I drove in hard and deep.

I knew Chasey was into it, loving every second of it, because she put her hands on the backs of her thighs and spread her legs wider.

Keeping one hand gripping the back of the couch, I let go with the other and brought my thumb to her clit. I couldn't not touch her. Having her like this, spread wide and open for me, it would have been torture not to touch.

I applied pressure with my thumb, gripped the back of the couch tighter, and relentlessly thrust my hips forward.

Chasey's sexy moans and little gasps for breath filled the air around us. There was an unbreakable connection between our gazes, and neither of us seemed able to look away.

God, I'd missed this.

I'd missed her.

And in that moment, connected to her in the most intimate way possible, I felt nothing but love for her.

I wanted this with her for a long time to come.

I wanted this and everything else she had to give.

Her lips parted, and the tight, almost tortured, sound of her moans came rapidly. She was on the verge of an orgasm.

"Are you going to come, babe?" I asked, still not tearing my eyes from hers.

"Beck," she panted her warning.

With both of my hands now at the back of the couch, I pounded my cock into her. Fast. Hard. Deep.

She was the first to break eye contact when her orgasm hit. Her head pressed back into the cushion as her eyes squeezed shut and her lips parted, allowing the sounds of her moans of pleasure to fill the room.

I already thought Chasey was perfection. Seeing her like this took things to a level I didn't think was possible.

And that was when I buried myself deep and groaned through my own climax.

Still hidden in the warmth between her legs with my forehead pressed against hers, I gently stroked over the skin at her cheek.

Her eyes sparkled, and she said, "I'm so glad you're back."

I closed my eyes and allowed the tip of my nose to drift up along the side of hers. Then I kissed her lips and replied, "Me too."

"You seem tense."

"What?"

Chasey and I were in her bed. We'd gotten up off the couch a little while ago and had taken care of getting ourselves cleaned up.

Now, we were here. And though it was late, I knew that neither of us was ready to fall asleep yet. There was no way Chasey was going to be able to drift when her body was wound so tightly. For me, I'd stay awake until I knew that she was okay and didn't have anything on her mind.

Thinking it was best to go into this with a lighthearted tone, I teased, "After those two orgasms, I would have thought you'd be a bit more relaxed."

"I'm relaxed," she lied.

"If I didn't know any better, I'd say you could pass for a statue right now," I countered.

There was a moment of silence before she rasped, "I just missed you a lot. That's all."

I wasn't quite sure that was all. In fact, I knew that wasn't all there was that was messing with her head. But I didn't want to force it out of her. I wanted her to feel comfortable enough to share. I wanted her to trust me enough to know that she could tell me the truth about her feelings. Even though she hadn't elected to tell me, I knew our lack of communication this past week bothered her. I wanted her to be the one to admit that to me.

There was another bout of silence, but this one lasted a very long time. So long that if I hadn't been paying attention to the way her body felt and knew otherwise, I might have believed she'd fallen asleep.

I didn't want this for her or for us so I urged gently, "You can say whatever is on your mind, Chasey. We can only work through things if we're honest with each other about them."

"I don't want to say the wrong thing," she returned softly.

I hadn't expected that.

Not only that, but I didn't like it at all.

"Telling me how you feel will never be the wrong thing, babe," I assured her. "Even though we met for the first time when Luna was only five weeks old, this thing between us is still very new. We both have to have a mind to one another in navigating this relationship. I can't promise you what's going to happen, but I can promise that this won't work if either of us feels like we can't say what's on our mind."

The silence stretched between us again, and I was convinced Chasey wasn't going to open up to me. But eventually, she shared, "It was different."

"Different? What was different?" I asked.

"The way it was between us before you spent the holiday weekend with us, and the way it was afterward," she clarified.

"In what way?" I pressed.

She took a moment to, presumably, collect her thoughts and figure out how she wanted to share this. I had been spooning her, so I kept my arm wrapped firmly around her body and simply allowed my thumb to continue stroking the underside of her breast. I didn't know if it was doing anything to help her, but I hoped it was providing some comfort and encouragement.

"We talked more," she began. "Actually, we just talked. While I knew you had to go home after the holiday, I guess I expected that we'd still have at least that."

"And we didn't," I stated, knowing that was the case.

"And we didn't," she agreed.

I didn't say anything as I allowed the weight of her disappointment to consume me. She'd been disappointed in her last relationship, and the last thing I wanted to do was give her more of the same.

"Beck?" she called.

"Yeah?"

"I don't want you to think that I don't respect the time you need to do what you do," she started. "I just don't think I had a clear understanding of how it would be. This last week really opened my eyes to what your life is really like."

I didn't, not for one second, think that she was begrudging the time I needed to do the work that I did. But it was clear that she thought I would think that.

"I should have checked in more often," I told her. "I'm sorry that I didn't."

"You were busy," she reasoned.

"And you weren't?" I countered. "There is no doubt in my mind that you had far more responsibilities to manage. Despite that, I have a feeling that if I had called you, you would have made the time for me. I should have given you the same."

The silence stretched a moment between us as Chasey took in my words. Then she cautiously asked, "Can I ask why you didn't?"

"You absolutely can ask me anything you want, babe," I told her. "Don't hold yourself back from that. There's no good reason why I didn't reach out because the truth is that I'd be feeding you a bunch of excuses. All I can say is that when we're in the studio, it's really tough to get out of that mindset. I don't like to be distracted, and considering everything else that was going on, we were already dealing with enough."

"Everything else?" she repeated.

I sighed. "Suffice it to say that we did not accomplish all that we had hoped to accomplish this week with Cash's song."

"Did something happen?"

"There wasn't one major thing that happened," I said. "It was just a bunch of little things. Walker seemed distracted, which was strange because he's usually very focused on the music. We asked him if everything was alright, and he insisted everything was fine."

"Do you believe him?" Chasey asked.

I didn't. I didn't believe him, but I respected him. If he had something going on that he didn't want to talk about, then I wasn't going to push it with him.

"No. I have a feeling I know what's bugging him, but I don't want to make any assumptions or start rumors," I answered honestly.

"Rumors?" Chasey repeated. "That doesn't sound good at all."

It wasn't.

That was why I refused to get involved or say anything about it until Walker was ready to share. I had a feeling, though, that there was something going on with him and Holland. Ever since the band had made the second trip to New Hampshire back in the summer, Cash put an idea in our heads. We all agreed that he might be right and that Walker and Holland might have had a thing going on between them. They always seemed to take off early whenever we all went out together. Sometimes, particularly after that trip, they exchanged awkward glances. I think they believed they were still fooling all of us, but that was no longer the case. It was so obvious now.

Of course, what didn't make sense was that while he seemed particularly distracted during our studio session all week, Holland was her typical self. Maybe she just did a better job at hiding whatever was bothering her. Or, maybe Cash, Killian, Roscoe, and I were making assumptions about Walker and Holland that were all wrong.

"It's not, but that wasn't all we had to deal with," I shared. "There was Roscoe, too."

"Did something happen to him?"

"Not exactly. He was just irritable and moody. And he said a lot of shit that was out of line," I explained.

"How do you guys record anything if stuff like that is happening?" Chasey wondered.

I let out a laugh and reminded her, "Well, we didn't get the song done. We figured out some parts of it, but there's still work to be done. And since this is a song Cash wrote for Demi, he's not willing to have it be anything less than perfect."

Chasey brought her hand up to cover mine at her breast. For a long time she didn't say anything. I had a feeling she was thinking about things, and I wanted her to have the time to think about whatever it was that was on her mind. So, I kept myself quiet.

Eventually, just as I had suspected she would, Chasey spoke.

"I'm sorry things didn't go well for you this week, Beck," she lamented.

"It's okay," I assured her. "I'm just really happy to be here with you right now. And I can't wait to see Luna in the morning."

At that, Chasey rolled over and pressed her chest against mine. She drove her fingers into my hair and kissed my mouth.

She didn't say anything else after that. She simply cuddled deeper into my body and drifted off to sleep.

After I worked out that she was simply showing gratitude for the fact that I had mentioned wanting to see Luna in the morning, I closed my eyes and fell asleep minutes after she did. And all the negative thoughts about the status of our relationship moving forward, especially with regard to how the band would affect it, faded away.

CHAPTER 20

Chasey

MY EYES FLUTTERED OPEN, AND I SMILED.

I was staring at the wall of Beck's chest, so there was no reason not to smile. There was also the fact that he was naked in my bed and had woken me up in the middle of the night to deliver another round of orgasms.

Mostly, I was smiling because even in his sleep, Beck was holding me close to him. And that notion—that he'd hold me close like that when he was asleep—made me believe that so much of what I'd been worried about over the last week was all in my head.

Of course, I knew it hadn't been in my head because Beck came right out and apologized for not making the effort to communicate with me. I didn't necessarily know what that meant for us moving forward, but the fact that he knew something was bothering me before I shared it and was willing to acknowledge that he could have handled things differently gave me a bit of confidence when it came to the future of our relationship.

This was new.

For me and for him.

And while I didn't plan to dig into Beck's past to learn about his former relationships, I had to believe that what we had was different than what he might have had with someone else. It was going to take time for the both of us to navigate through the murky waters to get to a place that had us both feeling good about where we were.

If how I felt right now was any indication of how that journey was going, it was safe to say that we were in a great place.

I tipped my head back slightly and took him in.

God, he was good-looking. Even in his sleep, he looked impossibly handsome. And a man that looked like him thinking I was beautiful made me feel like I was on top of the world.

But beyond the physical magnificence of Beck was something so much more beautiful.

His heart.

I'm just really happy to be here with you right now. And I can't wait to see Luna in the morning.

His words from last night rang in my head. He could have just about anyone in the world he wanted, and he chose me. He chose us.

Maybe it wouldn't last forever—I tried not to think about that—but we had him now. And he seemed, if nothing else, to adore us. I knew he adored Luna. He always included her in our conversations, he asked about her, and he wanted to see her this morning.

What man… what single rock star who could have his pick of the litter would be here right now if he didn't feel strongly about us?

I took in a deep breath and sighed with relief. I didn't know how I managed it, but I'd found a good man. Moving forward, all I wanted to do was make sure I held on tight to him.

Just as I had that thought, I heard Luna start to stir.

Then, the most amazing thing happened. Beck's eyes shot open. He looked down at me and said, "She's awake."

My heart exploded.

It had been the tiniest, sweetest little sound from Luna, and it woke him.

Yeah, I'd definitely found a good man.

"She's awake," I confirmed.

He smiled, shifted, and kissed me. "Good morning, babe."

"Good morning, Beck," I returned before I pushed the cover back and moved to get out of bed.

I'd just gotten out of the bed, slid on a pair of panties, pulled a shirt over my head, and taken two steps toward the door when Beck asked, "Can I get her and bring her to you?"

At Beck's question, I froze on the spot. "What?" I replied, convinced I'd misheard him.

"Would it be alright if I went in Luna's room this morning and got her?" he asked again, sitting up in the bed.

Nope.

I definitely heard him correctly.

He wanted to get my baby. He wanted to go in her room and let his face be the first she saw this morning. The magnitude of how much that knowledge affected me was beyond anything I could have imagined.

I had been so stunned by it that I remained quiet for entirely too long. My silence led Beck to making assumptions about how I was reacting to his question.

"I'm sorry," he apologized. "I just… I missed her and didn't want to wait to see her. I understand if you're not ready for that. It's okay. Maybe another time."

God, the disappointment in his voice was so palpable. He loved her. He loved my little girl in a way that she'd never be loved by her own father. If I had any doubt about it before, there was certainly none now.

"I think I love you, Beck Emerson," I blurted.

The minute the words had passed through my lips, my eyes widened and I slapped my hand over my mouth. I was only supposed to be thinking that.

Why?

Why did I just say that to him?

My stunned eyes watched as something moved through Beck's expression. He got out of the bed and moved toward me, completely unashamed by his nudity.

When he was inches away, Beck tipped his head to the side and looked down at me adoringly. He tugged my hand away from my mouth, and with a voice deeper and huskier than I'd ever heard it, he asked, "What did you say?"

I bit my lip nervously, wondering if I'd just made the biggest mistake of my life. It seemed I would soon find out because I couldn't pretend I hadn't just said what had to be the most powerful words anyone could say to another person.

"I think I love you," I murmured.

For several long moments, Beck didn't respond. My insides were a mess.

I ruined it.

I just ruined it, mere minutes after I realized just how lucky I was that I'd found a good man. I dropped my gaze to the ground, feeling nothing but a mix of terror and sadness.

"Chasey," he whispered. The sound of his voice made me close my eyes. This was it; he was going to end this. I did my best to brace myself as Beck urged, "Look at me."

Slowly, I brought my attention to him. Tears filled my eyes as a lump formed in my throat.

Beck reached out for my wrist and held on to it as he shared, "I think I love you, too."

My head jerked back. "You... you do?"

He nodded.

A sob escaped, and Beck immediately pulled me into his arms. He held me for a few moments as I tried to pull myself together. I should have been jumping for joy that he felt the same, but instead I was a blubbering mess in his arms.

"You're the most amazing man I've ever met," I cried, feeling overwhelmed.

Beck kept one hand wrapped around my upper back to the opposite shoulder while the other stroked up and down my spine. At the same time, he kissed the top of my head.

"Don't cry, babe," he said softly.

It took me a few more seconds, but I eventually pulled myself together enough to lift my face from his chest. When I looked up at him, he brought his thumbs to my cheeks and wiped away my tears.

Before either of us could say anything, Luna started to cry.

I smiled at Beck through my tears and said, "You can get her."

"Are you sure?"

Nodding, I confirmed, "I'm positive."

Beck didn't waste a single second. He stepped away from me, pulled on a pair of pants from his bag he brought back to my bedroom last night, and walked out of the room to get Luna. I stood there feeling stunned and unable to move.

Or, I hadn't been able to move.

But a moment later, when I heard Beck enter Luna's room, I slowly walked back toward my bed and lifted the monitor off the nightstand. I held it in my hand and listened.

"Good morning, princess," I heard him say to her.

I couldn't stop myself from smiling. Luna, obviously, did not respond; however, her crying had subsided. That's when I noticed that Beck had picked her up.

"Did you sleep good? Are you hungry now?" he asked as he walked out of the view of the camera. I heard a bit of rustling around, and I was unsure what he was doing, but since he continued to talk I focused on that. "Mommy is waiting for you," Beck went on. "She's going to feed you, and I'm going to make her breakfast. And then, after you've got a full belly, you're going to have to show me how your music skills are progressing. Okay? Does that sound good?"

I heard little whimpers come from Luna before I heard the distinct sound of Beck kissing her cheek.

"Come on," he declared. "I think I have everything. Let's go find your Mama."

The next thing I knew, Beck walked back into my bedroom carrying Luna, a diaper, and a container of baby wipes.

"I've never done it before, so I wasn't going to attempt it," he began. "Plus, I didn't know the rules for changing diapers of babies who aren't your own."

I wanted to tell Beck that he'd been more of a father figure than Luna's own father, but I didn't want him to feel any sort of unnecessary pressure to take on a role that he might not have wanted to fulfill.

"I'll take care of it," I told him as I set the monitor back down on the nightstand. "Thank you for bringing everything here."

As Beck moved toward me with Luna in his arms, I scooted myself back on the bed. When Beck stopped at the side of the bed, he tossed the diaper and wipes down onto the mattress. I looked up at my girl, held my arms out to her, and beamed, "Good morning, baby girl."

She squealed with delight and flashed me a big smile as she reached for me.

I took her from Beck and got to work on changing her diaper after I'd given her about a million kisses.

While I changed her diaper, Beck moved to the other side of the bed and started to dig through his bag. Much to my dismay, he yanked out a T-shirt and pulled it over his head.

By the time he got back to my side of the bed, Luna's new diaper was on and I was zipping up her pajamas.

"You're like a superhero," Beck declared.

"A superhero?" I repeated.

"You changed her so fast," he shared.

Smiling as I lifted Luna in my arms, I corrected him. "I'm not a superhero, Beck. I'm a mom."

He shrugged. "It's basically the same thing."

A brief moment of silence passed between us before I asked, "Can you wait?"

"Wait?"

"To make breakfast," I clarified.

Beck cocked an eyebrow. "You're not hungry?" he asked.

"I am. I just... I don't know how long I have you," I started. "I kind of want to keep you close while I've got you here."

Beck's expression softened, and he lowered himself down onto the bed. I took that to mean he was okay with waiting for breakfast.

Once I had Luna settled in my arms and nursing, Beck swung his legs around so they were on the side of the bed he'd slept on, and he rested his head on my thighs just above my knees. Never in a million years did I think Beck would cuddle with me like that, but the minute he was there, I couldn't deny how much I loved it.

As I smiled down at him, I drove the fingers of my free hand into his hair. My fingernails glided over his scalp while a look of contentment washed over Beck.

Finally, he said, "I'll be here for the rest of the weekend, but even after I leave, I want you to know you'll still have me."

The weekend.

I had the weekend.

I wanted so much more.

"You seem upset," he noted.

I swallowed my emotions down and admitted, "It just doesn't feel like enough time."

"I know. That's actually something I wanted to talk to you about this weekend," Beck shared.

"What?"

He exhaled deeply before he said, "Well, I hadn't intended to bring this up yet, but considering I didn't think we'd be sharing all those words we did this morning, I think this is good to do now. It's still just over two and a half weeks away, but I would really love for you and Luna to come to Pennsylvania and spend Christmas with me there."

My hand stopped moving in his hair. I didn't know what I expected Beck to say to me, but I certainly hadn't been prepared for that.

He wanted us to spend Christmas with him.

In Pennsylvania.

I didn't even know how I could make that happen. Where would Luna sleep? Did portable cribs exist?

I was in the middle of having a million thoughts about the logistics of making that happen when Beck interrupted them. "I checked and saw that the post office is closing early on Christmas Eve. And since Christmas is on a Friday this year and you are normally off on Saturdays, we could leave as soon as you get out of work on Thursday."

"Beck…" I trailed off. I didn't want to disappoint him, but I thought he needed to understand what he was asking. "Technically, I'm actually off on Christmas Eve. I realized a few weeks ago that Luna's day care would be closed for certain days around the holidays, which is why I had off the day after Thanksgiving. I put in for Christmas Eve as well. That said, even though I'll have that time off, there's a lot that I have to consider."

"Like what?"

I let out a laugh. "Like traveling states away with a baby," I told him. "Luna's crib is here. How many diapers will I need to pack? Will I have enough baby wipes? What about food? She's starting to eat solids now."

"Chasey?" Beck called.

"Yeah?"

"They have babies in Pennsylvania," he deadpanned.

I blinked in surprise. "Um... okay?"

"So, what I'm saying is that if there's anything she needs that we can't pack and take with us, we can buy it there."

He made it sound so simple.

But I didn't think it was that easy.

I mean, he wanted us to spend Christmas with him. To me, it should be about Christmas, not needing to run to the store for something I didn't think to pack because I didn't know we'd need it.

"What's going on?" he asked, obviously unable to miss how hard my mind was working.

"I don't want to ruin your Christmas," I said.

"Babe, being with you and Luna is what will make it special," he assured me. "If you don't want to come to Pennsylvania, we'll work it out. I'll talk with my family and figure something out so I can be here with the two of you on Christmas morning. It's okay. I don't want you to be upset worrying about something that should really just be fun and exciting."

He was going to work it out with his family so he could spend Christmas morning with us?

I couldn't let him do that. He'd already done that for Thanksgiving.

Shaking my head, I insisted, "I'll figure it out, Beck. Luna and I would love to take a trip to Pennsylvania."

"Are you sure?" he asked.

Nodding, I confirmed, "Absolutely. It'll be Luna's first vacation."

Relief swept through Beck's body, and it wasn't until it happened that I realized that he'd been so tense about this. Maybe I'd want to pull my hair out, maybe I'd feel like I was crazy for doing this, but in the end, as long as I was with Beck, I had a feeling I wouldn't regret going.

"I love you," he said after some time passed.

Warmth spread through me. "I love you, too."

For the next little while, Beck and I stayed like we were until Luna finished eating. Then we spoiled her with a bunch of attention in the bed since she had filled her belly and was feeling pleasant.

It warmed my heart to see the way Beck interacted with her. And he wasn't afraid to show her affection, either. I loved that she had that from him. Being on my own, it upset me that Luna didn't have any aunts, uncles, or grandparents to show her love. She'd only ever had me.

And Mara.

And Mara's family.

And now Beck.

If we were lucky, she'd have him for a long time.

And if I got my wish, she'd eventually have his family, too.

CHAPTER 21

Beck

"I CAN'T BELIEVE IT."

Those words came from me as I sat on the floor of Chasey's living room, where she was sitting beside me and Luna was on the blanket in front of us. Luna was busy showing me the improvements she'd made to her skills on the piano. If nothing else, she'd become much more sure of herself, banging away at the keys and giggling herself silly.

The three of us had just finished having breakfast together a little while ago, and I'd been living in a state of shock ever since.

"What do you mean?" Chasey asked.

"It's only been a week," I replied, staring at Luna in amazement.

"A week?" she repeated.

Nodding as I brought my attention to Chasey, I clarified, "It's only been a week since I was last here, and I feel like Luna has grown so much in that time."

Chasey's expression warmed. "They say it goes fast."

"Well, I don't like it," I shared. "She's sitting in her high chair, lifting tiny pieces of mashed avocado to her mouth to feed herself like she's all grown up. She's been babbling away all morning with so much to say. And she's obviously improved her skills on the piano."

No sooner did I get those words out when Chasey let out a laugh. "You might not like it, but these are all good things, Beck," she assured me. "It's all part of growing, and I love that she's learning all these new things. Of course, I'd love for her to stay this small forever, but that's never going to happen."

I shifted my attention back to Luna and watched as she got herself onto all fours and began rocking back and forth.

I'd been gone one week, and so much had changed.

"It makes me never want to leave again," I rasped.

I couldn't get over how much this was affecting me. Suddenly, it was making sense to me why Chasey had said from the start that all she ever wanted to do was be a stay-at-home mom so she could take care of her husband and raise her babies.

She didn't want to miss this.

Milestones.

Luna would grow quickly and learn new things. If Chasey was working when Luna decided to take her first steps, there was no doubt in my mind that she'd be devastated.

I wanted nothing more than to change that for her.

I loved her. I loved both of them, and despite how hard and fast that had happened, it didn't stop me from wanting to give them everything.

Everything.

Before I could figure out how to best communicate all that without scaring the living daylights out of Chasey, I felt her touch on my arm. "We love you, and we'd never kick you out," she said softly.

I placed my hand on top of hers and replied, "I love both of you, too. And while I appreciate your willingness to open up your home to me and would love nothing more, I can't stay."

"I know," she assured me.

"I hate the idea of having to leave you and Luna again,"

I told her. "But I've got to go back so we can finish recording that song. I hope it's not going to need much more than this next week."

"What happens then?" she asked.

I took in a deep breath to prepare myself to share it. Even though there was nothing set in stone just yet, Chasey was important to me. I thought she deserved to know what could be coming down the pipeline.

"We might head back into the studio to record a new album. Cash shared last week that he has been working on a lot of material. We also learned that Holland has been doing the same. So, that's a possibility. There were also discussions of us going back on tour."

"Is this an either or thing?" Chasey questioned me.

"It could be both," I answered. "It will likely be both. It's simply the timing that we haven't worked out. And if recording songs on the album go anything like the one we're currently trying to do is going, that could be a lengthy process. That said, talks of another tour came up when we were still on the last one."

I didn't know if I should admit the truth about where everyone stood with touring. The truth was, the only person who seemed to have any reservations about it when we'd been discussing it while on the last tour was Cash. At the time, he'd been doing the long-distance thing with Demi, and he hated being apart from her. I couldn't say I didn't now understand exactly how that felt.

Of course, now that Demi was living with Cash and she was going to be the My Violent Heart swag and merchandise manager, Cash no longer had anything to worry about. If we went out on tour, Demi would be going with us.

Unfortunately, the enthusiasm that I used to have about another tour was fading. It seemed I wasn't the only one either.

Throughout the course of the last week, when we'd all

been in the studio, the subject of another tour came up. While Cash, Killian, Roscoe, and Holland all seemed to be fired up about planning one, Walker's interest seemed to be waning. He didn't come right out and give any reasons why, but it was clear he wanted a bit of a longer break. Considering he hadn't felt that way just a couple months ago, I knew there had to be something else going on with him.

While I didn't know what Walker's reasons for wanting to delay the tour were, I couldn't say I didn't sympathize with him. I felt the same.

If we could push the tour back a bit, I'd be able to really get some quality time in with Chasey. We'd really have a chance to explore our relationship to see if it had what it took to go the distance.

Part of me already felt sure. The other part of me had some nerves. Those nerves all seemed to be attributed to Chasey, though. I simply wanted to make sure she didn't feel like she was rushing into something she wasn't ready for too soon.

"I'm sure you guys will work it out," she said in an attempt to be reassuring.

Just like that, I started to wonder where her head was at.

"How would you feel?" I asked.

Chasey's brows knit together. "How would I feel about what?" she countered.

"About me going out on another tour," I clarified.

She looked away a moment, directing her gaze to her daughter. Chasey wasn't giving anything away with her expression, but I could see her mind working hard. I felt myself getting a bit antsy as I waited for her to respond.

Eventually, she returned her attention to me and said, "I'd miss you. I'd miss you every single day, but I'd be happy for you."

As much as I liked her answer, it also surprised me.

"You mean, you wouldn't want me to stay?" I questioned her.

WISH

"Obviously, I'd love for you to be here with me," she said. "But I get the distinct feeling that your music fills you up the same way me being home with my daughter and raising her fills me up. I'd never, ever, want to take that away from you. We all need those things in our life that make us feel fulfilled, Beck. Sometimes, like with you, you get lucky enough to make your dreams come true right from the start. And other times, like with me, you have to hold on to that wish just a little bit longer."

God, she was incredible.

Instead of being bitter about how things had turned out in her life, she found a way to still keep her heart and her mind open. She didn't hold on to the disappointment of what her ex-husband's betrayal had done to upend all the plans she had for her future.

"How are you even real?" I asked.

"Why do you say that?"

Shaking my head in disbelief, I replied, "I just would have thought that you'd feel differently about everything, especially me going on tour. There's a certain stigma, one most of us haven't done much to combat, that goes along with the life of a rock star. I'm surprised you don't feel any worry about that given what you've been through."

For a long time, Chasey held my gaze. "You aren't my ex, Beck," she eventually declared. "If I sat here and told you that I wouldn't feel any jealousy or envy about thousands of women seeing you perform on stage night after night while I was here, I'd be lying. But when it comes down to it, I've had to take a long hard look in the mirror. You've given me no reason not to trust you, and you do everything you can to make me feel like you care about me. I mean, yeah, I've had moments where I've doubted what I brought to the table in this relationship. But the bottom line is, you're still here. You're still driving six hours to see me. I can't dismiss that, and I have to believe that if you didn't want to be here, you wouldn't be."

Finally.

Now it felt like we were getting somewhere. Maybe it had been the declarations of love this morning, or maybe it was something else, but either way, we were making progress. Even if Chasey still hadn't quite figured out the reason why, it seemed she didn't need it. She knew how she felt—how I was making her feel—and that was all that mattered.

I lifted my hand to the side of her face, drove my fingers into her hair, and settled my palm at the back of her head. I tugged her forward toward me and kissed her.

Seconds later, Luna's hand landed on my leg.

I pulled back from Chasey, looked down at the little girl, and saw her staring up at us in awe.

Unable to stop myself, I reached for her, lifted her in my arms, and pulled her close to blow raspberries on her cheeks.

The sound of her giggles filled the room and made something squeeze in my chest. There was nothing better.

Chasey

I completely forgot.

It should have been at the forefront of my mind, but it wasn't.

I mean, how could it possibly remain there when I'd been experiencing some of the very best moments of my life?

It was Thursday, and I had been having a great week. Ever since Beck left to head back to Pennsylvania for at least another week while he worked with the band to finish recording the song Cash had written for Demi, he'd proven to me that my feelings mattered.

The discussion we'd had not long after he first arrived last Friday wasn't simply a means to smooth things over.

He actually wanted to make a change and improve the situation.

So, I'd received a call from him every night since he'd returned home. Some nights, we spoke longer than others, but the point was that he found a way to connect with me. Knowing he had something incredibly important that he was doing and still made the time to reach out to me because he knew it meant something to me was beyond what I could have expected from him.

And after the incredible weekend I'd had with Beck where he shared so many wonderful things with me and we both told each other that we loved one another, I wasn't exactly sure how I could have possibly stopped relishing all the good vibes.

I was the happiest I'd ever been in my life.

Luna was growing by leaps and bounds, learning new things all the time.

Beck and I were in love.

Nothing could mess with that.

Or, so I thought.

And that was my mistake.

Because instead of taking measures to ensure that I handled things that needed to be handled, I seemed content to remain in my fantasyland where nothing bad happens.

I'd just finished helping a customer at the window when my coworker, Tyler, said, "Hey, Chasey, there's a call for you."

"Me?" I asked.

Nobody had ever called me at work. As soon as I realized that, it hit me that someone who was calling me at work might have something important to say, somebody like Mara or a member of the staff at Luna's day care.

Today, Luna was at home with Mara.

Oh, God. What if something happened?

"Yeah, it was a woman, but I didn't catch her name," Tyler answered.

Shit.

Shit. Shit. Shit.

"Thanks."

I moved away from the front window since there was only one customer waiting in line. That customer could be helped by Brianna, who'd been working alongside me all morning and afternoon long, when she finished with the customer she was currently helping.

I got to the phone and answered, "Hello?"

"Chasey, it's me," Mara's voice came through the line.

In an instant, my stomach dropped. A cold feeling settled over me as it felt like my chest was being squeezed. I could barely breathe just imagining what was happening.

"Tell me what's wrong?" I demanded.

"Aaron's here. Aaron's here, and he wants to take Luna with him," she shared.

"No. He can't."

"I know. I know that, but he's demanding to see her. I closed the door on him and won't let him inside, but Chasey, he's not going away. He said he's calling the police."

Fuck.

Fuck!

"I'm leaving right now," I told her. "I'll be there as soon as I can. Don't let anyone in. Just stay with my girl until I get there."

Without waiting for a response, I slammed the phone down and found Tyler.

"Whoa," he said as I nearly ran into him. "Are you okay?"

I shook my head. "No. I'm really sorry, but I need to leave now. There's an emergency at my home with Luna. I have to go."

"Sure," he replied as he nodded his head. "Go. I'll cover for you."

WISH

"Thank you."

If I had more time, I'd probably have taken a minute to think about what nice thing I could do for the people I worked with. But I didn't have time.

I had to get home to my daughter.

I had to make sure they didn't take my baby away from me.

CHAPTER 22

Chasey

MY HEART WAS POUNDING.

I couldn't breathe. I hadn't taken a full breath since Tyler told me I had received a call at work.

This was my very absolute worst nightmare.

Though it was a short distance from my job to my apartment, every second that passed as I sat in the car and drove home felt like an eternity.

No.

It hadn't been driving. It was racing.

Everything was racing. My heart. The car.

To say I was panicking as I made my way home to my daughter would have been an understatement.

He couldn't have her. He couldn't take her away.

What if I was too late?

Would they just take her away? Would Mara open the door for the police if they arrived before me?

Oh God. If I returned and found Luna wasn't there, I was positive I'd die.

I continued to blink my eyes rapidly to prevent the tears

from pooling there and clouding my vision. The pain I felt in my throat was unbearable. It felt as though I'd swallowed a baseball.

The realization I'd had months ago that my husband was cheating on me should have been the most painful experience of my life.

Compared to this, compared to what I felt now, that didn't even rank on the scale.

Luna.

My Luna.

I didn't know how I could feel such a battery of emotions all at once, but they were coming at me from all angles.

Panic. Terror. Frustration. Confusion. Anger.

Luckily, by some miracle, I made it home and didn't see any police cars yet. It was lucky for me only in that I knew Luna was still safe inside the apartment with Mara. It was not lucky for me *or* Aaron that Aaron was still here and I was feeling all that I was feeling.

No way was I going to be able to hold myself back.

I tried to call on the smidgen of relief I felt knowing I'd made it here before he had the chance to take Luna, but my efforts were futile.

I was no longer a woman scorned. I was a mama bear on a mission to protect her little cub, even if the man I was protecting her from was her own father.

This wasn't about him wanting to spend time with Luna. If there was one thing I knew for sure, that was the truth. There was something else going on, and I intended to find out exactly what it was.

After parking my car, I turned it off, got out, and marched in Aaron's direction. He hadn't seen me when I first arrived, but once I was moving toward him, he noticed me. His lips moved as he said something into his phone, and a moment later, he disconnected the call.

Perfect timing.

"What the hell do you want?" I seethed.

"I'm here for my daughter," he said.

"Since when, Aaron?" I countered. "In all these months, you haven't wanted a single thing to do with Luna. Now you want her. What's this really about?"

He narrowed his eyes at me. "It's about you not giving me the time I'm entitled to with her," he answered.

I was seriously going to lose my mind. I wasn't giving him his time?

"Excuse me?" I countered. "Are you crazy? You must be crazy. You walked out of our place months ago, and you never came back. You didn't ask about her. You never came to see her. I *did not* keep her from you. You chose to stay away."

He crossed his arms over his chest and shot me a smug look. "Well, I guess we'll just have to see what the police say when they arrive. I'm not leaving here without her."

As though on cue, police sirens filled the air around us.

I couldn't actually believe I was dealing with this right now.

"How dare you do this? You don't know *anything* about her!"

"I will once I'm able to spend time with her," he shot back.

Dropping my head back to look up at the gray sky, I realized it was December in New Hampshire and I couldn't even feel the cold. I'd been in such a rush to get out of work so I could get here that I didn't take the time to even put on my coat.

Apparently, I was immune to the bitter temperature because I was running on adrenaline and anger.

Whatever.

Just then, two patrol cars pulled up and the officers stepped out.

"Officers," Aaron declared as they moved toward us. "Thank you for coming out here."

"It's no problem," one of the officers returned. "Can you tell us what's going on?"

Aaron glanced at me briefly before returning his attention

to the officers. "I came by to pick up my daughter since today is supposed to be one of my days with her," Aaron began. "But my ex-wife is refusing to give her to me."

The officers looked around and asked, "Where is your daughter?"

"She's inside my apartment," I said. "She's with my best friend, who babysits her on Mondays and Thursdays while I'm at work."

Confusion washed over their faces, and one of the officers looked at Aaron and stated, "But I thought you said Thursdays are supposed to be one of your days with her."

"They are," Aaron insisted. "But my wife has been keeping her from me."

"Oh, you're such a fucking liar, Aaron," I spat. "Officers, I'm sorry he called you here. The reason my friend is with my daughter today is because from the very moment I caught my husband cheating on me months ago, he's had no relationship with his daughter. None."

"I've got a court order that states that she's supposed to be with me on Thursdays," Aaron announced.

"Really? Guess what? I've got one, too. And you know what else that court order says?" I retorted. Without waiting for him to respond, I answered for him. "It says that you're supposed to pay child support, but I haven't seen a dime of that, have I?"

"Oh please," he scoffed. "It's not like you need it now with your rich boyfriend, do you?"

I jerked back.

Is this what this was all about?

Was he pissed because he'd seen me out with Beck when Beck had insisted on getting decorations for my place?

"Luna is not his daughter or his responsibility," I noted.

"Oh. So you want my money, but you won't let me spend any time with her?" Aaron questioned me.

I let out a frustrated groan. This man was impossible.

"What time does Luna take her naps, Aaron?" I asked him.
"What?"

"What foods does she eat? What words does she say? Do you know if she's crawling? Do you know what her favorite toys are?" I shot one question after another at him. When he stared at me, completely dumbfounded, I went on, "Do you have a crib for her to sleep in? Do you have a car seat? What about if she gets fussy? Do you know how to calm and soothe her? You've n*ever* changed her diaper let alone given her a bath."

I could have gone on and on and on, but I had a feeling he got my point. He knew nothing about his daughter. Not one single thing. I was half tempted to ask him if he even knew her birth date but decided against it. I wasn't sure I wanted to know if he could forget something so incredibly important.

"I can figure that all out," Aaron returned. "I'm her father."

"You could have fooled me," I muttered.

"Folks?" one of the officers interrupted us.

Both Aaron and I turned our attention to the officers. They exchanged looks with one another before one came toward me and the other went toward Aaron.

The moment the officer was beside me, he suggested, "Why don't you talk to me for a minute?"

I sighed and nodded my agreement.

"What's your name?" he asked as he pulled out a pen and his small notepad.

"Chasey," I answered. "Chasey Rivers."

"Okay, Miss Rivers, I'm Officer Martinez," he began. "Can you tell me if I'm understanding this correctly? The man standing over there with Officer Robinson is your ex-husband and the father of your child."

"Yes, that's correct," I answered.

"Right. And there's a court order regarding the custody of your child that states your daughter should be with him on Thursdays?" he pressed.

I nodded. "Yes, but—"

He held his hand up and cut me off. "Relax, Miss Rivers," he urged me. "I can very clearly see that this isn't sitting well with you, but I have to ask if you're prepared to violate the court order because it could result in fines or worse."

Nodding again, I insisted, "My ex hasn't followed that court order either, so I'm willing to take my chances. He knows nothing about our daughter, and I'm terrified about what would happen to her if he took her."

"Has he ever been violent?" Officer Martinez asked.

I shook my head. "No. No, it's not that. I just… I have little faith in his ability to care for her when he's spent virtually no time with her. We separated when she was only five weeks old, and he wasn't exactly a hands-on kind of dad back then, either."

"How old is she now?" he questioned me.

"Just over six months old," I replied.

"And you said she's inside?"

"Yes."

The officer jotted a few notes down before he asked, "Would you mind if we went inside so I could see her?"

Immediately, I went on alert. "Are you going to take her?" I worried. "Are you going to let him leave here with her?"

"Ma'am, I just want to confirm that she's not in any danger," he explained. "As long as I can verify that she's safe and with one of her parents right now, I'm not removing her from where she is. This is something that you and your ex-husband will need to work out with the courts."

My body sagged so hard with relief, it was a wonder I remained standing upright.

For the first time since I'd gotten the call at work from Mara, I felt like I could breathe. She'd be here with me tonight and for the foreseeable future until this went to court. I couldn't ignore that possibility any longer and needed to make sure I came up with a game plan.

"You can follow me inside," I told him.

Not more than a minute later, I was opening the door to my apartment and allowing Officer Martinez inside. We made it to the living room where Mara was seated on the couch with the monitor in her hand.

"She's asleep?" I asked.

Mara nodded and held the monitor out to me. I took it from her as she replied, "Yeah. She's moved around a few times but hasn't woken up."

Glancing up at Officer Martinez, I said, "I can show you to her bedroom."

He shook his head. "It's okay," he assured me. "I'm not going to disturb her. It's clear to me by the state of your apartment that your daughter is not in any danger and is well cared for. I'm just going to get a few more pieces of information from you, and then we'll see to it that your ex-husband understands he needs to go through the court to resolve this matter."

"I appreciate that," I rasped.

For the next few minutes, I spoke with Officer Martinez and answered his questions. Before I knew it, he was moving toward the front door.

"Good luck, Miss Rivers," he said when he put his hand to the doorknob.

"Thank you, Officer."

"Oh my God. Tell me everything that happened," Mara demanded once I'd closed and locked the door behind him.

I made my way back to the living room and flopped down on the couch. No longer having the adrenaline running through me, the exhaustion hit hard.

"Aaron's being spiteful," I remarked.

"Spiteful?" she repeated.

As quickly as I could, I told her the whole story and everything that Aaron had said to me when we were outside. When

I finished, I said, "So, you see, this isn't about Luna for him. It's about Beck."

"You think so?" she asked.

I nodded. "Absolutely. At first, I was unsure, but then he said something that indicated that's what this was all about."

"What did he say?"

"That I shouldn't need his child support money now that I had a rich boyfriend," I replied.

Her eyes widened. "He's jealous."

I nodded. "Or his ego is bruised," I offered. "He probably never thought I'd move on and find someone else. Better yet, he probably assumed nobody would want me, especially not someone like Beck Emerson."

"It's a sad day for Aaron when he realizes he's being replaced like a set of dead batteries," she declared.

At that, I burst out laughing. It was then that I said a silent prayer of thanks that I had Mara. In that moment, even though Luna wasn't going to be going anywhere, I needed something else to lift my mood.

Mara made that happen for me.

And while I didn't like to think about Beck being a replacement for Aaron because I wholeheartedly believed our relationship was our own, the sentiment behind Mara's words made me feel good.

Months ago, I'd been so depressed and downtrodden at the harsh reality of what my life had become. While things were currently very far from being perfect, they were so much better than I could have ever imagined they would be.

Part of it was my determination to be the very best I could be for my daughter, but the other part of it was all thanks to Beck. He'd brought something special to our lives, and I didn't know how much we needed it until we had it.

"You're the best," I declared when I finally settled down.

She grinned proudly at me. A moment later, she asked, "So what are you going to do now?"

I sighed and shook my head. "I don't know," I admitted. "I'm guessing that considering this seems like it's about to get ugly, I'm going to need a lawyer."

"What a nightmare," she said.

"Tell me about it," I mumbled. "I don't need this headache right now."

"You'll get through it," she insisted. "Whatever you need, you know you can count on me. And if you've got things to deal with when I'm at work, you know my parents love Luna."

I nodded and smiled. "Yeah, I do. Thanks, Mara."

"Anytime, Chasey."

Before I could say anything else, Mara and I heard Luna on her monitor. Only, instead of waking up crying or feeling fussy, she did something else.

She sang.

Or, that's what I told myself she was doing.

Obviously, she wasn't saying any real words, but her voice had this clear melodic tone. It was delicate and sweet, and I instantly felt my eyes fill with tears.

"You might have a hell of a battle in front of you, but there's no denying that you're still one lucky mama," Mara noted.

Just as a tear spilled down my cheek, I swiped at it and agreed, "Yeah, I am."

With that, Mara declared, "I'm going to go and let you have your time with your girl. Call me when you know more about what's happening with Aaron. Otherwise, I'll see you on Monday."

I dipped my chin in acknowledgment and asked, "Do you have anything fun planned for this weekend?"

Her face lit up. "There might be a guy I'm going on a date with," she shared as we made it to the front door.

"What? Why didn't you tell me?" I asked.

"It's only the second date," she explained. "We'll see what happens this weekend. Then I'll fill you in."

"Okay. Have fun."

Not even a minute later, I walked into Luna's room, saw her smiling and happy face, and felt my whole day turn around. Truth be told, it had started to turn around once Officer Martinez told me he wouldn't be removing Luna from my care tonight. It got even better when I talked to Mara about the whole situation with Aaron. So, already feeling better about the day before I even walked into Luna's room, it wasn't going to take much.

The fact that she was still singing up a storm and smiling at me... well, that right there was the reason I'd fight every day. I never wanted her to feel anything but utter joy like that.

But once I picked her up, held her close, and inhaled, I had to admit that there was one small part of me that was terrified that I'd end up in court with Aaron, and suddenly, I wouldn't see my daughter's beautiful face every day.

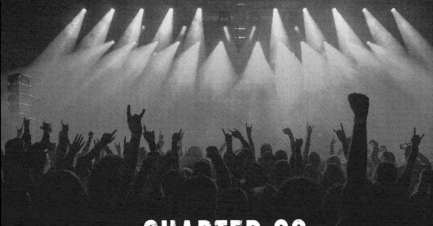

CHAPTER 23

Beck

"HELLO?"

One word was all it took for me to know that something wasn't right.

Just one word.

I was suddenly on edge as I shot up off the couch in the studio and walked out into the hall for a bit more privacy.

"Chasey?" I called. "Babe, is everything okay?"

It was later in the evening, around the time I usually called, so I hoped that with whatever was wrong, Luna was already asleep.

Chasey's forlorn voice shared, "The police were here today."

"What?" I asked, feeling utterly alarmed. "Are you okay? Is Luna okay?"

"Physically, we're fine," she answered. "And Luna is totally oblivious to anything that's going on. She was actually sleeping when the police were here. But I can't say that I'm doing okay."

None of this was making sense. "What happened?"

There was a long pause, and I braced myself for whatever Chasey was going to share. It felt like I'd been waiting for hours before she said, "I might not always have Luna here."

My body tensed. "Why would you say that?" I asked.

"Mara called me while I was at work today," she began. "Aaron showed up at my apartment demanding to have his time with Luna."

"Are you serious?"

Truthfully, I didn't think this was the kind of thing that Chasey would ever make up, but I was in too much shock to really know what else to say.

"Yes." There was another pause before she continued, "I've never been so terrified in all my life. I thought for sure that the police were going to make me hand Luna over since the court order states that Thursdays are one of the days that Aaron is supposed to have her."

"Babe, why didn't you call me?" I asked.

"What could you do?" she countered, her voice feeling defeated. "You're there, and I'm here."

Fuck, I hated this.

"I assume Luna is still there with you?"

"She is. They wouldn't remove her from here since she wasn't in any danger. But the officer I spoke with told me that this is something that's going to have to be worked out in court," she shared. "He told me I could be facing some serious trouble for not adhering to the court order."

"Isn't child support part of the court order, too?" I pressed.

"It is. So, I'm hoping that helps my case."

I swallowed hard, feeling myself get emotional about whatever struggles Chasey would be facing, and asked, "What do you want to see happen?"

"I want things to stay the way they are," she began, her voice soft. There was another lengthy pause before she cried quietly and added, "But if I'm being realistic, I don't think I'm going to get my way."

"Babe..." I trailed off as I listened to her cry. Her heart was breaking, and I was here.

I had to go to her. I had to be there for her.

Just as I was going to tell her that I was going to get there to be with her as soon as I could, Chasey asked, "Am I wrong?"

"What?"

"Is it wrong for me to not want to give up any time with her?" she clarified. "Beck, I swear, if he had been in her life from the start, I would have figured it out and accepted it. But he hasn't been there, and I just… I just can't let her go."

"Chasey, I think what you're feeling is completely normal," I began. "You're used to always having her there, and I can't say I'd feel differently if I were in your situation."

She sniffled. "Do you really mean that?"

"I do. If he hasn't been around for the first six months of her life, he doesn't know anything about her," I said. "I saw how she responded to him when we went out shopping. I'd hate for her to feel like that again."

That was the truth.

The mere thought of that baby feeling any kind of unhappiness or stress or anxiety didn't sit well with me. I would do whatever I could to make sure she never felt an ounce of pain. And while I wasn't saying that her father would physically harm her, he'd already done plenty of damage by not being around all this time. If there was anything I could do to save her from that, I would.

And I'd do it for her mother, too.

"I don't know what I'm going to do now," she murmured. "I think my best bet is to contact an attorney."

I didn't want her going through this alone. We hadn't finished recording—Cash was being particularly picky about this song—but I couldn't stay here.

"Don't do anything yet," I instructed. "For tonight, why don't you take a warm bath and try to relax a bit. Get a good night's sleep because you have work tomorrow morning. I'll leave here tomorrow and get there by the time you get off from work. We'll figure everything out then."

"Beck, that's not necessary," she argued. "I don't want you to have to be involved in this mess."

"Chasey, you're mine," I told her.

She didn't respond.

I continued, "You and Luna are *my* girls. And it's my job to take care of you. I don't care if you think this isn't something I need to be involved in. I'm already involved because I'm with you, and I love you. Whatever affects you is my responsibility."

"Beck..." She trailed off. "I don't know what to say."

"Just tell me you love me and that you'll see me tomorrow," I urged.

"I love you, and I'll see you tomorrow."

"And you're going to go relax now, right?" I pressed.

"Yes."

I smiled, feeling marginally better about the situation. I hated that I wasn't there when she needed me, but I hoped that knowing I'd be there for her tomorrow when she got home from work would help her to feel reassured and confident that she'd get through this.

"No matter what it takes, Chasey, we'll figure it out," I promised. "Okay?"

The silence stretched between us. Then, with her voice just a touch over a whisper, she said, "Okay, Beck."

"Good. I love you."

"I love you, too."

With that, we said goodbye and disconnected.

I made my way back into the studio to fill the rest of the band in on what I had to do. If any of them had an issue with it, they didn't say. And at that moment, I couldn't have been more grateful for them.

The minute I saw her car, I got out of mine, leaving my bags inside. I could get them later after I knew she was taken care of.

By the time Chasey parked and turned hers off, I was already there by her door.

Just as I'd promised, I was here for her when she got home from work.

I opened her door, and she didn't hesitate to get out and throw her arms around me. I held her close as she declared, "I'm so glad you're here, Beck. Thank you."

"Anything, babe. Anything you ever need, you know I've got you."

She tightened her hold on me, and I allowed her to have that for just a bit longer. But eventually, I grew concerned.

"Chasey, let's get Luna inside," I urged. "It's cold out here."

At that, she loosened her arms and let go. I opened the back door, peeked inside, and saw my favorite little girl staring back at me.

Smiling, I greeted her, "Hi, princess."

Her face lit up. She returned the smile, and that's when I noticed something. My eyes widened. "Are you getting your first tooth?" I asked her. I twisted my neck to look back at Chasey. "She's got a tooth coming in."

Chasey nodded. "Yeah. Isn't it crazy?"

Mind blowing.

I mean, I knew this was the natural order of things for children, but seeing it happen to one that I knew was unbelievable. Just like that, she had a tooth coming in.

Not wanting to prolong her exposure to the cold air, I quickly removed her seat from its base and carried it in one hand while I wrapped my other arm around Chasey's back to her opposite shoulder.

Once we were inside, I worked on getting Luna out of her seat while Chasey took care of her own jacket and Luna's diaper bag.

"Thank you for helping," she said once we were settled in the living room.

I sat down and held Luna in my arms while she played with one of her toys.

With my attention focused on Chasey, I replied, "You're welcome, babe. Are you okay? Did anything crazy happen today?"

She shook her head. "Everything was fine," she answered. "But I'd be lying if I said I was okay."

"Tell me what's going on," I encouraged her.

I wasn't surprised. She'd had some time to think about everything now, so it seemed only natural that she was experiencing some new emotions.

"I feel guilty," she confessed.

This surprised me. "Guilty?" I repeated. "How so?"

She shrugged. "No matter what I do, I feel guilty for how this all could affect Luna. Part of me believes that I'm doing the right thing by not wanting to just give Luna up on the days Aaron was supposed to have her because this is completely out of the blue. I'm worried she'll spend her time with him feeling just like she did in that store. I can't bear to think about putting her in that position."

I understood that. That was exactly what I'd imagined she was feeling. Apparently, that wasn't all there was, though.

Because a moment later, Chasey added, "But the other part of me keeps questioning what kind of a mother am I to deny my child the right to know her father? I mean, maybe she'll be upset for just a little bit, but if she gets used to him, doesn't she deserve to know him? Doesn't she deserve to have a relationship with her father?"

Now, I could see why she was struggling so much with this. It was easy to look at this from her initial perspective. He hadn't been around, Luna didn't know him, and it was going to cause a lot of anxiety all the way around.

But if the guy wanted to be a real dad—one who was there

for his daughter and had a genuine relationship with her—didn't Luna deserve that?

The answer I came up with in my head surprised me. Because while I knew it was going to be the most difficult thing for Chasey to do, while I knew she'd suffer not having her daughter with her all the time, Luna's happiness mattered more. Deep down, I knew Chasey would see it that way, too. That's why she was struggling.

"Why don't you call him?" I suggested.

She jerked her head back. "Aaron?" she asked.

I nodded.

Chasey blinked at me. She was in complete disbelief.

"Why are you looking at me like that?" I asked.

"Because… you… I… you want me to call my ex-husband?" she questioned me.

"Yes."

"Why?"

"I think you should try to set up a time to meet with him," I answered. "Before you get attorneys involved, the both of you should try to see if you can work this out."

Her brows shot up. "You want me to meet with my ex?"

"Babe?" I called.

"What?"

"First, I'm not the least bit concerned about your ex being any sort of competition for me," I began. "I trust you, and I'm confident in what we have. Second, this isn't about me. This is about Luna. We need to figure this out for her. And last, I'm not worried about you setting up a meeting mostly because I'm going to be there with you."

"You are?"

Nodding again, I said, "I'm not leaving New Hampshire until we get this sorted for you and for her. I think it's best for you to call him, see if he can meet tomorrow, and then we can see what he wants to have happen."

WISH

"I... I don't... I don't think I can just hand her off to him," Chasey stammered.

"Nobody expects you to do that," I insisted. Then, because I didn't really know what her ex-husband expected, I corrected myself. "I don't expect you to do that. But maybe you can get him to agree to a couple of meetings where you're both present. He can spend some time with her, she can get used to him, and you can rest easy knowing she's not going to be somewhere that's causing her stress. If this is really about his daughter, he should want to do what's best for her. You two have to co-parent for the next seventeen and a half years, Chasey. You should try to see if you can come to some kind of reasonable arrangement that makes you both happy."

For a long time, Chasey didn't respond. To top it off, I couldn't read the expression on her face.

Maybe she was pissed at me. Had I overstepped? I loved her, and I loved Luna. I only wanted what was best for them.

But maybe Chasey didn't think I needed to be sticking my nose into something like this, especially when I likely wasn't saying what she wanted to hear.

When she finally opened her mouth to speak, I never could have guessed she would have responded the way she did.

"I'm not thrilled with any of this, but you're right, Beck. I need to do what's best for Luna. So, if I can work it out with Aaron and avoid court, that's what I should do," she said.

"Go ahead and make the call," I urged her. "After you finish, I'll order dinner, and we can have a quiet night in. Okay?"

"Okay," she agreed.

At that, Chasey got up and moved to get her phone. I spent the next few minutes focusing my attention on the little girl in front of me. It blew my mind to think that anyone could ever walk out on her, but I knew it could happen.

It had happened to me, and it had happened to Chasey.

And I think that's why I had a feeling that if Chasey took a

A.K. EVANS

minute to really think about the situation, she'd suck it up and do what she had to do. She might not like having time without Luna—I couldn't say I blamed her—but she knew her daughter deserved to have a relationship with her father if he was offering one.

A few minutes later, Chasey walked back into the room.

"Well?" I asked.

"He's willing to meet tomorrow morning," she said.

"Good. Let's hope we can get it all sorted for you tomorrow then," I replied. "For now, let's enjoy the rest of our night. Okay?"

Chasey moved toward the couch, sat down beside me, and cuddled close. I threw my arm around her back to her opposite shoulder again, just like I'd done when we first walked from her car to the front door of her apartment.

Then, before I ordered dinner for us, I spent the next fifteen minutes holding both of my girls in my arms, and I knew it was exactly where I was supposed to be.

CHAPTER 24

Chasey

MINUTES.

There were just minutes left.

It was Saturday morning, and Beck and I had just dropped Luna off with Mara's mom. Last night, we discussed it and decided it would be best to leave Luna with a sitter. I didn't have a lot of options, and since Mara had already gone above and beyond for us earlier in the week and she had a date this weekend, I didn't want to disturb her.

So, I called Mara's mom.

Ruth was beyond excited to hear from me and was more than willing to spend a couple hours with Luna this morning. I couldn't have been more grateful.

Now, Beck and I were just a few minutes from the coffee shop, where I'd arranged to meet Aaron. The coffee shop was the best option for us because not only was it public, which would hopefully discourage any over the top arguing, but also because I was too nervous to think about going to a restaurant where I'd have to order some food.

I'd already experienced enough public humiliation to last a lifetime, so I really hoped Aaron was willing to communicate and cooperate in order for us to come up with a reasonable agreement.

"Thank you for being here for me today," I said to Beck.

His hand, which had been resting on my thigh, gave me a squeeze. "Anything you need, Chasey. I've said that from day one," he reminded me.

He had.

He had said that the very first day I met him.

Why I didn't believe he was being honest with me back then was beyond me. But I knew differently now. He had proven it over and over again.

Even facing this horrible situation, I felt incredibly lucky because I knew that regardless of what came of all of this, Beck would be by my side through it all.

We finally arrived at the coffee shop. As I got out of the car and Beck linked his fingers with mine, I felt the mounting nerves.

"It's going to be okay, babe," Beck assured me. "I promise."

I knew I needed to trust him, but it was hard.

Obviously, Luna was fine for now, and there was no indication that she'd be immediately whisked off somewhere with Aaron. If this went back to court, it would take time. But I was hoping to avoid that at all costs.

Beck and I walked inside the café, and I immediately spotted Aaron. He saw me, shifted his attention to Beck, and something moved through his features.

Great.

I could already tell this wasn't going to go well.

"You couldn't meet me on your own?" he asked when we approached the table.

"You had your girlfriend sitting in your car outside my place two days ago, Aaron," I reminded him. "Let's not go there."

He rolled his eyes at me. "Alright. Well, you wanted to meet. What do you want to say?"

I took in a deep breath. Then I said, "I think we should try to figure out a way to do this that's going to be best for everybody involved."

"I'm not exactly sure I understand what you mean by that," he replied. "That might be because you seem to think that keeping Luna away from me is best."

Shaking my head, I insisted, "Aaron, that's not the case. But you haven't spent any time with her from the beginning, and I know that you don't know much about taking care of a baby. So, forgive me, but I can't just willingly hand her over without knowing that you know how to provide her with the care that she needs."

"I'm sure I can figure it out. Besides, Laura's sister has two kids, so she has experience," he countered.

Laura?

I had to assume he was referring to his girlfriend. If he'd said something like that to me months ago, I might have been upset by it. In this case, I wasn't. I had moved on, and I had Beck.

"That's great, but that doesn't change the fact that Luna doesn't know you," I pointed out. "I'm sure you remember what happened at the store a few weeks ago."

He nodded. "I do."

"Okay, so what I'm saying is that I think we need to ease ourselves into this," I began. "Look, the last thing I want to do is deny you or her the right to know each other, but you have to reasonable about it."

He sat back in his chair and crossed his arms over his chest. "What are you suggesting we do then?" he asked.

I took a moment to make sure I had my wits about me and to brace myself. I had a feeling Aaron was not going to like what I had to say.

"For the first few meetings, I was thinking we could both be there," I told him. "We can find neutral places to meet, so you can spend time with Luna. This way, she'll have time to adjust to being around you."

"I'm her father," he clipped.

Nodding, I confirmed, "You are, but you haven't been around for the last seven months of her life, Aaron. I'm trying to be reasonable and work out something that's going to make it easy on her. Quite frankly, I'm making it easy on you, too."

"Oh, so I should be thanking you?" he retorted.

I shook my head. "No. You should be *listening* to me," I pleaded. "Aaron, please, think about her for a minute. Not you. Not your ego. Trust me when I say I don't want her away from me at all, but I'm going to sacrifice what I want to give her what she deserves. You should be willing to do the same."

"The court order has already made it clear that she deserves time with me, and it does not say anything about that time being for a couple hours while you supervise," he noted. "I'm not going to agree to this."

"The court order also states that you should be paying child support," I reminded him, though I wasn't certain he needed that reminder.

Throwing his hands out to the side, he declared, "You can't prevent me from seeing her simply because you haven't received any money."

"No, you're right. I can't. But if I have to go to court and fight you to make sure that she gets everything she deserves, I will absolutely do that. I don't care if it bankrupts me."

"Man, just listen to what she's saying and consider what's in your daughter's best interests," Beck interrupted.

My head snapped in Beck's direction, but he didn't look at me. His eyes were pinned on Aaron. Prior to arriving here, Beck and I had discussed the situation and decided that he was going to let me work it out with Aaron. Beck did note that if things started to get out of control, he might not hold himself back. But he had promised he'd only step in if he thought it was absolutely necessary.

I wasn't sure we had reached that point yet.

Clearly, he felt differently.

And in that instant, the conversation took a dramatic shift, one that I was convinced was heading into a bad place.

"Oh, you think you know what's best for her?" Aaron spat.

Beck shot Aaron a look of disbelief. "Are you serious right now? Listen to yourself. I'm suggesting you calm down and see reason here. Chasey isn't saying you can't see your daughter and spend time with her so that you can have a relationship with her. She's saying that you need to consider how suddenly throwing Luna into this instead of easing her into it is not in Luna's best interests. You're supposed to be her dad. She should be the priority here for you."

"What? You want to be her dad now?"

"That's not what I'm saying at all. I'm simply telling you that if she were mine and I'd been stupid enough to do what you did and suddenly realized the error of my ways, I'd bend over backward to fix those mistakes and prove I was worthy of being that little girl's father," Beck explained.

"So, do it then," Aaron challenged him. "How much are you willing to pay?"

My brows pulled together as I tried to figure out how this had suddenly turned into a negotiation between Beck and Aaron and at the same time I tried to work out what Aaron was even talking about.

"What?" Beck asked. "How much am I willing to pay for what?"

There was a long pause. In fact, it had been so long I started to wonder if Aaron even heard the question.

But a moment later, Aaron leaned his forearms on the table, pinned his eyes on Beck, and dropped his voice. "You give me half a million dollars, I'll sign over all my rights to you."

I gasped and jerked back in my chair.

Beck's hand on the arm that had been wrapped around my back connected with my shoulder and squeezed me gently.

Aaron didn't just say that.

I must have misheard him.

With a firm hold on me, Beck's eyes narrowed as he leaned toward Aaron. "I'm sorry. I think I missed something there," he started. "Because I could have sworn I heard you say that you wanted to sell your daughter to me for half a million dollars."

"That's exactly what I said."

My eyes widened, my stomach was in knots, and my heart was aching.

I couldn't believe I loved him once. What kind of a man would ever say something like that?

Visions of my daughter danced in my head. My beautiful girl deserved so much better than this, so much better than him.

Even if I had wanted to step in and say something I couldn't. My body was trembling with a mix of sadness, heartbreak, and anger.

The next thing I knew, the sound of Beck's chair scraping across the floor filled my head. A moment later, he was standing and tugging me up beside him. Looking down at Aaron, he deadpanned, "I'll pay for all the attorney's fees. You'll hear something from that attorney sometime this coming week. Until then, you don't come near Chasey or Luna. Am I understood?"

"You're going to pay me, right?"

Yep. Those words came from Aaron. There was no backpedaling, no remorse. He had not one ounce of regret for what he'd just suggested. Luna didn't matter to him at all.

I was gobsmacked.

Shocked.

Hurt.

Beck seemed to be in a state of disbelief, and he proved that when he said, "You're unbelievable. You don't deserve her. You didn't deserve Chasey when you had her, and you definitely don't deserve Luna now."

Without another word, Beck turned toward me and said, "Let's go, babe."

"But—"

"Babe," he warned.

I held his gaze a moment, understood the silent screams in his eyes, and nodded my head in understanding.

With that, Beck led me out of the coffee shop and right to the car. The minute we were both inside, I burst into tears.

"I hope you're not upset with me."

That came from Beck.

I couldn't say I didn't understand why he'd said those words. I hadn't exactly been very talkative since we walked out of the meeting with Aaron.

Beck tried talking to me on the way to pick up Luna, and I shut it down.

"Chasey, I—"

That was all he got out before I cut him off. "Not now, Beck. Please. I just want to get Luna right now."

There was an extended pause, and I used that time to focus my attention outside the window. Tears filled my eyes. A moment later, Beck's voice filled the cabin of the car, and it was incredibly sweet and tender. "Anything you need, babe."

Anything you need.

I wanted to scream and shout at the top of my lungs that I needed to understand how I had failed so badly at choosing a partner. What had I missed? There was one question I continued to ask myself from the moment we got into the car.

How had I ever fallen in love with a man like Aaron?

Luna was going to be just like me. Just like Beck. A child raised in a single-parent home. My heart broke for her.

After we picked her up at Ruth's house, Beck drove us back to my apartment. I'd spent the rest of the afternoon focusing my attention on her. I didn't discuss what happened with Beck. I barely spoke to him at all.

But now that Luna had gone down for her afternoon nap, it seemed Beck wanted to try again.

But since I'd spent so long recalling everything that had happened this morning, namely the fact that my ex-husband wanted to *sell his daughter*, I hadn't responded to Beck.

He was quick to apologize. "Chasey, babe, I'm so sorry if I was out of line," he lamented. "I just… he wasn't listening to anything you were saying and seriously considering it. I wanted to fix this for you. And I'm still going to do whatever I can to make that happen."

"I know you had your heart in the right place," I assured him. "There's no need for you to apologize because you didn't do anything wrong."

"Maybe I pushed too hard," he reasoned. "It wasn't my place to step in like that."

I sighed. "He doesn't want to be her father, Beck. This was about money. It was about money right from the start. He saw us at the store, realized we were together, and saw it as his opportunity for a money grab. I questioned his motives when I got his calls, and I knew for certain when he showed up here two days ago."

"His calls?" Beck asked.

Crap. I just realized I hadn't shared that bit of news with Beck. "He left two voice mail messages for me," I told him. "The last one came in on Friday. I listened to it not long before you got here."

"Why didn't you tell me?"

Suddenly, I felt bad about not telling him. I hadn't wanted to burden him with it, but it was clear he ended up in the mix of it anyway.

"Well, when you first got here, we were a bit busy," I began. "But then we talked about other stuff before we went to sleep. And when we got up, I told you I loved you. Mostly, I'd forgotten about his calls, but even if I had remembered, I'm not sure I would have said anything. I would not have wanted any of his nonsense ruining such a special weekend."

Beck's eyes searched my face in silence for a bit. Eventually, he asked gently, "How are you feeling right now?"

I felt a flood of emotions. I wasn't sure I could effectively communicate all that was in my heart. So, I went with the simplest ones.

"I'm devastated for Luna, I'm angry at myself, and I'm embarrassed for what Aaron said to you," I shared.

"I get your feelings about Luna, but I'm not sure I understand the anger or the embarrassment," he replied.

After taking in a deep breath, I explained, "I'm angry at myself for not seeing him for who he was a lot sooner. And I'm horrified that he took one look at us together, knew what you did for a living, and actually had the audacity to suggest you pay him. I'm so sorry about that."

"Chasey, come here," Beck urged.

I moved to the opposite side of the couch and settled myself next to Beck. He wasn't satisfied with that, so he lifted me and placed me in his lap. Then he said, "You do not apologize for *anything* he did. He's responsible for everything that came out of his own mouth."

I nodded my understanding. "Why did you tell him that you're going to have an attorney contact him?" I asked.

"Bottom line, babe, he doesn't want to be a father," Beck began. "I hate that for Luna, but she'll be better off in the long run if what he showed me today is any indication of the kind of man he is. I'd be terrified for her to be in his care. So, I wasn't joking when I said I'd be having an attorney contact him. I'll do what I can over this weekend to find the best attorney for this case, and we'll meet with him or her as soon as that's possible."

"Beck, this is a lot," I started. I couldn't continue speaking because he had pressed his finger to my lips.

"I'm doing this, Chasey," he insisted. "I'm doing it partly because I can but mostly because I love you and I love Luna. I'm going to take care of this just like I promised."

His voice indicated I shouldn't argue with him, so I didn't. If he wanted to take this on, and he had the grit to do it, I'd let him. I was still barely functioning as it was. Clearly, I was going to need his help.

"Thank you," I rasped.

Beck leaned forward, pressed a kiss to my cheek, and responded gently, "Anything you need."

Anything I need.

There was no doubt about it.

Beck was a miracle.

CHAPTER 25

Chasey

"**H**E TRIED TO SELL YOU HIS DAUGHTER?"

At least we weren't the only ones who thought it was ludicrous.

It was Thursday afternoon, about a week before Christmas, and I'd taken a half-day at work today. Beck and I were sitting in the attorney's office.

This was the very expensive, highly sought after, and best family attorney in not just the small town of Finch, but in the state of New Hampshire. And Beck had hired her.

He meant what he said when he told me he'd give me anything I needed.

I wasn't sure I deserved him.

We'd just finished filling her in on everything that had happened from the time Luna was born up through our meeting with Aaron this past weekend. Unsurprisingly, she was shocked by what she'd learned Aaron wanted to do.

"That is correct," Beck confirmed. "Half a million dollars and Luna would be mine."

"Wow," she marveled. "I've heard a lot of crazy things in all my years as a practicing attorney, and this has got to be in the running for the top ten."

There we had it.

I wasn't exactly sure her words were making me feel any better.

"What recourse does Chasey have in this scenario?" Beck pressed.

God, I was so glad he was here. I could barely think straight anymore.

"Well, there are a few options," she began. "Some will be easier than others. Some might take longer. In the end, I think we'll have a very good chance at getting this handled in a favorable manner. The easiest option, Chasey, is to have your ex-husband surrender his rights. If he's willing to do that without any hassle, this will be a relatively painless process as far as the logistics go."

She paused a moment, directed her attention to Beck, and added, "Of course, I should probably just confirm first, though, that I'm not out of line when I say that you are interested in adopting Luna. Would that be a fair assumption?"

Oh man.

Now the attorney was putting Beck in this horrible position. I didn't know where she'd gotten that idea from, and I didn't need him feeling like he was on the spot and now obligated to do this. I needed to put a stop to it immediately.

"Excuse me, Ms. Wexler," I interrupted. When she returned her gaze to mine, I explained, "Beck is here to support me with this, but what you're suggesting is a bit much. I don't see what that would have to do with my ex-husband surrendering his rights?"

I could feel a profound shift in the room—a shift that came from Beck sitting beside me—but I didn't look in his direction as I waited for Ms. Wexler's response.

She nodded. "I'm sorry for the confusion," she began. "In

this case, having someone who wants to adopt Luna would be necessary. The court won't simply allow your ex-husband to surrender his rights, which gets him out of any financial obligation for his child, without ensuring that there's someone prepared to take on that responsibility."

"But… but there are single parents everywhere," I argued.

"There are," she confirmed. "But in most of those cases, it's simply a matter of one parent doing all the work much like it was for you for the first several months of Luna's life. Technically, one parent is doing all the work while the other does nothing for the child. Luna's father still had rights to see her, and he was technically responsible for supporting her financially. The court won't force him to see her or spend time with her, but they will require him to provide for her. He can't just get out of that because he wants to, and you can't be okay with him doing that without having someone prepared to adopt her."

I slumped back in the chair. This was beyond frustrating.

"The other option, if adoption is out of the question here, is that we do have the ability to file for termination of parental rights," she began again. "This will be a much more arduous process. To top it off, it doesn't always go the way we hope. That said, we do have some damning evidence against your ex that could help the case. We could file for the termination of parental rights based on the notion of abandonment. If a parent has no contact with their child for at least a six-month period in New Hampshire, it constitutes child abandonment. We're just over that six-month mark now, so that will work in our favor."

I perked back up.

Okay. Maybe this wasn't completely hopeless.

"Right, well, then that's what we'll have to do," I said.

"Chasey?" Beck called from beside me.

I finally tore my attention from Ms. Wexler and looked over at him. "Yeah?" I replied cautiously, unable to read the expression he was wearing.

There was an extended pause as he simply stared at me, searching my face. I started to grow concerned, but just then, he said, "Babe, you're it for me."

"I'm... it?" I asked curiously, not sure I understood what he meant.

"It," he repeated. "The one. And I love Luna as though she were my own. It's up to you, but I would love nothing more than to adopt her."

"What?" I gasped.

He couldn't be serious. My heart couldn't handle this. In one instant, he was telling me I was the one, and in the next, he was telling me he wanted to adopt my daughter.

This couldn't be real.

"I love you, Chasey," he said softly. "I love you in a way I know I'll love you for the rest of my life. I don't want anyone else. There's nothing I want more than to have you and Luna with me in a way that's permanent."

Tears filled my eyes. "You want to adopt Luna?" I rasped.

He nodded.

I couldn't believe it. This wasn't about the financial support I had no doubt he'd want to provide. For me, it was the fact that he wanted to give Luna something that neither one of us had in our own lives.

A father.

Not just a father figure.

A real father.

Because there was no doubt in my mind that's precisely what he would be.

I spent so long thinking about how much I loved Beck for wanting to be this man in my daughter's life that he spoke again.

"And Chasey?"

"Yeah?"

"If there weren't all kinds of moral and legal issues surrounding what your ex suggested to me over the weekend, you should know that I would have easily paid him five times what he was asking. I'd have done that not only to give Luna a stable, safe, and secure family but also to be sure that you don't ever have to worry about sleeping a single night without your daughter living under your roof. I'd have done that so you wouldn't have to worry about taking the long, difficult road through this process."

Five times?

Did Beck just admit that he'd have paid two point five million dollars to Aaron just so he could take on the responsibility of providing for Luna for the rest of his life?

"Beck..." I trailed off.

What was I supposed to say? This was a lot. We had barely been together for a month yet. I didn't even know how it was possible we could be having a conversation like this.

"I'm going to step out for a minute," Ms. Wexler interrupted. "I'll give you two a chance to talk privately. I'll be back."

For the next few seconds, I simply stared at Beck. He did the same with me.

Once we were alone, he said softly, "Chasey, I love you, and I hate that it feels like you're freaking out right now."

"Beck, this is a lot," I told him. "And it's fast. Really fast. I don't want there to be any regrets."

Tipping his head to the side, he returned, "You're unsure about me?"

"No, but we have such very different lives," I remarked. "Is this what you really want?"

I hated that I had to ask him that question, but it was unavoidable. There wasn't anything I didn't love about Beck, and this situation right now was making it impossible to control how I felt about him.

I was terrified that I'd get lost in him, I'd sink deeper into the good I had with him, and once he realized he'd jumped into this too soon, I'd be left to pick up the pieces.

There was a bit of an incredulous look on Beck's face as he asked, "Do you think I'd ever do something like this without being absolutely sure it was what I wanted? Do you think I'd do that to you? Do you think I'd do that to Luna?"

"Not intentionally, but Beck, this is a big decision," I noted.

"I know that, Chasey," he insisted. "But I'm not the kind of man who makes a commitment to someone and walks away. For months, I hoped my phone would ring and your voice would be on the other end. I thought about you all the time, even when I knew little more than just your name. I spent months wishing for a call that never came. Seeing you again at Granite, getting that second chance, I knew I couldn't let you get away. And I'm so glad I didn't."

Wow.

Beck had shared before that he had wanted to hear from me, but I don't think I ever realized just how much he had wanted it to happen.

Even still, I worried about whether this was going too fast. "What if you change your mind?" I began to fret. "This is fast."

"Babe, listen to me," he pleaded. Something in the sound of his voice made me stop thinking about every worry and concern I had. It made me put all of my focus and attention on him. "I've been trying to figure out how to tell you this without making you want to run in the opposite direction. The truth is, I hate going home. Not because I don't love where I live or my family and friends who live there. I hate it because you're not there. Luna is not there. I'm sick and tired of going home and feeling like I've left a piece of me here. I want you and Luna to come home with me."

Oh God.

Beck wasn't messing around.

I hated that he hated going home. Beck deserved to love going home. The man he was, the way he made me feel and how he took care of both my daughter and me, he earned the right to love going home.

I wanted to give him that.

But before I could tell him that, he spoke again. "Chasey, I'm not going to change my mind about you. I want you in my life in a way that's permanent."

Tears filled my eyes. I never thought I'd get another shot at something so beautiful in my life, but here it was. Beck was in front of me wanting to give it all to me. All I needed to do was trust him to do what he said he was going to do.

"Okay," I rasped.

His brows shot up in disbelief. "Okay?" he repeated.

I nodded.

Leaning toward me, bringing both of his hands up to frame my face, Beck kissed me. Right there in the office of the attorney he'd hired for me, Beck landed a hot and heavy one on me. I let him, hoping I was giving him one back that communicated how much he meant to me.

A moment later, the door opened, and Ms. Wexler declared, "Well, that can only mean good things."

Beck smiled against my lips as I let out a laugh.

We separated ourselves from one another—begrudgingly, of course—and turned to face her as she sat back down at her desk.

"So, have we made a decision?" she asked.

Beck and I glanced at each other, and I swear it was a wonder I didn't melt into a puddle right there on the floor at the bright, shining look in his eyes and the smile on his face.

"We have," Beck answered.

With that, we spent the remainder of our time with Ms. Wexler going over everything that we could expect over the next few months.

While there was still the hurdle we needed to overcome

with regard to convincing Aaron to actually sign over his rights, I felt the best I had in days about the whole situation.

And I had Beck to thank for that.

It was later that evening when it happened.

It was after Beck and I had left the attorney's office, and he dropped me off at home.

It was after he stood at the front door to my apartment and he told me to go inside to fill Mara in on everything and spend time with Luna.

It was after I asked him if everything was okay, and he confirmed that he needed to make a few calls and run a couple of errands.

It was after I accepted he was telling me all that I needed to know at that moment and would tell me whatever else I needed to know whenever it was time.

It was after he kissed me at my front door before waiting to walk away until I was safe inside.

It was after I'd gone in and filled Mara in on everything that had happened with Beck at Attorney Wexler's office.

It was after I'd admitted I felt so good about all of it and was happier than I thought I could be but still believed Aaron would find a way to be difficult.

It was after Beck returned to my apartment, spent time with Luna and me, and had dinner with both of us.

And finally, it was after I'd given Luna her bath, put her down for the night, and walked into my bedroom prepared to take a shower.

Beck was sitting on the edge of my bed with an expression I couldn't read on his face.

"What is it?" I asked.

"It's done."

Confusion washed over me. "It's done?" I repeated.

"Aaron is going to surrender his rights to Luna," Beck shared.

Confusion turned to surprise. "What?"

"I had some things to take care of this afternoon, and that was at the top of my list," he started. "We met, had a discussion, and he's agreed to surrender his rights."

Slowly, cautiously, I moved toward the bed, which meant I moved in that manner to Beck. When I stood in front of him, he reached a hand out to me. I took it, and he tugged me into his lap.

"What happened?" I asked.

Beck's eyes searched my face. "I don't want you to worry about the details of it," he said. "I just want you to know that I took care of it, and you don't have to worry any longer."

I didn't know how I felt about that. I kind of wanted to know the details. Mostly, I wanted to be sure that Beck wasn't agreeing to pay him off.

Unable to hold myself back, I begged, "Please tell me you did not agree to give him any money."

"I did not agree to give him any money," Beck assured me.

I eyed him curiously. This seemed too good to be true. "Did you threaten to hurt him or do anything illegal?" I pressed.

Beck chuckled. "No, babe. I didn't."

"I don't understand. He just agreed to it without any hesitation?"

Beck didn't respond.

Okay, so there had been some tentativeness on Aaron's part. What changed his mind?

As I sat there trying to work out what happened, I must have made it clear I couldn't just forget about the details. This was huge, and Aaron liked to win. I couldn't understand why he would suddenly agree to this if no money was involved.

Likely noting the concern on my face, Beck let out another laugh. "Looks like I need to share more," he mumbled.

"It would be appreciated," I remarked.

"I promise there was nothing shady that happened, Chasey," he said. "I simply told him that your attorney was going to need a bit more time before contacting him. He was actually more than happy to talk to me because he had indicated that he'd changed his mind and no longer wanted half a million dollars to sign over his rights."

"What? Now he wants to be a father?"

Beck shook his head. "No, babe. I'm sorry, but he actually asked me for more money. A million to be exact."

What a dirtbag.

Beck must have noticed that sharing that bit of information did little to help my mood, so he continued, "I told him he wasn't going to be getting a dime. In fact, I made it very clear that if he didn't wise up and really think about what he was doing, he stood to lose a lot. I explained exactly what we wanted him to do. He wasn't okay with that, but it's not because he's interested in being a father. He's just being a dick at this point."

"Well, how did he suddenly go from being a dick to agreeing to surrender his rights?" I wondered.

"I told him I loved you," Beck stated.

I cocked an eyebrow. "What does that have to do with it?"

The corners of Beck's mouth twitched as he struggled to hold back a grin. "Let's just say it became very clear to him that he was going to be facing a long and very expensive legal battle, one that I am very willing and able to sink my money into. And while I don't like the idea of essentially pushing a man out of his daughter's life, your ex-husband is not a man who wants to be a father. If he was willing to sell her, it makes me physically ill to think what lengths he'd be willing to go to if she were in his care, so I have no regrets or reservations about this."

It wasn't until Beck said those final words that I even

considered that. Suffice it to say, the thought made me physically ill, too.

Not wanting to allow my mind to linger on those horrific thoughts, I asked, "So, he realized what he was up against and decided to get out while he could?"

"I figure it's mostly that," Beck returned.

My shoulders sagged with relief. Was this really going to be this easy?

"Are you okay?" Beck asked me.

Nodding, I confirmed, "Yes. I just... I hate his indifference to his daughter. In the end, I know she'll be better off, but it's still sad."

"I'm sorry," he lamented.

"You shouldn't be apologizing, Beck," I told him. "You've only made our lives better since the beginning. And this? Taking care of this for us is beyond what I ever would have expected you to do."

Beck's hand came up, drove into my hair, and landed at the back of my head. "You remember what I told you, right?"

"What?"

"Anything you need, Chasey."

"I love you," I said.

"I love you, too."

At that, Beck crushed his mouth to mine.

Then he lifted me in his arms and carried me into the bathroom where we showered together.

CHAPTER 26

Chasey

"THIS IS TOO MUCH."

"It's not."

"Beck, she's never going to remember all this," I announced. "She won't even know it happened."

He cocked an eyebrow as he looked at me and said, "Then it's our job to make sure she does."

I looked away from him and returned my gaze to the sight before me. "How did you even do all of this?" I asked.

It was as though he had magical powers. Because even though some of this could have been done before Beck arrived in New Hampshire just over a week ago, he hadn't come back to Pennsylvania until he brought Luna and me with him yesterday afternoon.

And now it was late on Christmas Eve, and Beck and I were standing in his massive family room of his humongous house staring at the gigantic Christmas tree that had more presents around it than I'd ever seen in my entire life.

Initially, I had assumed that Beck was simply a generous man. I mean, I already knew that he was. Seeing those gifts, I no longer had any doubts.

But upon closer inspection, which I'd done mostly to see how far Beck's gift-giving extended and refresh my memory on names of people who were important to him, I realized that the vast majority of those gifts had nametags indicating they were for Luna.

Yes, there were some for other people, like his mom and his sister, but at least eighty percent of what was there was for Luna.

He'd gone overboard.

I didn't know when he'd done it, nor did I know how. I just knew that he hadn't spared any expense.

And it didn't stop there.

Beck had gotten *everything* we needed for Luna. He fully furnished an entire room in his house for her, complete with a crib, changing table, dresser, and glider for me to rock and nurse her in.

There was a high chair for her. A stroller. Loads of diapers. All of her favorite solid foods he'd been seeing her eat over the last several days.

No matter where I looked, and there were a lot of places to look in his house, there was something there for Luna. It was as though she'd been living here her whole life instead of just coming for a few days for the holiday.

"I'm a determined and resourceful man," Beck shared.

"Beck, this is—"

"Chasey?" he called, interrupting me.

"Yeah?"

"Babe, I want to enjoy this time with you tonight. I don't want you worrying about things that you don't need to worry about. I love you, I love Luna, and I want this Christmas to be special," he said.

My heart melted.

"It already is," I returned quietly. "And the reason for that has nothing to do with all of this."

He smiled and replied, "I agree. Come on."

With that, he urged me away from where we were standing in front of the tree to sit on the floor in front of the couch, where he had done what he'd done while I was busy giving Luna a bath and nursing her before putting her down for the night.

The entire coffee table was covered with food and non-alcoholic wine, and the space was extra cozy due to not only all the pillows and blankets he'd set out but also to the fire from the fireplace.

It was sweet, romantic, and my every wish come true.

As we ate tasty food and drank delicious wine, Beck and I talked about everything. I focused a lot of my attention on learning about his mom, her boyfriend, and his sister. I wanted to be sure that I wouldn't make a fool of myself when I met them tomorrow.

"This was lovely, Beck," I told him after I'd taken a sip from my wineglass, set it down, and sat back to take the pressure off my belly that was now full.

"I'm glad you enjoyed it," he said.

I looked around the room and sighed, leaning into him. "You've spoiled us," I murmured. "Going back to work is going to be the worst."

"So don't."

I let out a soft laugh. "It doesn't work like that," I noted.

"For you, it does."

I lifted my head from his shoulder to look him in the eyes. "What does that mean?"

He held my gaze a few moments before he shifted himself out from behind the coffee table and toward the tree. He plucked a gift off of the top of one of the many stacks of them and walked on his knees back in front of the fireplace.

"Come here," he urged gently.

I didn't delay.

I went to him, doing it crawling on all fours since he was still down on his knees. When I made it to him, I settled my booty back on my heels, my shins pressed into the floor beneath me.

Beck held out a gift and said, "This is for you."

My brows pulled together as I took it from him. I unwrapped the small box, unable to miss the nerves in my belly.

When I had it opened, I took the lid off the plain white box, flipped it over, and shook the leather-wrapped, cream-colored jewelry box into the palm of my other hand. Once it was there, I looked up at Beck, saw the anticipation in his face, and opened the box.

A ring.

A diamond ring.

It was just sitting there, sparkling and huge and absolutely stunning.

I returned my attention to Beck. He lifted the box out of my hand, pulled the ring out, and took my hand in his.

"If you don't want to go back to work, Chasey, you don't have to," he said.

"Beck," I whispered.

"I want to give it to you," he continued. "I want to give you the thing you've wanted all your life. Marry me, Chasey. Marry me and take care of me, Luna, and all the babies I'm going to give you. If you do that, I promise I'll always take care of you."

Beck wanted to marry me. He wanted to marry me so I could take care of him and Luna and all the babies he wanted to give me.

It hadn't been long. I hadn't even officially met his family yet.

It felt fast.

Very fast.

But I didn't care.

Because even if it was all those things, it was also something else.

It was wonderful. It was lovely. It was the most selfless,

loving, and wonderful man I'd ever met promising to love me
and Luna and all of our babies forever.

He was going to make my wish come true.

So, I wasn't going to stop him.

"Okay, Beck, I'll marry you," I rasped.

A smile spread across his face as he slipped the diamond on
my finger. I looked down at the ring sitting at the base of my
finger and felt something warm move through me.

I was Beck's.

He was mine.

Looking up at him through hooded eyes, I knew he was
thinking the exact same thing.

"When?" I asked.

"When what?"

"When do you want to get married?" I clarified.

He looked around the room briefly before he brought his
attention to me and confessed, "I'd do it right now if we could
make that happen."

Wow.

He was very serious about this.

"What about babies?" I pressed.

"What about them?"

"When are you going to give me lots of babies?"

His expression softened. "We get everything settled for you
and Luna in New Hampshire and my girls move here permanently, I'll make it happen."

He'd make it happen. Just like that. As soon as everything
was settled and his girls were here permanently.

"I love you," I told him.

He leaned forward, drove one of his hands into my hair,
and brought his mouth to mine. "Love you, too."

Once he kissed me, that was it.

I was completely caught up in the warmth, the heat, the
passion, the desire, and the love I had for this man.

Our clothes were gone almost instantly. Beck got me to my back on the floor in front of the fire. He lifted one ankle in his hand and began kissing his way up my leg. When he made it to the top, getting dangerously close to my pussy and making me ache with anticipation, he pulled back and lifted the other ankle in his hand.

Beck's mouth moved up my legs as his hands explored every inch of them. By the time he made it to the top again, I was dying for him to put his mouth on me.

He didn't.

He skipped over the most intimate part of my body and allowed his lips to drift over to my hip. His tongue darted out to lick me there before he moved to my abdomen and continued his ascent up my body.

"Beck," I pleaded, feeling desperate and needy.

He gave me the tiniest bit of relief when he made it to my breasts and captured one in the palm of his hand while his mouth claimed the other.

As he played with my breasts, licking and teasing them, I urged my hips up into his body.

I didn't care if it made me seem desperate. I was desperate. I'd take any friction I could get, even if it wasn't his cock, which is what I really want.

Whether it was the moaning, the begging, or the movement of my hips, I'll never know, but eventually, Beck brought his mouth up to mine and asked, "Are you covered with birth control for now?"

I shook my head.

He stared at me, looking pensive, with the tip of his cock at my entrance. I did not want him to get up. I did not want him to move away. But I wasn't on birth control, and he wasn't ready for a baby.

"Would you be upset if you got pregnant now?" he asked, completely surprising me.

"Not at all," I answered.

"I'll pull out to increase our chances of avoiding it for now, but if it happens, I won't be upset," he said.

"I won't either," I assured him.

Not a moment later, he pushed inside.

My fingertips dug into his shoulders as my neck arched. "Baby," I breathed.

"Fuck, fuck, you're beautiful," he hissed.

He dropped his face into my neck, where he licked, kissed, and nipped at my skin. He did that while driving his hips into me in a slow, steady rhythm.

With his body against mine, my hands on him, his cock driving inside me, and his ring on my finger, I was lost in him.

In us.

He rolled us so that he was on his back. He allowed me to take the lead for a bit. I kept it slow and steady. Something about it this time was so different, so wonderful, that I didn't want to rush it.

At the same time, climbing higher and higher to that point of no return was almost unavoidable. There was too much there between us.

Eventually, Beck rolled me to my back again, and it was only a matter of a few slow, languid strokes of his cock into me when I started to feel it take hold. My fingernails dug into his skin, preparing because I knew this was going to destroy me in the most beautiful way possible.

Then it happened.

I moaned through the delicious pleasure splintering across my body as Beck worked me through my orgasm. He held on just long enough to see me through.

Once he did, he pulled out, fisted his cock, and came on my belly.

It was the best night before Christmas of my life.

WISH

This was the best.

The absolute best.

It was Christmas Day, and I was engaged.

Luna had had a bounty this morning, what with Beck taking his time to go through each of the presents he'd gotten for her. No doubt she was slightly overwhelmed with all the excitement, but she trucked right along with Beck encouraging her all the way.

My heart exploded with joy seeing him with her this morning. Obviously, I'd joined in with all of it because it was my girl's first Christmas, but in more than one instance, I simply sat back and stared.

This man.

This amazing man came into my life and made me fall in love again, and he did it while giving my daughter something he didn't have to give to her.

I thought he deserved to know it.

"You're going to be amazing," I told him as Luna sat in front of him playing with one of the many toys he'd gotten her.

A look of confusion washed over his face. "What do you mean?"

"As a father, Beck," I clarified. "You're going to be an amazing father. Luna is so lucky to have you in her life."

"Babe," he replied.

That was it. He didn't say anything else, and I understood it. What I'd shared hit him somewhere deep, got him a little choked up, and he couldn't get out more than just that single word.

But even with that word, I knew what it meant to him to hear me communicate my thoughts and feelings about the kind of man he was. I moved close, touched my mouth to his, and the two of us spent our morning with our girl.

Our girl.

Those two words left me feeling like I was floating.

And it was good I had that because if I gave myself a chance to forget about all the good that was happening inside my head and my heart with Beck and Luna, I'd start to think about what was happening with Beck and me.

It should have been good.

We were engaged.

But I couldn't stop myself from feeling a bit of worry creeping in.

"Chasey, what's wrong?" Beck asked after I'd put Luna down for her morning nap.

"What?"

"Something is on your mind," he noted. "Tell me what's wrong."

That was another thing that told me Beck was the man for me.

He knew. He could take one look at me, know something was wrong, and then he set out to fix whatever it was.

Coming to a stop in front of him, I said, "I'm just nervous."

"About what?"

"Meeting your family."

"They're going to love you," he assured me. "And they're going to adore Luna. Be prepared to see her spoiled."

I tipped my head back, looked up at him, and pressed deeper into him. "You already do that," I noted.

His lips twitched. "Okay. Then prepare to see her be even more spoiled."

I rolled my eyes.

"Don't be nervous," he urged gently, giving me a squeeze.

"But we're engaged," I reminded him.

"I know that. You say that like it's a problem."

How was it possible for him to take one look at me and know something was wrong, and yet, he couldn't understand why this was an issue?

"Beck, baby, I haven't even met your family yet, and we're engaged. Not only that, but we've only been officially together since Thanksgiving," I said.

"I haven't stopped thinking about you since I saw you in the summer," he declared. "And we might not have been intimate with one another before Thanksgiving, but we'd been talking to each other regularly since the beginning of November."

"You're talking about a matter of weeks," I argued.

Nodding his agreement, he replied, "Weeks where we got to know one another better and I hated being away from you. What does the amount of time we've been together have to do with this? We know what we feel. That's all that should matter."

He was right. The more I thought about it, the less it bothered me that this had been quick between us. Beck was an incredible man. He made me feel good, he made me happy, and he loved my daughter so much, he was willing to adopt her. Time would not change the way I felt about him. At least, it would not change in a negative way.

But I was still concerned.

"I don't want them to get the wrong impression of me," I murmured.

He tipped his head to the side. "What impression is that?"

My eyes shifted to the side and moved through the plethora of gifts strewn about. Beck must have seen that, realized where my head was at, and ordered, "Get that thought out of your head right now. I told you this that day I took you out for an early dinner and you forgot your wallet. I knew what kind of woman you were then, Chasey, and that hasn't changed. You didn't ask for any of this. I did this. Better yet, while we were still in Pennsylvania over the last week, who do you think I called to help me pull this off?"

I blinked in surprise as my lips parted in shock. His family? His family had gone through all of this trouble to do this?

"They did this for you?" I asked.

He tipped his head back and forth, thinking. "I mean, I guess you could say they did it for me because I asked, but the truth is that they did it for you and Luna because I've told them all about my girls. They know how I feel about you."

"But will they trust that how I feel about you is genuine?"

"Why wouldn't they?"

Shooting him a look of disbelief, I said, "You're Beck Emerson, member of My Violent Heart."

Beck features warmed. "Chasey, my family is going to spend about two minutes with you and realize that you're every bit the woman I already know you are," he shared. "Please don't worry."

What else could I do?

He was insistent that I had nothing to be concerned about, so I decided it was best to listen. If things didn't go as he had hoped, I could always go back to fretting later. So, we got to work on preparing some of the food.

And later had now arrived.

Luna was awake and playing, food was in the oven, and the doorbell rang.

Beck appeared in the kitchen with Luna tucked tight to his body in one arm while he extended his free hand to me. "Ready?"

I nodded and took his hand.

Seconds later, the front door was open and two women and one man stood before us. Their eyes moved between Beck, Luna, and me several times before the older woman of the two broke out into a full-blown grin and declared, "Merry Christmas."

"Merry Christmas, Mom," Beck replied.

Beck's mom stepped forward. She was carrying more bags in her hands than she had arms, but she still managed to hold her arms out wide and embrace her son.

"Is this Luna?" she asked when she let him go.

"This is her," Beck confirmed.

"Merry Christmas, Luna," she said to her.

Luna stared at Beck's mom for a few seconds before she

twisted her body and plastered her body to Beck's, hiding her face in his neck.

God, I loved that. I loved that she recognized when she was feeling unsure that she could trust him to protect her.

I might have continued to think on that if Beck's mom hadn't turned her attention to me and said, "You must be Chasey."

"I am. It's so nice to meet you. Merry Christmas, Ms..." I trailed off and instantly grew nervous. What was I supposed to call her? Surely, she wasn't Mrs. Emerson any longer, right? Oh God, why hadn't Beck prepared me for this?

"Sandy," she said.

"Right. Ms. Sandy."

Beck, his mom, and the two other people standing there all let out soft chuckles.

I was beyond confused at what was so funny when Beck's mom explained, "It's just Sandy. My name is Sandy. We don't need to be formal."

"Oh," I replied, feeling a flush hit my face.

She shuffled toward me, pulled me in for a hug, and said, "It's so nice to finally meet you, darling."

"You too," I responded.

When she stepped back, Beck introduced, "Chasey, this is my sister, Sadie."

She gave me a hug and said, "Merry Christmas."

I returned the same sentiment before she moved on and did the same with him. Then, Beck said, "And this is Glenn."

"He's my boyfriend," Sandy declared proudly.

"Woman, must you always call me your boyfriend?" he countered. "We're not teenagers anymore."

"Could have fooled me," Sandy murmured.

There was a very clear indication in her tone about the ways in which Glenn reminded her of a teenager.

"Oh God, this is more than I need to know," Beck muttered. "And may I remind you that there's a baby in the room?"

I bit my lip to stop myself from laughing. I loved them all already.

"It's wonderful to meet you, Chasey. Merry Christmas," Glenn said as he moved in close, carrying a bunch of bags. He gave me a one-armed hug as I returned my own version of that sentiment.

Everyone shuffled inside and eventually made it to the family room. Glenn set down all the bags he was carrying and said, "I've got a few more I need to get from the car."

More?

Were they crazy?

"I'll help," Beck volunteered.

He lifted Luna away from his body, kissed her cheeks, and said, "I'll be right back, princess."

Once Beck held her out to me and took off with Glenn to get more of whatever was left in the car, I stood there staring at Sadie and Sandy.

Sadie's mouth was agape.

Sandy had tears in her eyes.

"Is," I stopped and cleared my throat. "Is everything okay?" I asked.

"Holy crap," Sadie declared.

"He's… I… I've never seen him do something like that ever," Sandy rasped. "He's a natural."

I smiled. They'd just witnessed Beck being incredibly sweet and gentle with Luna. They were seeing, for the first time, how easily he fell into a role and filled shoes that he didn't need to fill.

"He's the most amazing man I've ever known," I told them.

Their stunned gazes came to my tear-filled eyes. I hoped they knew how lucky I felt to have him.

"He's in love," Sadie announced, surprise and a bit of something else evident in her tone.

"Yes, he is," his mother agreed, her emotions getting the best of her as a tear rolled down her cheek.

I wanted to think this was all good stuff, but I just couldn't be sure.

"You have *no idea* how happy this makes me," Sadie said.

Well, there it was. It was good news.

A moment later, Beck's voice filled the room. "What the heck happened?" he asked. "We weren't gone more than a minute."

"You're so good," Beck's mom told him.

"What?"

"With Luna," she clarified. "You're so good with her."

Beck's body relaxed. "That's good considering in a few months she's officially going to be mine," he said.

"I'm so happy for you, Beck," Sadie told him.

"Thanks, Sadie. But there's something else you should know," he said.

"What?"

Beck brought his eyes to mine. They were shining. I knew precisely what he wanted to do, so I gave him a slight nod. He looked back at his family and shared, "Last night, I asked Chasey to marry me and she said yes."

"You're engaged," his mother gasped.

"Yes."

Any control she'd gotten over her emotions had vanished as she rasped, "I'm getting a daughter-in-law and a granddaughter all at once?"

Oh my heart.

I placed my hand on the back of Luna's head to distract myself because I was on the verge of losing it.

"I don't know what the timing of it all will be, but essentially, yes," Beck answered. "Quite frankly, they're yours for the taking now, Mom."

Sandy's eyes remained on her son for a few more seconds. Then she turned them toward Luna and me. The next thing I knew she stripped off her jacket, let it fall to the floor, and moved close to us.

"Can Nonnie hold you?" she asked Luna.

I was done.

Gone.

Nonnie.

She *wanted* to be Luna's nonnie.

I didn't know where she'd come up with the name, but I didn't care. Just as her son had stepped in to fill the role of Luna's daddy, Sandy wanted to be her nonnie.

Luna hesitated, but she eventually must have decided that Sandy was okay because she leaned her body in her soon-to-be nonnie's direction. The minute Luna was in her arms, Sandy kissed and hugged her.

"Aunt Sadie is next," Sadie declared, moving close.

At that declaration, I couldn't hold back. A sob escaped. And while Beck's family gave Luna more love than I ever thought she'd have, Beck pulled me into his arms.

He lowered his mouth to my ear and whispered, "I told you."

He did. He had told me.

I never should have doubted him for a single second. I tipped my head back and whispered, "I love you."

Beck smiled and touched his mouth to mine, either forgetting or not caring that his family was standing right there.

I had a feeling it was the latter because there was no way Beck could ever possibly forget people who loved like his family did.

All the nerves I'd had were gone, and by the end of the night, there was one thing I knew for sure.

This had been the best Christmas of my life.

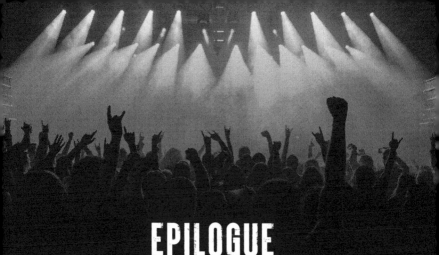

EPILOGUE

Beck
Ten months later

"**D**ADDY!"

I'd just walked in the door, and that sound was like music to my ears.

I stopped moving, crouched down, and braced myself for what I knew was coming. Sure enough, seconds later, she came into view.

Wearing pink, with a head of blonde hair like her mother's, Luna was sprinting toward me with something in her hand.

"Daddy!" she shouted again as she got closer.

Right in the gut.

Every single time from the very first time she called me that.

I didn't think I'd ever feel anything better than what I felt when I signed the papers that officially made Luna mine months ago, but I was wrong. Every day she called out my name like that, it just got better and better.

Her little body collided with mine, and I instantly lifted her in my arms and gave her a kiss on the cheek.

"Hi, princess."

"Surprise!"

I looked at Luna's hand and found another art project curled in her grasp. Yes, another one.

As I had expected, my sister adored her niece. That meant she spent a lot of time with Luna, and she spent a good chunk of that time doing all things art.

Luna loved it.

I loved that she loved it, and I loved that Sadie had that with her.

But when Sadie wasn't around, it meant that I had to do art projects. Art projects gave me anxiety. It was a wonder I didn't break out in hives every time Luna wanted to do one with me.

I often tried to convince my daughter to play the piano. Not surprisingly, my girl gave me that. If I asked her to play the piano with me, she'd play with me.

I loved that she loved art, but even more than that, I loved that she loved the piano. It was ours. Nobody else played piano with Luna.

"Surprise!" Luna shouted again.

Just then, I looked up and saw Chasey standing there looking at us.

My wife.

My beautiful wife.

Chasey and I had gotten married in a small ceremony earlier in the year with my family, the band, Mara, Mara's boyfriend, and Mara's parents there. It was intimate, small, and completely perfect for us. Mara and Sadie stood beside Chasey and Cash and Walker stood beside me as Chasey and I committed ourselves to one another in the official capacity.

Needless to say, she never went back to work. She called into work the first day the post office was open after the Christmas holiday and told them. Part of her felt bad for not giving them notice, but the other part of her was relieved. She hated the job, hated leaving Luna, and she wanted to stay here in Pennsylvania with me.

We made a few trips back to handle the legal business, pack up her things she wanted to bring here, and give her time with her best friend.

But once Chasey made that call to quit her job, for the first time since I met her, I finally saw her completely at ease. There was no longer any tension or lingering stress in her. I hadn't realized until she made that call just how much working and being away from Luna was affecting her.

Now, she was extraordinarily happy. She was going to let me give her the life she'd always wished for. It was a job I was honored to have; that was how happy she made me.

Holding Luna in my arms now, I smiled at Chasey and moved toward her.

"Surprise, surprise, surprise!"

I chuckled. "What's that all about?" I asked.

"She has a surprise for you," Chasey said after I'd greeted her with a kiss.

My eyes shifted to Luna and the project she had in her hand. It was approaching Halloween, so it wasn't hard to figure out that she'd spent the day making Halloween-themed art projects. She had a pumpkin that seemed to be made out of tiny pieces of orange tissue paper crumpled up and glued to a thick piece of card stock cut out in the shape of a pumpkin.

"Did you make me a pumpkin, princess?" I asked her.

"Her shirt, Beck," Chasey declared.

My brows pulled together as I lowered my gaze to Luna's shirt. I had to adjust her body in my arm so I could pull down her shirt and read it.

Two words and my body froze.

Two words.

My eyes shot to Chasey's. "Are you serious?"

She nodded.

Big sister.

Luna was going to be a big sister.

Chasey was pregnant.

The feeling of utter joy and surprise washed over me. My throat grew tight; my eyes got wet.

I reached my free arm out to Chasey. She didn't hesitate to move close.

"Baby," Luna said as I kissed Chasey. "Baby, baby, baby."

Everything was said in threes these days.

Chasey laughed against my lips. "I'm so glad I kept repeating the word surprise before you got home."

"When did you find out?" I asked.

"I took a test today. When it came back positive, I took Luna shopping for her shirt."

"We made a baby," I said.

"We made a baby, Beck."

I held her gaze for a few more seconds. Then I declared, "I love you."

"I love you, too."

"Let's go out for dinner to celebrate," I decided. "What do you think, Luna? Should we go out for dinner?"

"Yes!"

Chasey and I both laughed. So much shouting all the time.

I had a feeling we were in for more of that.

I couldn't wait.

With that, we got ourselves ready and went out to celebrate.

And the following year, we had another reason to celebrate when our family grew by one with the addition of Rosie.

I was one happy man with all my girls.

I couldn't have hoped for a better life than the one I got. And with all the bounty I'd already received, I felt a bit selfish about it, but I also knew I'd wish for more.

Preview of

CLOSER

Rock Stars & Romance Book 3: Walker & Sadie

PROLOGUE

Walker

THIS WAS SUPPOSED TO BE A HAPPY OCCASION.

I guess for everyone else it was. For me, it was anything but happy. I was miserable, a feeling I hadn't been a stranger to over the last few months and had only gotten worse over the last two days.

"So, are you going to be going on tour, too?"

I tried not to react to that question. The likelihood was that I was overthinking things, though. Considering that question came from Demi and was aimed at Chasey, the truth was that nobody would have been paying attention to me anyway.

Demi was Cash's girl, and Chasey was Beck's fiancée.

It was New Year's Eve, it was late, and we were all at Beck's house.

As it turned out, once Beck and Chasey got serious—or more serious than they already had been—he wanted her to meet the rest of the band.

So, we were all here now.

In fact, it was more than just the band. Not only were the remaining members of the band—Holland, Killian, Roscoe, and myself—here but so were quite a few others. My brother,

Raiden, who was our road manager had arrived along with a few other roadies. Beck's sister, Sadie, and some of our security staff were here were also here. And Killian and Roscoe had each brought a woman with them.

There was a full house, but it wasn't rowdy. Several smaller groups of individuals had huddled together to talk, drink, eat, and have a good a time. We'd been here for a couple hours now, and it had been nice.

Well, nice for everyone else. On the surface, I was sure I looked like I always did. Not overly enthusiastic not exactly sulking either. That was the beauty of how I'd lived for a long time. I'd learned to control my reactions.

It seemed most of the band had congregated in one area.

And now, the subject of touring had come up.

Chasey, sitting beside Beck on one of the oversized chairs, perked up beside him and said, "I didn't know the tour had been scheduled."

"It hasn't been," Beck assured her.

That's when Demi clarified, "Sorry, I worded that wrong. If the band decides to do another tour, do you think you'll go?"

"It's not a matter of if," Cash interjected. "It's a matter of figuring out how soon we want to do it."

"Well, you did just finish one up not that long ago," Sadie chimed in.

That was the truth.

We'd just finished up a tour at the beginning of November. Technically, it was finished at the end of October, but Cash had asked us if we'd play one more show back in Demi's hometown in New Hampshire.

We all agreed. What was one more show?

But now we were back, and there had been talks of planning another tour. Not only that, but the discussion had been leaning toward that tour starting soon.

Unfazed by that fact, Roscoe note, "Yeah, but life on the road is nice. New places, new people. It's a pretty sweet life."

That was Roscoe. He loved this life.

Truthfully, we all did.

But where I believed we'd all get to a point when we'd want to settle down—something I didn't expect to have happen any time soon—Roscoe could probably make music and go on tours until the day he died.

"So, what do you think, Chasey? Would you come on tour?" Demi pressed, returning the conversation to where it had started.

I was mildly curious about what her reaction would be. Chasey had a daughter named Luna who wasn't even a year old yet. It was one thing to have her sleeping soundly in the room Beck had set up all for her in this house while a party was happening downstairs, and it was something else entirely to take a baby on tour.

That's not to say that it couldn't be done or that nobody in the industry hadn't ever done it. It was just that I couldn't imagine it would be easy.

"As I told Beck already, I don't think I'll go on the tour," Chasey started. "Of course, that doesn't mean I won't ever go to any show that's close or that I won't consider flying to a location when there's a longer break, but I'm planning to spend my time here with Luna. She's still very young, and I want to be with her and keep her where she's most comfortable."

"That's really amazing that you're so supportive of his career," Demi declared.

Chasey shrugged. "I don't think so," she replied. "I'm content to see Beck do his thing while I do mine. Obviously, I'll miss him terribly, but I'd never want him to give up his passion."

That was nice to hear. I was glad that Beck had found someone who supported his career like that. I knew there had been a point in time, only a few weeks ago, where the topic of touring had come up, and everyone had been wondering how things would play out with Beck considering he'd gotten involved with a single mom.

"So, if we know that Chasey and Beck aren't a problem, I think we should just get on scheduling something to start up again," Roscoe put in. "I'm ready."

"Me too," Killian added.

Those responses had been expected. If they could have their way, I had no doubt Killian and Roscoe would have had us out performing next week.

"That's cool with me," Cash said. "I've got my girl, so I'm good to go whenever, wherever."

That was the truth because after discussing it with the rest of us first, Cash had offered to have Demi come on board as an official employee for My Violent Heart. Her best friend from when she lived in New Hampshire designed T-shirts had worked on creating some designs for the band, and Demi was going to now be the official swag and merchandise manager.

Demi leaned her torso into Cash's body. He effortlessly took her weight and curled his hand around her shoulder.

Just then, Holland walked up and joined the conversation. She sat down between Sadie and Demi as Killian asked, "What about you Holland?"

"What about what?" she said.

"You up for another tour?" he clarified.

"Totally," she answered.

I had to speak up. Instantly, I chimed in for the first time since the conversation had started. "I'm thinking we should take a break for a little."

"What's a little while?" Roscoe wondered.

I shrugged. "I don't know. Maybe a year?" I threw out.

I hadn't really considered a time frame. I just knew I wanted time. Actually, I needed it so I could sort things out.

"A year?" Cash repeated.

"Yeah."

"Walker?" Beck called.

I brought my attention to him. "Yeah?" I returned.

"We all know."

My body went solid. There was no way they knew. Not wanting to jump to conclusions about it, I asked, "What?"

"We get it," Beck replied, his voice oddly reassuring. "You guys took a chance, kept it quiet, and it didn't work out. If she can move on from it, I know you can, too."

My eyes narrowed on him. He wasn't making any sense. "What exactly are you talking about?"

Beck shot me an incredulous look, and I could feel everyone else's eyes had been darting back and forth between us.

"You and Holland," he blurted.

Holland gasped.

I cocked an eyebrow as my gaze shot to the side where Holland was sitting. My focus moved through the entire group, and I was suddenly very angry.

"Are you shitting me?" I clipped.

I didn't get angry. Not ever. Never with the band. And yet, right now, I was fuming. Because of that, I lost my temper. "You think I've been fucking Holland? You think I'm in some secret relationship with her?"

The look on Beck's face indicated that that was exactly what he thought.

"You aren't?" Cash asked.

"Fuck no," I fumed. "She's like a sister to me."

"So, what's going on with you?" Roscoe asked.

What was going on with me?

This was bullshit. All of them, all of these people that were my family, had made some assumption about me and had discussed this all at some point behind my back.

Shaking my head in disgust, I barked, "Fuck this. I'm out of here."

"Walker, man, don't leave," Killian jumped in, yanking his arm free from the woman who'd been hanging on him since the moment they arrived.

I didn't listen. I took off toward the front door.

I'd been dealing with enough over the last several months, even while we were still on tour. The last two days had been the worst of all. I didn't need to add this to it.

Though, that was the problem.

I'd been keeping a secret from them for years now. If it got out, it was likely that I'd have to make an impossible choice.

Either the band and my passion or the woman I loved.

OTHER BOOKS BY
A.K. EVANS

The Everything Series
Everything I Need
Everything I Have
Everything I Want
Everything I Love
Everything I Give

The Cunningham Security Series
Obsessed
Overcome
Desperate
Solitude
Burned
Unworthy
Surrender
Betrayed
Revived

Hearts & Horsepower
Control the Burn
Behind the Wheel
Far Beyond Repair
How to Rebuild
Out of Alignment

Archer Tactical

Line of Fire

Collateral Damage

Silent Target

Rock Stars & Romance

Fragile

Wish

Closer

Underneath It All

Terrible Lie

Complication

Road Trip Romance

Tip the Scales

Play the Part

One Wrong Turn

Just a Fling

Meant to Be

Take the Plunge

Miss the Shot

In the Cards

Only in Dreams

Break the Ice

ABOUT
A.K. EVANS

A.K. Evans is a contemporary romance author of over twenty published novels. While she enjoys writing a good romantic suspense novel, Andrea's favorite books to write have been her extreme sports romances. That might have something to do with the fact that she, along with her husband and two sons, can't get enough of extreme sports.

Before becoming a writer, Andrea did a brief stint in the insurance and financial services industry and managed her husband's performance automotive business. That love of extreme sports? She used to drive race cars!

When Andrea isn't writing, she can be found homeschooling her two sons, doing yoga, snowboarding, reading, or traveling with her family. She and her husband are currently taking road trips throughout the country to visit all 50 states with their boys.

For new release updates, sign up for the A.K. Evans newsletter: http://eepurl.com/dmeo6z

Be sure to follow Andrea on all social media platforms, too.

Facebook
www.facebook.com/authorAKEvans

Facebook Reader Group
http://bit.ly/2ys50mU

Instagram
www.instagram.com/authorakevans

Goodreads Author Page
www.goodreads.com/user/show/64525877-a-k-evans

Bookbub
www.bookbub.com/authors/a-k-evans

Twitter
twitter.com/AuthorAKEvans

Made in the USA
Monee, IL
19 April 2022